SERENDIPITY

Praise for Kris Bryant

Home

"*Home* is a very sweet second-chance romance that will make you smile. It is an angst-less joy, perfect for a bad day."—*Hsinju's Lit Log*

Scent

"Oh, Kris Bryant. Once again you've given us a beautiful comfort read to help us escape all that 2020 has thrown at us. This series featuring the senses has been a pleasure to read…I think what makes Bryant's books so readable is the way she builds the reader's interest in her mains before allowing them to interact. This is a sweet and happy sigh kind of read. Perfect for these chilly winter nights when you want to escape the world and step into a caramel-infused world where HEAs really do come true."—*Late Night Lesbian Reads*

Lucky

"The characters—both main and secondary, including the furry ones—are wonderful (I loved coming across Piper and Shaylie from *Falling*), there's just the right amount of angst, and the sexy scenes are really hot. It's Kris Bryant, you guys, no surprise there."—*Jude in the Stars*

"This book has everything you need for a sweet romance. The main characters are beautiful and easy to fall in love with, even with their little quirks and flaws. The settings (Vail and Denver, Colorado) are perfect for the story, and the romance itself is satisfying, with just enough angst to make the book interesting…This is the perfect novel to read on a warm, lazy summer day, and I recommend it to all romance lovers."—*Rainbow Reflections*

Goldie Winner *Temptation*

"This book has a great first line. I was hooked from the start. There was so much to like about this story, though. The interactions. The tension. The jealousy. I liked how Cassie falls for Brooke's son before she ever falls for Brooke. I love a good forbidden love story."—*Bookvark*

"This book is an emotional roller coaster that you're going to get swept away in. Let it happen…just bring the tissues and the vino and enjoy the ride."—*Les Rêveur*

"People who have read Ms. Bryant's erotica novella *Shameless* under the pseudonym of Brit Ryder know that this author can write intimacy well. This is more a romance than erotica, but the sex scenes are as varied and hot."—*LezReviewBooks*

Tinsel

"This story was the perfect length for this cute romance. What made this especially endearing were the relationships Jess has with her best friend, Mo, and her mother. You cannot go wrong by purchasing this cute little nugget. A really sweet romance with a cat playing cupid."—*Bookvark*

Falling

"This is a story you don't want to pass on. A fabulous read that you will have a hard time putting down. Maybe don't read it as you board your plane though. This is an easy 5 stars!"—*Romantic Reader Blog*

"This was a nice, romantic read. There is enough romantic tension to keep the plot moving, and I enjoyed the supporting characters' and their romance as much as the main plot."—*Kissing Backwards*

Goldie Winner *Listen*

"Ms. Bryant describes this soundscape with some exquisite metaphors, it's true what they say that music is everywhere. The whole book is beautifully written and makes the reader's heart go out to people suffering from anxiety or any sort of mental health issue."—*Lez Review Books*

"The main character's anxiety issues were well written and the romance is sweet and leaves you with a warm feeling at the end. Highly recommended reading."—*Kat Adams, Bookseller (QBD Books, Australia)*

"I was absolutely captivated by this book from start to finish. The two leads were adorable and I really connected with them and rooted for them…This is one of the best books I've read recently—I cannot praise it enough!"—*Melina Bickard, Librarian, Waterloo Library (UK)*

"This book floored me. I've read it three times since the book appeared on my Kindle…I just love it so much. I'm actually sitting here wondering how I'm going to convey my sheer awe factor but I will try my best. Kris Bryant won Les Rêveur book of the year 2018 and seriously this is a contender for 2019."—*Les Rêveur*

Against All Odds

"*Against All Odds* by Kris Bryant, Maggie Cummings, and M. Ullrich is an emotional and captivating story about being able to face a tragedy head-on and move on with your life, learning to appreciate the simple things we take for granted and finding love where you least expect it."—*Lesbian Review*

"I started reading the book trying to dissect the writing and ended up forgetting all about the fact that three people were involved in writing it because the story just grabbed me by the ears and dragged me along for the ride…[A] really great romantic suspense that manages both parts of the equation perfectly. This is a book you won't be able to put down."—*C-Spot Reviews*

Lammy Finalist *Jolt*

Jolt "is a magnificent love story. Two women hurt by their previous lovers and each in their own way trying to make sense out of life and times. When they meet at a gay- and lesbian-friendly summer camp, they both feel as if lightning has struck. This is so beautifully involving, I have already reread it twice. Amazing!"—*Rainbow Book Reviews*

Goldie Winner *Breakthrough*

"Looking for a fun and funny light read with hella cute animal antics and a smoking hot butch ranger? Look no further…In this well-written first-person narrative, Kris Bryant's characters are well developed, and their push/pull romance hits all the right beats, making it a delightful read just in time for beach reading."—*Writing While Distracted*

"It's hilariously funny, romantic, and oh so sexy…But it is the romance between Kennedy and Brynn that stole my heart. The passion and emotion in the love scenes surpassed anything Kris Bryant has written before. I loved it."—*Kitty Kat's Book Review Blog*

"Kris Bryant has written several enjoyable contemporary romances, and *Breakthrough* is no exception. It's interesting and clearly well-researched, giving us information about Alaska and issues like poaching and conservation in a way that's engaging and never comes across as an info dump. She also delivers her best character work to date, going deeper with Kennedy and Brynn than we've seen in previous stories. If you're a fan of Kris Bryant, you won't want to miss this book, and if you're a fan of romance in general, you'll want to pick it up, too."—*Lambda Literary*

Forget Me Not

"Told in the first person, from Grace's point of view, we are privy to Grace's inner musings and her vulnerabilities…Bryant crafts clever wording to infuse Grace with a sharp-witted personality, which clearly covers her insecurities…This story is filled with loving familial interactions, caring friends, romantic interludes, and tantalizing sex scenes. The dialogue, both among the characters and within Grace's head, is refreshing, original, and sometimes comical. *Forget Me Not* is a fresh perspective on a romantic theme, and an entertaining read."—*Lambda Literary Review*

Whirlwind Romance

"Ms. Bryant's descriptions were written with such passion and colorful detail that you could feel the tension and the excitement along with the characters."—*Inked Rainbow Reviews*

Taste

"*Taste* is a student/teacher romance set in a culinary school. If the premise makes you wonder whether this book will make you want to eat something tasty, the answer is: yes."—*The Lesbian Review*

By the Author

Jolt

Whirlwind Romance

Just Say Yes: The Proposal

Taste

Forget Me Not

Touch

Breakthrough

Shameless
(writing as Brit Ryder)

Against All Odds
(with Maggie Cummings and M. Ullrich)

Listen

Falling

Tinsel

Temptation

Lucky

Home

Scent

Not Guilty (writing as Brit Ryder)

Always

Forever

EF5 (novella in Stranded Hearts)

Serendipity

SERENDIPITY

by
Kris Bryant

2022

ISBN 13: 978-1-63679-224-8

This Trade Paperback Original Is Published By
Bold Strokes Books, Inc.
P.O. Box 249
Valley Falls, NY 12185

First Edition: September 2022

Credits
Editors: Ashley Tillman and Shelley Thrasher
Production Design: Stacia Seaman
Cover Design by Kris Bryant

Acknowledgments

I love creating stories around music. We've all dreamed about being rock or pop stars at some point in our lives. I never outgrew the dream, but I can't sing or read music, so I write about it. I have attended concerts ever since I was old enough to drive myself to venues, and I have seen some incredible shows. Music touches our hearts in a way that nothing else does. It's designed to pull out emotions that we either hide or nourish, and it makes us vulnerable. Love, anger, happiness, sadness, euphoria, rage, peace. The list goes on. Isn't it wonderful that one little four-minute song can lift us up or shred us? While it's wonderful to create music and words that reach a lot of people, success comes at a price. I wanted to write that aspect. What sacrifices does somebody make to reach their dreams? Why can't people have both?

I'd like to thank Ashley for being a stellar editor as always. We're such a good team. Trust me when I say that without her, my books wouldn't be as smooth. Thank you, Bold Strokes Books, for publishing my books. I'll never get tired of telling my stories, so I'm thankful you still want to publish them.

Thank you to Deb for creating my beautiful and wonderfully simple covers. I love that she knows exactly what I'm envisioning even if my words don't come out right.

Molly is still by my side as I write these books, but I know that won't always be the case. Having her in my life is such a blessing.

Thank you to my parents and my sister for their love and support. Nope, they still aren't allowed to read my books.

I love my friends! Thank you, Fiona, for our chats and all the beautiful photos you send me of the g. snaps. K.B.—we need more writing dates—even if they're at the lake and we're on the boat. I'm sure it's the perfect time to write! Encouragement is so important during the writing process, so a big heartfelt shoutout to the people who check on me, including Paula, Carsen, GFB, Mellie B, Morgan, Friz, and so many others.

Another big shout-out to my online friends who read, tweet, post, and share our books with their friends. I love our community of readers and writers who lift one another up.

My patrons are doing great things on Patreon for animal shelters and sanctuaries around the world. I'm proud that what we are doing is making a difference. Animals give us unconditional love, and even though we can't keep them all, we can at least give them food, beds, and toys until they can find their forever homes.

Thank you to everyone who reads this book and continues to support our LGBTQIA family. You are the real superstars!

For all the pop and rock stars who never made it to the stage.

CHAPTER ONE

"Big turnout tonight, huh?" Charley asked.

Annie adjusted the microphone stand and smiled at her best friend. "I can't believe how many people signed up." She absently wiped her hands on her black pants before pushing a blond curl behind her ear. Her curly hair always managed to slip out of the confinement of the hair tie, giving her a messy "I just woke up" look no matter how many times she tried to tame it. She slipped her phone into the docking station and took a deep breath. In eight minutes, she was going to livestream *Coffee & Chords*, a popular show for her YouTube channel. Wednesdays were open-mic night at Charley Shock's coffee bar, The Night Owl. It always amazed Annie how many people drank coffee late at night, but there was a need, and The Night Owl was the only coffee bar that stayed open until eleven.

"Go get ready. I'll get the stage set up." Charley pointed to her clock.

Annie went into the back room to slip into her jacket, throw product on her hair, and touch up her makeup. She sat on the single bar stool onstage and adjusted the mic. Wednesday nights were her absolute favorite. Most people loved Friday nights, but not Annie. That was her night to order takeout, curl up on the couch with a good book, and fall asleep until Raven Elizabeth, her rescue cat of eight years, pawed her on the face for a late-night snack or a game of fetch. Brainpower and creative juices flowed best for her on Wednesdays.

She contracted work as a jingle writer for several local advertising agencies. The rest of her time was spent at The Night Owl doing solo gigs, which allowed her to work out new songs and practice in front of crowds. She was thankful Charley gave her the stage whenever she wanted. "Okay, everyone. We're going live in one minute. I'm going to start off by playing a quick song, and then first on the list is Harmony Hannah." She stumbled over the name and bit her lip to keep from laughing at the horrible alliteration. Annie always played the first song to give her viewers enough time to pop on. She had over twenty thousand followers, and open mic was good exposure for local artists, especially queer ones.

"Is everyone ready?" The loud applause made her smile. She was in her happy place. She strummed a few times to tune her guitar, and once she felt comfortable, she hit the live button but turned off the tip jar. She didn't feel comfortable taking money for other people's performances, and trying to divide the online tips was a nightmare. "Welcome to another episode of *Coffee & Chords*. We're coming to you live from open mic at The Night Owl, the best coffee bar in the Denver area."

Most of the people or small bands played soft, easy-listening music because the venue was a coffee shop, not a concert arena. Country was also popular, but after scanning the crowd and not seeing cowboy hats or cowboy boots, Annie figured tonight would be a night of folk and pop music. The stage wasn't big enough for head-banging bands with tons of equipment, so most artists were low-key.

"We have a great night in store for you. Over fifteen musicians have signed up, so sit back and enjoy the show." Annie didn't introduce the song she was playing. She didn't have to. It was a cover of a popular pop tune on the radio, but she slowed it and gave it a personal twist. Several people in the audience sang it with her, which always made her smile. When she was done and saw the number of viewers was where she wanted it to be, she introduced the first guest to the onstage. "First up is Harmony Hannah. Let's give her a warm welcome." Annie scooted offstage and waited for Hannah to finish her song so she could come back onstage and introduce the next guest, Loco Motion.

"What's your number tonight?" Charley put her arm around Annie's waist and rested her cheek on her shoulder.

Annie checked the app on her watch. "Just over three thousand." Annie loved the closeness she and Charley shared. They had been best friends since high school, forming a strong bond initially over music and then over their love of books, junk food, and scary movies. Despite what people assumed, Charley was straight and had a boyfriend of three years, but fully supported Annie's queerness.

"I bet by the end of the night, you'll have five thousand viewers," Charley said.

"I hope so. Half of the sign-up sheet is new to me. My viewers really appreciate fresh sounds."

"Harmony Hannah isn't horrible," Charley said.

Annie nudged her in the ribs. "Shh. The phone picks up everything. We don't want people to hear you." She turned around to watch Hannah. "But you're totally right. She's pretty decent, just not comfortable in front of a crowd." Hannah's glittery rainbow guitar strap reflected the spotlight, blinding everyone in the crowd when she strummed.

"High school. Who didn't have anxiety then? She sounds like she's wrapping up. Go save her before she melts into a puddle of awkwardness," Charley said.

Annie quickened her pace and slid up beside Hannah right when she strummed the last note on her guitar. Annie started applauding, and the crowd picked up her cue. "Thank you, Harmony Hannah. Was that an original song?" The young musician nodded and blushed. She now understood why Hannah asked to go onstage first. Sometimes it was easier to get it over with and sit back and enjoy the rest of the night without the anxiety of counting down the minutes until stage time. "Great job." She waited until Hannah shuffled off the stage. "Next up is a new-to-us band, Loco Motion, that just formed a month ago." Annie ignored the rest of the biography they handed her. They were pressed for time, and this was an open mic. "Let's give them a warm welcome."

"They sound pretty good for being new," Charley said when Annie returned to her spot next to the stage.

"I think so, too." Annie liked their youthful energy. They were only a minute into their song, but she heard something she liked. Maybe it was the lead singer's vocal agility or the way his fingers glided so smoothly along the strings of his guitar. His chord transitions were flawless. With practice, she imagined Loco Motion could go far, or the lead singer could strike out on his own. He was good enough. Since she started open mic two years ago, three performers had gone on to sign contracts with record labels. Not because of her, but Annie liked being able to say, "I knew them when."

"What's your schedule for tomorrow?" Charley asked softly.

"I'm headed to the hospital to play for a bit. Then I'll be here after lunch, if that's good?"

Charley nodded. "That works. How's Peyton?" Her fingers pressed into Annie's waist when she asked the question.

It wasn't a secret that Peyton suffered from retinoblastoma. Annie just hated that it defined her niece already at such a young age. There was always the underlying message when people asked about Peyton because the question was never about her being a kid. It was never about how she was doing in preschool or if she liked playing soccer or if she wanted to be in tumbling. It was always about if she was going to survive the cancer or if her sight would ever be normal. "She's good. You know how she is. So resilient." When Peyton was diagnosed at four, a late age for the disease, the prognosis was grim. The tumor behind her right eye had been growing at such an alarming rate the doctors feared the cancer had already spread to other parts of her body. Thankfully, it hadn't, but her treatment plan was still aggressive.

"How many days is she in for?"

"Sarah will probably keep her overnight." Annie's older sister was head nurse of the pediatric wing of the university hospital. Years ago, they joked about how it was a good idea to take the job in case Sarah and her husband had accident-prone children. Little did they know how important that decision would turn out to be.

"I think it's great that you play for the kids. It gives them something to look forward to every week." Charley pointed to the bar. "Looks like they need me over there, but stop by before you head to the hospital tomorrow, and I'll give you some freshly baked cookies for Peyton."

"She'll love it. Go. I've got this." Annie turned back to the stage. She spent the next few hours welcoming the next thirteen guests until it was time to say good night and end her livestream. "Thank you to everyone here and those watching from somewhere else." She stopped the stream and broke down the stage as people were leaving. It was almost midnight, but Annie felt so alive. She helped Charley close and walked to her apartment two blocks away. It was tough having no outlet for the inspiration that had swelled after tonight's performances, but it was late, and she knew her neighbors were asleep. There was always tomorrow. Tonight, she'd crawl into bed and read the comments on tonight's livestream.

"Hello, baby." Annie squatted and rubbed Raven's ears. The

soft, silky triangles were bright pink against her black fur, and Raven preferred having them rubbed more than her belly. "Did you miss me tonight? Are you hungry?" A quick check of the food bowl let her know that not only did Raven eat all her kibble, but she had used her bowl as a hockey puck on the kitchen floor, her way of demanding more. Annie opened a can of wet food and scooped half into Raven's dish. "We're celebrating. Tonight was a good night." Raven meowed her approval and rubbed against Annie's legs, ready to devour the seafood pâté once it was in her bowl. Annie changed into her pajamas, spent a few minutes on her nightly routine of brushing her teeth, exfoliating her face with a new sugar scrub her sister had recommended, and applying a new leave-in conditioner that promised to tame her curls overnight. She scoffed at the guarantee on the box but followed the directions just in case it worked. It was almost one in the morning. She crawled under the covers and pulled up her YouTube channel. The comments were mostly positive, but one or two people always had cruel words about talent or about the LGBTQ community. She quickly deleted the hateful posts in case anybody who was onstage tonight was doing the same thing she was. She couldn't control the like or dislike feature, but she could eliminate the rude words. It amazed her that people wanted to get noticed, even if it was at the expense of others. After doing a first run-through of cleanups, Annie closed her laptop, tossed a mouse toy around for Raven, and drifted off to sleep.

"Hello, everyone." Annie peeked into the children's chemotherapy room and waved at the tiny faces that lit up when they saw her. Annie had made her musical visits weekly. She also made it a point to play for any child who spent their birthday at the hospital, which, sadly, was a lot. The kids loved it, and since her sister was in charge, she let Annie play whenever she could fit it into her schedule.

Peyton yelled when she walked in the room. "Auntie Annie!" She waved her arms frantically, as though Annie wouldn't notice her fifteen feet away.

"Good morning, big girl. How are you feeling?" Annie gave Peyton a tight hug and would have kissed her on her head if she wasn't wearing a mask. Since their immune systems were compromised, Annie wore blue tear-away coveralls and a see-through mask. She could still sing fine with it, and the children could see her mouth.

"Okay."

"I'm going to play a few songs, and then we'll go back to your room and hang out there." Annie leaned down and whispered, "I have a surprise for you." Peyton clapped her tiny hands together with delight, and the clear tube attached to her arm swung slightly. Annie swallowed her sadness and kept a smile on her face. "Who wants to hear a few songs?" At their cheers, she sang a quick little nursery rhyme to get them in the mood. By the third one, every single kid in the ward was smiling, even the ten-year-old girl who scowled at her when she first showed up and strummed the childish song.

"Can you play something from the radio?" the girl asked.

"I can. What's your name?"

"Zoey, but you can call me Zee," she said.

Annie smiled even though her heart broke. The navy-blue beanie hat that rested just below her brow emphasized the translucent half-moons under her solemn brown eyes. "That's a lovely name. Any requests?"

"What about anything by Bristol Baines?"

Annie thought about it and grabbed her capo. "Do you like the song 'Let Love Through'?" She adjusted it on the neck of her guitar and strummed a few seconds before she liked the sound. "Want to sing it with me?" Zee nodded. Who didn't know Bristol Baines? She was all over the pop chart, and while her music was too poppy for Annie's tastes, she liked the bones of her songs. Since Zoey had agreed to sing with her, Annie decided to keep the song true to form. "Everyone, Zee is going to sing with me. And if you know the song, feel free to jump in and sing it with us."

Annie looked up when Sarah and a woman slipped into the room. Annie barely gave the woman standing next to Sarah a second glance. Wearing coveralls and a mask, she was completely unidentifiable, but she gave off powerful energy. She assumed it was a parent of one of the children and waved to both before she started playing. It was a faster song, and Annie liked the challenge of the playing the different notes. It was one that Bristol played on the piano, but Annie had learned it on her guitar.

She smiled when Zoey slowly, quietly joined in. By the end of the song, they were both belting out the lyrics. The entire room applauded when they were done. Annie walked over and fist-bumped Zoey. "That was amazing. Had Bristol heard that, she would have been super impressed."

"We have time for one more song, Annie," Sarah said.

"One more song. Got it." She pretended to think hard. "This is a tough one. Is there one that we all want to sing? Maybe 'You Are My Sunshine' or something like that?"

"'Party in the U.S.A.,'" one of the tiny patients yelled, and everyone else cheered.

That song was older than the patients in the room. How did they even know it? It wasn't that Annie didn't appreciate Miley Cyrus's talent; she just didn't like her music. She smiled and started strumming. These kids deserved happiness, and if that's the song they wanted, then that's what she was going to give them. "Everybody put your hands up like the song says." She waited for them to put their hands up. When they all had their hands up as high as they could, given their treatment restrictions, Annie continued. She sang the rest of the song and ended it with a whoop of delight. "I have to go now, but I had a wonderful time with all of you." Annie went around the room and fist-bumped all ten kids. She met Sarah on the other side of the door.

"Guess what?"

"What?" Annie asked, peeling off her mask and coveralls. She let Sarah fix the collar on her shirt.

"I just met the most amazing person, and you're going to love me."

Annie held up her hands and waved them at her sister. "Oh, no. You are not playing matchmaker with me. I'm fine on my own."

"Oh, hell, no. She's way out of your league anyway."

Annie playfully smacked her sister's arm. "That's not a nice thing to say."

"I'm teasing. Besides, she's straight anyway."

"Like you were with her for what? Ten minutes? And you talked about her sexuality? Weird." Annie slung her soft case over her shoulder and held up a small brown bag. She didn't want to talk about the secret woman who'd watched her play. "This is from Charley for Peyton. I can only assume it's nothing but sugar and frosting and is guaranteed to put a smile on her face."

Sarah put her hands on Annie's shoulders and looked her straight in the eye. "I know you're ignoring me, so let me put it to you another way. You just played a song by one of the hottest artists of our time, the legendary Bristol Baines, in front of her manager."

Annie could only stand there and gape at her sister. What were the odds?

CHAPTER TWO

Y ou have to listen to this."

Bristol groaned and chucked her pillow at Lizzy, her manager and friend. "I was almost asleep."

The bed bounced as Lizzy plopped down next to her. Lizzy held her hand and squeezed. "I found your opening act."

"I have an opening act already."

"But you need two. At least until the end of the tour. Here. I want you to watch this little video and, if you like her, head over to her YouTube channel. She's good. She does covers and original stuff," Lizzy said.

Musicians begged to open for Bristol. Fast Cars was a concession to the studio because they were on the brink of stardom and Top Shelf wanted them onstage right before her, but Bristol purposely left the opening spot for musicians she believed in.

"If I do this, will you leave me alone?"

"As long as you say yes."

Bristol struggled into a sitting position. "Show me." She hit play and watched the woman in the blue coveralls perform a stunning rendition of "Baby Shark" that made Bristol perk up even though she didn't want to, sing an amazing cover of one of her own songs, and finish with a Miley Cyrus Top 40 song that was making a comeback on the kids' music circuit. She was good, but anyone could sing kids' songs. "She sounds okay, but I need more before I make a decision." She handed the phone back to Lizzy and waited for her to pull up more videos.

"Here's one she did last night. It's the most recent. Oh, she's really cute behind the coveralls and the mask," Lizzy said.

Bristol snatched the phone away. "She has great hair. Her voice is good. Does she only do covers?"

"Would I recommend her if she did? Go back to last weekend's stream. She mentions originals. She has an EP on iTunes, and it's downloadable from her website." Lizzy put her head next to Bristol's to get a better view of the phone screen. "She's got the look. And she has a ton of followers, so it's not like she's a nobody."

Bristol turned her head and frowned at Lizzy. "My little brother has two million followers on TikTok, and he's just a regular kid."

"Your little brother makes stupid teenage boy videos about blowing up things and scaring your family. He has all those followers because people are hoping to get a glimpse of you and your spectacular life," Lizzy said. She scrolled to the next video. "Besides, all kids are doing that now. But Annie Foster? She's somebody who deserves to be heard. And we should let her stream from the stage."

Bristol gave Lizzy the look, the one that told her to chill out. "Maybe she doesn't want to. Maybe being in front of tens of thousands of people will freak her out. You know this lifestyle isn't for everyone," she said.

Lizzy held up her hand. "I know you're struggling right now, but you used to love giving opportunities to underrepresented artists. Maybe if you make somebody else's dream come true, you'll be able to focus on something positive." Once she heard Bristol take a deep breath, she quickly added, "Just because you're done with it doesn't mean somebody else wouldn't love the chance. Just give it some thought. We have two nights here and twenty more shows in six weeks. Would you rather trust the studio to send someone you like?"

Bristol sighed and took the phone from Lizzy. She listened to two original songs and another cover. Annie Foster's voice was crystal clear. It was pure and beautiful. Bristol knew she was a good fit for their tour but didn't like how sure Lizzy was. Besides, she was in a bad mood and wanted to wallow for a bit longer.

"I can see in your eyes that you want to sulk for the rest of the day, and I totally get it, but since we're pressed for time, I, as your manager, friend, and publicist, need to jump on this," Lizzy said.

Bristol tamped down her tantrum. "Can I go with you when you talk to her?"

"I need to find her first."

"Can't we just go to The Evening Eagle, or whatever it's called, and find her there?"

Lizzy laughed. "The Night Owl, and why don't I just call there and get her contact info? Maybe we can do a Zoom or a FaceTime call. I can also leave a message at the hospital for her sister." She didn't have to remind Bristol that it was almost impossible for her to be out in public without causing a massive disturbance. Social media was a blessing and a curse. They could be in front of millions with a simple post in a matter of minutes. They parked the tour buses at a different hotel to throw off the fans, but the diehards knew what she was doing, and they always found her.

Bristol growled. "I need a day out. Just a quick dash. I'll put my hair under a cap and wear a business suit or a hazmat suit, whatever you think will hide me. I just need to be around people." The effects of almost eighteen months on the road, performing the same songs over and over and being around the same people day in and day out were starting to take their toll on her mental health. She needed to do something normal, like have lunch in a restaurant again or window-shop for something she didn't need. She missed strolling in public and feeding off the energy of people. She frowned. That hadn't happened since she was a teenager, and that was eight studio albums ago.

"This never turns out how we want," Lizzy said. Her voice held a gentle warning, as though Bristol could forget what happened the last time she was out in public. An eleven-year-old kid got trampled as a mob chased Bristol. Not only was it an eye-opening experience, but it also made Bristol retreat further inside herself. She'd refused interviews and public appearances except for the stage until a month ago.

"Can we at least try?" Bristol asked.

"Of course. Let me make a few calls and see what I can do." Lizzy waited.

"Why are you staring at me?"

"I'm going to need my phone in order to do that." Lizzy held out her hand until she dropped the phone into her palm.

Bristol picked up her own and googled Annie Foster. It was a wholesome name. And she was pretty. The all-American girl-next-door. Women with guitars were a dime a dozen. But the number of subscribers was impressive no matter what she'd told Lizzy. Bristol pulled up a video of one of Annie's most viewed videos. She was engaging, comfortable in front of people, and had a smile that was both infectious and sexy. Bristol downloaded her EP and clicked through her website. It was fun and flirty, with a ton of queer content. She'd played at Denver Pride and performed several times at The Center, Denver's LGBTQ organization and safe place for queers. Bristol was impressed with how involved Annie was in her community.

"Okay, so the woman who owns The Night Owl said she's going to contact Annie now and try to get her to meet us at the place in an hour." Lizzy rested her head on the pillow next to Bristol.

"So, you're saying we're going on a field trip? Oh, my God, I can't wait." Bristol jumped up and raced to her suitcase. Most of her clothes were on the bus, but she always had an overnight bag of casual clothes to wear in the hotel suites. She pulled out a pair of leggings and an oversized T-shirt. "Can I get away with this?"

"No. You look too much like you," Lizzy said.

"It's summer. I can't hide in a trench coat or sweatshirt. I'll sweat to death."

Lizzy piled Bristol's long, chestnut-brown hair up on her head. "If we find a cap that says something like Rocky Mountains and you wear my oversized sunglasses and sit in a corner, then maybe we'll have a few minutes."

"I'll take a few minutes of normalcy. Give me ten minutes to get ready." Bristol was filled with a giddy energy she hadn't felt in a long time. Lizzy never let her go out. She needed this outing. Even if it was for five glorious, boring minutes. She changed clothes, put on her favorite sneakers, and tied a windbreaker around her waist. One of her security guys knocked on the door and gave Lizzy a Colorado Rockies hat from their gift shop. Bristol gathered her hair and tucked it up.

"You look like a soccer mom," Lizzy said.

"Then I freaking nailed the look." Bristol slid Lizzy's large, black sunglasses on her face. "I don't look like me."

"You look like the quintessential middle-America soccer mom who's hunting a cup of java to keep herself sane from too many soccer and T-ball games," she said.

"As long as I don't resemble Bristol Baines." She stared at herself in the mirror and wiped off the lipstick. "Soccer moms don't have time for lipstick."

"We might be underselling soccer moms," Lizzy said. She picked up her bag from the coffee table. "Let's go before I change my mind."

The coffee bar was larger than Bristol expected. She followed Lizzy in, put her head down, and tried to appear as casual and inconspicuous as possible. Nobody gave her a second glance.

"Hi. We're looking for Charley. Is she available?" Lizzy asked the barista behind the register.

"I'm Charley. Are you Lizzy?"

Charley was attractive, with black hair that was shaved short in the back and fell in chunks across her forehead. She wore a black T-shirt with The Night Owl logo across her chest. Her blue eyes widened in shock when she realized Bristol Baines was standing three feet away. Instead of making a big deal, she flipped the countertop open and motioned for her and Lizzy to follow her to the back of the store to a very small but private office.

"It might be better if we chat back here," Charley said. She motioned to two chairs opposite a desk with a small stack of papers and a coffee mug that said "Life Happens, Coffee Helps" above their logo. It was obvious Charley was proud of her business.

"Thank you for the discretion," Bristol said. She slipped off her sunglasses but kept the hat on.

Charley nodded and wrung her fingers nervously until everyone focused on them, and then she stopped. "I'm sorry. I didn't put two and two together. I didn't realize you repped Bristol Baines. When you called and said you wanted to book Annie for a show, I recognized Top Shelf, but not your name." She gave Bristol a nervous smile. "I can't imagine how hard it is for you to get out and about."

Bristol nodded thanks. If Charley only knew how hard it really was.

"So, Annie should be here shortly. I told her somebody from Top Shelf wanted to talk about participating in an upcoming performance."

"Thank you for helping set this up," Lizzy said.

Charley smiled. "Well, even if I knew who you were, I would have done the same thing. I think she needs to hear it directly from you." She nodded at Bristol.

All three turned when they heard a soft knock on the door.

Charley cleared her throat and stood. "Come in."

Annie breezed into the small room and stopped. "I'm sorry I'm late."

She was even prettier in person. Her eyes were bright, and her gorgeous hair was full of curls and shine. It hung past her shoulders, and Bristol wondered if it was as soft as it looked. "Oh, my God. You're Bristol Baines. Hi. I'm Annie Foster." She turned to Lizzy. "You were at the hospital, right?"

"Hi, Annie. I'm Lizzy. Bristol's manager."

Bristol could tell she was confused, excited, but also completely comfortable in the room with them. That never happened, but both Charley and Annie treated them like normal people. Annie's handshake was soft but firm. She unfolded a metal chair stacked against the wall and sat next to Charley.

"I don't even know how to ask this, but what can I do for you? Charley said Top Shelf was looking to book me for a night or two." She folded her hands in front of her and smiled at Bristol and Lizzy.

"Do you know Ali Hart?"

Annie nodded. "She's great. She had a few hits earlier this year. I like her music a lot." She cocked her head inquisitively at them as though the information was in front of her, but she needed their help getting the puzzle pieces to fit.

"Her wife went into early labor, so she had to leave the tour," Lizzy said. "We had two opening acts for Denver—Ali and Fast Cars—but now we're down to one."

"Lizzy showed me your videos on YouTube and thinks you would be a great fit for us. You're from here, so people will be excited to see you onstage. One of their own. We know it's last minute, but would you be willing to open tonight and tomorrow for me?"

If Annie was surprised, she hid it well. "Of course. It sounds like the opportunity of a lifetime. What do you think, Charley?" She turned to her friend, and an adorable look of disbelief passed between them.

"Will she get paid?" Charley asked.

Annie gasped, and Bristol laughed.

"Definitely. Not only will you get paid, but you are more than welcome to livestream for your channel," Lizzy said.

A slight blush feathered across Annie's cheeks, as though she was embarrassed that they watched her. "That would be wonderful."

"We know it's last minute, and we'll try to market it the best way we can. We'll promote it on all social-media platforms. Can you be at the arena at five today? That'll give you a few minutes to practice before going on."

"Of course. This sounds amazing. Just tell me where and I'll be there," Annie said.

Lizzy slid a laminated pass at her. "This will get you in the VIP parking lot and into the arena. Head to the south entrance and show them this. Here's my number. Just text when you're there, and I'll send one of my assistants to get you. You'll take the stage at seven thirty and will have a twenty-five-minute set. Fast Cars will perform after you. You're more than welcome to stay backstage during the concert, and we'll give you VIP seats for your family and friends. How many tickets would you like?"

Annie sat back and looked at Charley. "What are you doing tonight?"

"I'm going to watch my best friend open for Bristol Baines tonight. That's what I'm doing." Charley put her arm around Annie and gave her a side hug. "I'm so happy for you, Annie. This is such an amazing opportunity."

"I'd love to take my sister and niece," Annie said. She turned to Bristol. "Peyton just turned five. She has headphones for concerts."

"Why don't we give you four backstage passes, and everyone can either take a seat in VIP or stay backstage. And we can give everyone ear plugs," Bristol said.

"I'm so honored. Thank you so much. I look forward to tonight and tomorrow," Annie said.

"Let's get a picture of you two together so I can start promoting," Lizzy said.

"Try to blur out the background. I know it's a mess," Charley said.

"No worries. We'll just do closeups," Bristol said. She removed her hat and shook out her hair. "I picked a bad day to not wear a lot of makeup." She stood when Annie did, and they moved toward one another, cautiously and shyly. "Do you mind if I put my arm around your shoulders?"

"I don't mind at all," Annie said.

Bristol felt a slight quiver when she touched Annie. Honestly, she wasn't sure if it was her or Annie who shook. Maybe it was both of them. Bristol smiled because, of course, the All-American girl would smell like cinnamon and apples. "I'm sorry this is so last minute. We're normally very organized."

Annie's straight white teeth peeked out when her full red lips blossomed into a smile. "I get it. Sometimes babies want to get here sooner than we're ready for them. I feel for your friend, Ali."

"Do you have any children? It sounds like you're speaking from experience," Bristol asked. She wasn't sure why, but Annie didn't strike her as somebody who had kids.

"I just have a niece."

"You're going to have to scooch closer together. I know it's tight in here, but I need just your faces," Lizzy said. She snapped several photos and handed her phone to Bristol and Annie. "Scroll through them and mark the ones you like."

Immediately, Annie moved closer and pulled her hair over her shoulder. "You're very photogenic. The camera loves you."

"I could say the same for you. Looks like we take good pictures together," Bristol said.

Annie nodded and moved away. "Okay. I'll see you all at five, and I promise to not disappoint. I'll play my most popular songs, and if they don't sound great, we can switch them up tomorrow."

"Her music is amazing. Don't listen to anything she says right now. That's her anxiety talking," Charley quickly pushed Annie out the door. "Go get ready. I'll see you later. Text me the tickets, and I'll round everybody up."

"Thank you for letting us use your office." Bristol hated that everyone accommodated her so quickly because it was disruptive, and she hated being that person.

Charley waved her off. "Are you kidding me? Annie is my best friend, and she deserves a break. Thank you for finding her and giving her the opportunity. You won't be disappointed."

"I don't think we will either," Bristol said. She piled her hair back under the hat and slipped on the dark sunglasses. "Now I want a coffee. It smells so good in here."

"I'll make it for you personally, and it's on the house. It's the least I can do for you," Charley said.

Bristol and Lizzy had about eight minutes of uninterrupted small talk at a table near the back before somebody approached them.

"No, I'm not her, but I get that a lot," she said and grabbed her cup. "See you later, Charley."

Charley waved back as though Bristol and Lizzy were regulars who had stopped by for an early afternoon caffeine jolt. She smiled all the way back to the car, holding on to the feeling of normalcy. This was what she missed. This was exactly what she wanted. This was what she was willing to give up everything for. Normalcy.

Chapter Three

Annie raced to her car. It was after one. She had four hours to decide on a set list, get her equipment ready, find something to wear, and have her hair and makeup done. This was a job for a professional. She called her salon and waited on hold for five minutes.

"This is Jazz."

Annie wished she had Jazz's voice. It was raspy and sexy and everything hers was not. "Jazz. It's Annie. I have an emergency."

"Hair or makeup?"

"Both."

"I can work you in right now, but once my two o'clock gets here, I'll have to work on her."

"Jazz, I'm opening for Bristol Baines tonight." Annie knew she sounded winded and overly excited, but she was, and she didn't care.

"*The* Bristol Baines? Are you kidding me?" Jazz hissed her questions as though this were a secret.

"No. I have to be at the arena at five, and I don't trust my hair with anyone else. Plus, you know how bad I am at makeup."

Jazz yelled, "Bex. Push all my appointments back thirty minutes. We have an emergency."

"I love you, and I'll see you in five minutes," Annie said.

"I want every single detail. I'll be waiting with coffee," Jazz said.

Annie disconnected the call and checked her time. Jazz wouldn't let her leave until she was perfect. She'd already decided to wear her tight black pants, her Doc Martens, and a sapphire sleeveless top that emphasized the color of her eyes. What if she wasn't good enough or what if she had a meltdown on a stage that big? She needed to calm down. She did the only thing she knew what to do when life got overwhelming. She called her sister.

"What are you doing tonight and/or tomorrow night?" she asked.

"Hey, sis. What's going on?"

Annie tried hard to keep her voice even, but the excitement kept bubbling up. "How would you and Peyton and Chase like to go to the Bristol Baines concert?"

Sarah paused. "How did you get tickets? That sounds amazing. Chase is working, but if Peyton is feeling up to it, I say yes. Does this have anything to do with Lizzy? Did she offer you tickets? When did you talk to her?"

Annie smiled at her sister's excitement. "Oh, I got backstage passes and VIP seats because I'm going to be an opening act!"

Sarah howled into the phone. "Oh, my God! Are you serious?"

"Yes! I'm on my way to see Jazz so she can do my hair and makeup."

"Okay, okay, okay. Deep breath. What are you going to wear?" Sarah asked.

"Something black. I'm more concerned about my hair and makeup," Annie said.

"Don't they have somebody to do that for you?"

"Don't put the cart before the horse. I'm not about to go in there and start demanding things. I've got a twenty-five-minute gig and no time to practice, so I'm freaking out."

"What do you need me to do?" Sarah asked.

Annie loved that her sister was the first to jump in as though she wasn't the busiest person Annie knew.

"I need you to show up and have a great time."

"So, what happened? How did they find you? Did they call you? I mean, I gave them my business card, but I never got a call." Her sister sounded dejected.

"They called The Night Owl. This wouldn't have happened if you hadn't brought Lizzy into the ward," Annie said.

"Talk about fate that you sang a Bristol Baines's song when her manager was there," Sarah said.

"It's serendipitous," Annie said. She believed things happened for a reason and those reasons were mostly good.

"I'm so proud of you. Maybe this will be your big break," Sarah said.

"I'll just be happy to live in the moment," Annie said. She respected Bristol's success. It was the ultimate goal—all the fortune and fame at her fingertips. Annie didn't struggle financially like most musicians, but she dreamed of top-tier success. How would she do in front of thirty thousand people? Would she do her best or freeze onstage? "Okay. I'm at the salon. I'll text you later with the details."

"I'm so proud of you."

Annie disconnected the call and burst through the door of the salon.

Jazz was ready at her station with a hair straightener in hand. "Over here." She waved her to a chair in the back of the salon. "Have a seat. Tinks is going to help." She spun the chair around and pointed for Annie to sit.

"Thank you so much for getting me in. I'm so nervous." Annie bit her bottom lip and rubbed her hands on her pants out of nervous habit.

"I'm so excited for you. Let's get you ready for center stage," Jazz said.

Annie put her hand to her stomach and took a deep breath. "When you put it like that, I feel sick."

Jazz turned her chair so they were facing one another. "You'll rock the stage. You've been training for this for years."

"That's just me and a phone. And the coffee shop has maybe fifty people on a good night. This is a stadium. Playing in front of my city is exciting but also frightening," Annie said. She looked at herself in the mirror when Jazz turned the chair back around. Her brow was furrowed with determination. "Okay, Jazz. Make me look like a star."

"I'm supposed to check in here, I think."

Annie handed the security guard the pass Lizzy had given her. He inspected the front, the back, and finally pressed his lips against his shoulder walkie to read off the number on the tag to somebody who was probably in Bristol's security.

"Okay. You're clear to go in. Just turn left. Someone will meet you there to escort you where you need to be."

This was really happening, Annie thought. She reached the end of a short corridor, and a young man with an impressive pompadour, stylish glasses, and a killer smile greeted her. She returned his infectious grin.

"Annie Foster?" he asked. She nodded. "I'm Vaughn, one of Lizzy's assistants. Follow me." She could hear music and wondered who was warming up. Was it the band who was slated to go onstage after her, or was it Bristol Baines? She wanted to walk down one of the corridors that opened to the stadium and see, but Vaughn was on a mission to get her to where she was expected.

"Hi, Annie. Come on in." Lizzy greeted her as people with defined roles buzzed about. It was wild. Annie wasn't sure when Lizzy spoke if she was talking to her or somebody in her headset. "Bristol's warming up onstage now, and then you'll have a few minutes to practice."

Annie nodded. "Thank you."

"I have to go to the tech booth. Want to go with me? You can leave your guitar right there." Lizzy pointed to a corner and ordered one of the people darting around to stop what they were doing and stay with it. Annie smiled a silent thank you to them and followed Lizzy out the door and down to the open-air arena.

"She sounds amazing." Annie couldn't believe that in just two hours, she would be up there on that stage singing for everyone in the arena to hear. Bristol was wearing light blue shorts, sandals, and a sweat-drenched, long-sleeved T-shirt. "She looks great but also hot."

"The long-sleeve helps get her ready to perform under all the lights. Summer concerts are the worst. If she doesn't stay hydrated, she'll drop after the concert."

Annie stood beside Lizzy and watched as Bristol marched down the walkway of the stage belting out words to one of her major hits. Impressive was too mild a word to describe Bristol. She was remarkable. Annie couldn't wait to see her in front of her fans. "She's a real powerhouse." It was an observation, one she didn't realize she'd said out loud until Lizzy responded.

"There's a reason her fans have loved her for years. She's been doing this half her life."

"It must be so rewarding to do what you've loved your entire life," Annie said. Lizzy rolled her eyes, but Annie pretended not to see. It wasn't her place to question anything. She was thankful she was here and wasn't going to do anything to jeopardize her shot.

"It's been a journey," Lizzy said.

"Have you been with her the entire time?" Annie asked. Her gaze never left Bristol, and when Bristol gave her a wave from the stage, Annie looked around to see if the wave was for her or somebody else. She shyly waved back.

"Since day one. I heard her playing at a fair when she was fourteen and had her signed within the week. She didn't cut her first album until she was sixteen. We had to get her voice and piano lessons. Natural talent goes only so far. We had to polish the rough edges."

Annie couldn't believe that. Bristol had a range that all singers envied. That talent wasn't taught. It was discovered.

"Okay. Let's get you onstage. How are you feeling?"

Annie took a deep breath. "I'm excited. I hope I'm well received." What she really meant was that she hoped she didn't crash and burn or get booed off the stage.

"You're good. Come on. Let's kick her off so you can get some playing time," Lizzy said.

The palpitations in her chest became more pronounced the closer they got to the stage. She wasn't worrying about screwing up. She knew her own songs forward and backward. She was worried about people not liking her. She was worried that her music wasn't good enough to open for Bristol Baines.

"Sondra's bringing your guitar so we don't waste any time. I hope you don't mind," Lizzy said loudly over Bristol's voice that reverberated throughout the stadium. Would her voice be that strong?

"That's fine." The guitar was in a hard case, so she wasn't afraid of somebody banging it up. She stood by as Lizzy said something to the sound technicians, pointed to something on one of the computers, and motioned to Bristol to wrap it up by spinning her finger in a circle. Lizzy guided her to the side of the stage just as Bristol finished her song. She exited with her band and stopped in front of them. Her energy was so large that Annie took a step back.

"You sounded great," Annie said.

Bristol gave Annie a smile that made everything inside her turn to mush. She was sweating, breathing hard, but looked so beautiful and totally in her element. Annie's bones felt soft and her knees weak at the sheer power she exuded.

"Thank you," she said.

Bristol took the towel from Lizzy and wiped her face and brow. "Looks like you're up now." She motioned for Annie to take the stage.

Annie didn't remember walking to the microphone or how her guitar managed to work its way around her neck. Reality didn't set in until she strummed the first chord. She made a few tweaks on the tuning pegs out of habit and had her first flutter of anxiety on a stage bigger than any she'd ever been on before.

"Start strumming and we'll adjust your sound."

She couldn't tell who was advising her because the sunlight was sharp against her eyes, and she couldn't see past the stage. She randomly strummed a tune until she realized she was playing a jingle she'd created for an all-natural toothpaste last week. She quickly flipped to a faster song, closed her eyes to find her center, and started singing. The feedback was too much. "Can you raise the mic and lower the amp?" she asked. She gave the techs a thumbs-up when she liked what she heard. She sang one song from start to finish and whirled around when she heard applause coming from behind her. Bristol and Lizzy were behind her onstage.

"That sounded great. You're a natural onstage," Bristol said.

"I had no doubt," Lizzy said.

Annie blushed even though she knew they would be watching at some point, just not in rehearsals. "Thank you again for the opportunity. I think I'm ready." Annie wasn't sure she'd ever be ready for something this large, but she wasn't going to shy away from it. It was her dream.

"Do you have a favorite party anthem? Like a cover song that you like playing that really gets your audience pumped up?" Bristol asked.

Annie laughed. "Yeah, yours."

A smile and blush spread across Bristol's face. "Okay, besides one of mine, and not 'Baby Shark' because I saw that video. What's another song?"

Annie chuckled at the thought of Bristol bellowing out the lyrics to the earworm kid song. "Is this to get the audience pumped for the next band?" Her mind drew a blank on the name. Something like Kicking Tires or Burning Rubber. It had something to do with cars.

"No. I was thinking I could sneak out onstage and sing maybe half a song to get the crowd pumped up with you. If you want," Bristol said.

"I can't believe this is happening," Annie said. She smiled as Bristol and Lizzy laughed. "Okay, seriously, I love a lot of classics from the Beatles to U2, The Pretenders, anything Pat Benatar."

Bristol held her hand up. "Do you know 'Brass in Pocket'?"

Annie tuned her guitar and started playing. It was a sexy song and easy to play on the guitar. Bristol nodded and grabbed an electric guitar from one of her roadies. She played but let Annie sing solo until the chorus. She jumped in, and their voices fused in such a beautiful way that Annie felt it all the way from her fingertips to her toes. She couldn't take her eyes off Bristol. Her voice was sexy and confident, as if she was born to be in front of a microphone. Even though Annie knew Bristol preferred the piano, she didn't make a single mistake on the guitar. She honestly couldn't remember when the song ended, only that her fingers stopped strumming.

"Wow. That was amazing." Lizzy clapped and stood beside them onstage. "That should be the song you end with. People will be screaming."

Annie broke eye contact first. "That felt right." She struggled with the strap of her guitar while Bristol returned the electric guitar to the stand.

"I liked that a lot," Bristol said. She looked at her watch. "We should go. I need to shower and get ready. Plus, Fast Cars needs the stage. The doors open in thirty minutes." Bristol's sexy smile gave Annie such a rush. "We're going to do great things tonight."

CHAPTER FOUR

S he's really cute, and talented to boot," Lizzy said.
Bristol slipped into jeans and a fresh tank top. Her long hair was pulled up into a ponytail. She looked relaxed and carefree, when she was anything but. The only thing exciting about tonight was Annie. "I'm glad you found her."

"Who knew that getting fluids at a hospital would lead to us finding unknown talent," Lizzy said.

"She's only unknown to us." Bristol's need to defend Annie was completely unwarranted. But she didn't want to talk about why Lizzy needed hydrating. Alcohol on tour had been a sore subject, and Bristol was trying to keep her shit together and not mother hen Lizzy. Her job was to sing her songs, play her music, and sell out stadiums, not babysit her crew. "She has quite the local following. Not to mention her online presence." She rolled the bottom of her jeans and kicked off her flip-flops. "I think going out onstage barefoot sends a casual message, and I want the crowd to have fun tonight." Bristol had insisted on twice the amount of crowd security this tour. Fun was great, but she hated when people fought or got too rowdy. Her music wasn't like that, but some people thought all rules went out the window if a concert was in town.

"It's the perfect look. Let's get out there and watch Annie. I want to see how she does," Lizzy said.

They left Bristol's dressing room, followed closely by four personal bodyguards who flanked them the moment they shut the door. The halls were filled with arena workers and Bristol's own staff. People shouted, "Break a leg" or "Have fun." The well wishes echoed in the walkway as she made her way to the stage.

Annie had just started strumming her guitar. Bristol could tell she was slightly nervous but had the attention of the people who were ready for the show to start.

"Hello, Denver! How excited are you? I'm Annie Foster, and I'm going to play a few songs to get you ready for Bristol Baines."

Annie paused as the crowd applauded politely. "Most of you don't know this, but I'm from Denver. This is my hometown."

The crowd whooped and whistled, and Bristol could see Annie smiling from ear to ear. She kicked the set off with a faster song, and most of the crowd paid attention. Bristol knew the opening act could keep the crowd's interest for only about twenty minutes. After that, fans left to replenish their drinks or go to the restroom.

The first two rows were reserved for VIP. Half of the people hadn't made it to those rows, but some of those people were backstage watching the concert from the wings, a perk of backstage passes. Across the stage, Bristol saw Charley, a little girl wearing an eye patch, who she assumed was Annie's niece, and an attractive woman holding the little girl's hand. The woman looked like Annie, only she wasn't as crisp and fresh. Bristol waved to Peyton, and once Peyton saw her, she jumped up and down, waving back with excitement. Her mouth and nose were covered in a mask, but her excitement was unmistakable. Seeing children appreciate music always made Bristol's heart soar. If she could make a difference in just a few children's lives with her music, she would consider herself a success.

"Look at the crowd. Most of the time they don't give a shit about the opening act," Lizzy said.

"It helps that she's from here." Bristol knew local people helped keep the concert flowing. Her Instagram post of her and Annie blew up. Ninety-nine percent of the comments were positive. Bristol had her social media manager delete all comments that weren't kind. That was a full-time job. Bristol had access to the accounts but rarely engaged. It sucked the energy from her when she did, so she hired someone else to do it. "How many songs is she doing?"

Lizzy looked at her list. "Five, with the last one being the duet. She's on number three now."

"They're pretty impressed with her. Mostly everyone in their seats is paying attention." Bristol was far enough away that fans couldn't see her, but she could see them. All eyes were on Annie. She wasn't cocky, but she was sure of herself, and that was sexy. Her music was good even if it was a little slow for Bristol's taste, and her comfort level in front of the crowd improved with each passing minute.

"This is my last song. I want to thank you all for being so nice to me. I'm Annie Foster, and if you like my music, please subscribe to my YouTube channel." She tuned her guitar while a roadie quickly set up another microphone.

That was Bristol's cue. She slipped the electric guitar around her neck and started strumming from behind Annie. The crowd couldn't see her yet. She waited until Annie started singing and moved to center stage. The crowd shrieked once they realized who had joined Annie. Annie kept singing, and when Bristol came in at the chorus, the audience was deafening. Bristol smiled at Annie while they sang. With her raspy voice and Annie's crystal-clear one, their sound combined was incredible. It was as if they'd been singing together for years, though this was only their second time.

"Bristol Baines, everyone!" Annie shouted.

"Annie Foster, everyone!" Bristol shouted. She gave the guitar one final strum and left the stage for Annie to wrap up her set.

"Thank you, Bristol, for inviting me to sing on this tour. I'm opening again tomorrow night, and I hope to see you all. Next up is Fast Cars from California. They'll take the stage in twenty minutes, so you have time to get that concert swag you regretted not buying when you walked in. Thank you for such a warm welcome."

Bristol watched as Annie walked over to where her sister and niece were standing. Her niece threw herself against Annie and hugged her. Bristol turned to Lizzy. "Have somebody bring me a child's concert shirt and a few Angel/Devil tumblers." Lizzy immediately called for somebody in her headset and held up two fingers, indicating it would be only a couple of minutes.

"You need to get back to your dressing room and get ready for the concert. You're on in an hour," Lizzy said.

"I will. I just want to give Annie's niece a great concert experience."

Lizzy looked at her watch. "Okay. We'll wait."

"Can you have somebody escort them over?" Bristol asked. She knew Annie's friends and family wouldn't be able to get close unless she or Lizzy gave the okay. Having bodyguards was nice when she needed them, but she was getting tired of them around her twenty-four seven. She watched as one of Lizzy's three assistants approached them. "She did a remarkable job. We should ask her to finish the tour with us. Six weeks on the road would give her a ton of fresh exposure."

"We already have people lined up in Albuquerque, Santa Fe, and San Francisco," Lizzy said.

"We have twenty-one concerts left, and only six have full acts. Why don't we ask Annie if she wants to pick up shows where we don't have an opening act?"

"I think she's great, but maybe let's wait until the reviews come in before we make a rash decision."

Bristol bit her lip to keep from screaming at Lizzy. She loved her, but every time Bristol wanted something, Lizzy was always there to tell her why she didn't need it. She turned to Lizzy and folded her arms across her chest. Very quietly, she said, "I'm not asking. I need you to make it happen."

Lizzy visibly bristled. "Fine. I'll ask. Same salary and all the perks?" Her tone was cold.

Bristol knew she'd have to tread lightly. They had less than six weeks on the road, and tensions were high. This always happened. They got snippy near the end of the tour, spent time apart, missed one another, and came back stronger. It was a cycle.

"Yes. Offer her a seat on one of the buses. Fans are going to eat her up."

Lizzy turned slowly. "Are you changing the lineup after one set? Because that's going to piss off Fast Cars. Make sure you're doing this for the right reasons."

"What's that supposed to mean?" Bristol asked.

"Let's give her a week or two. Let's see how she does when she's not playing to the home crowd. Oh. Here comes Clarissa with the concert goods. Let's get Annie and her family over here."

Bristol stared at Lizzy's back when she took a few steps away to bark commands on her headset. She didn't have a lot of time to get ready, but she wanted to make a good impression on Annie's family. It mattered what Annie thought of her. She smiled when she saw Annie's wild blond curls bob through the throngs of people between them. Her sister was attractive, too, but looked tired and slightly frazzled, as though life was pressing her shoulders down and she was struggling to stay afloat.

"I like your music," Peyton said.

Bristol knelt in front of Peyton and high-fived her. "I'm so glad you could make it tonight." Bristol gave the concert goods to Peyton. "I thought you might like a souvenir." She smiled harder when the little girl squealed with delight.

"Thank you so much for having us." Annie's sister, Sarah, introduced herself. Her nervousness was not lost on Bristol.

"I'm just thankful you and Lizzy ran into each other at the hospital, or I wouldn't have Annie on the venue tonight," Bristol said.

"We're so proud of her," Sarah said and wrapped her arm around Annie's shoulder. The smile on Annie's face was so pure that Bristol felt something inside her shift. Maybe it was the weight of the show and being on the road for months, but right now, in this moment, Annie's genuine appreciation made her heart soar.

"It shows," Bristol said. Lizzy pointed to her watch. "And I need to get ready for my set. Have a good time. Annie, thank you so much. You rocked tonight." Annie's face lit up with the pure joy of doing what she loved. Bristol remembered when she felt butterflies before each concert, when stepping onstage meant everything to her. It had been too long since she had such an uncomplicated feeling.

❖

Holding the final note at the end of the show always gave Bristol a rush. Onstage, she loved the attention. It empowered her and filled her soul with love. People were happy and having the time of their lives. She just wished once she stepped offstage, she could turn off the fame and just be a regular person.

"Good night, Denver! You're amazing!" She waved and skipped offstage, knowing that in about thirty seconds, she would be back to sing her latest smash hit "Forever." She would end the encore with her very first number-one song from when she was sixteen. Over a decade later her fans still loved it.

Lizzy handed her a towel to dab the sweat off her face and wipe it off her neck. She downed an entire bottle of water and jogged back to the microphone. She was singing the song a cappella. Last week, when somebody in the band accidentally kicked a cable loose from the sound system, Bristol sang the song a cappella, and it was a smash. Reviews of that concert, as well as social media blasts, revived the song, and it found its way back to the top one hundred.

Never say never
I'll love you always and forever.

It was a sad song that Bristol wrote after her first girlfriend dumped her, but it wasn't about their brutal breakup. Sterling was the daughter of Top Shelf Records president, Tyson Mayfield, and made it a point to meet all up-and-coming talent. Bristol thought the nineteen-year-old was sophisticated and fun. When they kissed for the first time, Bristol was deliriously happy. Her life was snowballing into perfection. She was cutting tracks for a debut album that she was assured was going to take the world by storm. She had a girlfriend who was encouraging and beautiful and gave her inspiration. They dated for three months before Bristol found out Sterling was sleeping with the lead singer of The Red Zone. It wouldn't have been so bad if she hadn't found out by seeing it on Sterling's Instagram. When Bristol confronted her, Sterling said she was a delusional kid. Their relationship had never meant anything to Sterling. Bristol was crushed.

On the heels of their breakup, her parents informed her they were divorcing. Her strong foundation crumbled, so she threw herself into writing songs. Emotions that were bottled up because of her parents' nasty divorce poured out onto the page, and five songs made it onto her debut album, including "Forever." People could relate to it with any kind of heartache.

"Thank you so much for coming tonight. Be safe out there!" She waved and jogged off the stage for the last time.

"Great concert, Bristol!" somebody yelled from behind the curtain.

She waved and pushed her way through the crew backstage. Her security team flanked her and got her safely to her dressing room. She kept her head down, and once she was behind closed doors, she exhaled deeply. If there was only a way to tune out everyone after each concert, she wouldn't feel so overwhelmed.

She plopped onto the couch and picked at the fruit and vegetable tray on the coffee table. Lizzy would be in soon with a recap, but the first twenty minutes belonged to Bristol alone. It was one of her demands. She needed the quiet after the storm of a two-hour concert. Sneaking out early to get to the hotel was impossible, as thirty thousand people were trying to leave the venue at the same time. She had an hour before traffic thinned enough for them to break free.

Plus, so many people hung around back to get a glimpse of her getting onto the tour bus. She was always on alert when out in public, even if it was just for thirty seconds. Her Instagram feed was nothing but pictures of the concert. It made her smile. She scowled at the knock at the door but didn't make a move to answer it.

"I know I'm early, but I talked to Annie." Lizzy's voice was full of excitement.

Bristol couldn't help but smile. That meant Annie was on board with her idea of finishing out the tour. She grabbed a slice of apple and sat back on the couch. "Come in."

"Great job tonight." Lizzy beamed. That was one of the good things about your manager being your friend. They forgave easily.

"Thanks. It felt like a great show. Fast Cars and Annie did a wonderful job."

Lizzy sat down and grabbed a few grapes off the tray. "No glitches, no issues. Only one person got arrested for disorderly conduct. Not bad considering you had a sold-out stadium."

Bristol wasn't in the mood for small talk. She wanted to hear about Annie. "How did you get Annie to commit so quickly?"

"Her sister answered for her after agreeing to watch her cat. Apparently, Annie's a jingle writer and can work remotely." Lizzy laughed. "I think she was in shock. She went from coffee-shop musician to opening for the largest pop superstar in a day. Sometimes it's about who you know."

Bristol knew luck was a part of it, but Annie had genuine talent, too. "And sometimes it's about being at the right place at the right time. Great find, Lizzy." Bristol was rewarded with the first warm smile from her all night.

CHAPTER FIVE

How is this happening?"

Annie could barely control her excitement. She muffled a scream into the palm of her hand and quickly looked in the back seat in case her outburst woke Peyton. Her sister reached over and squeezed her leg.

"It's because you're wonderful and you're finally getting much deserved recognition. I'm so happy for you, baby sis. And don't worry about anything. I'll take care of your plants, Raven, and your mail. Whatever you need. When do they want you to start the tour?"

"In four days. I don't know if I'm supposed to fly out to meet them or what. Her manager is supposed to meet with me tomorrow with the contract. Do I sign it? Should I have somebody look it over?"

"Of course you should sign it, but I can't believe they wouldn't let you seek professional advice first. I'm sure you'll be able to forward it to your lawyer. Bristol isn't going to screw you over."

"I didn't get that vibe either." Annie looked out the window at the sparse traffic on the highway. It was a late night for all of them, but Annie didn't think she could sleep tonight. Her dream, the one she'd never let blossom in her head because she never thought it was possible, was coming true. She pulled up her Instagram to see the comments on her quick post from earlier today when she informed her followers she would be opening for Bristol Baines. "Wow. My subscribers are so sweet. Listen to this. 'Congratulations. Well deserved.'" She laughed. "Okay. Listen to this one. 'Bristol Baines should be opening for you. Can't wait to see your beautiful music climb the charts.'" She turned to face her sister in the darkness. "I can't believe this is happening."

Sarah's voice lowered. "Mom and Dad would be so proud of you."

That was a zinger to her heart. "Thanks, sis. I know they're proud."

"And we're all proud of you, too. Oh, hell. Charley was probably your second biggest fan there," Sarah said.

"I saw her dancing away. I love my family. You're all so supportive."

"Promise you'll buy me a loaded SUV when you become as big and famous as Bristol," Annie said. She patted the dashboard of the ten-year-old minivan lovingly. "But I will forever love you, Karen."

"I've never understood that. Why Karen?"

"Because she's temperamental and bossy and an overall pain in the ass."

Annie laughed. "I promise to buy you the best car ever. You definitely deserve it." Her phone dinged. It was Charley.

Are you home yet, superstar, or are you out partying with Bristol?

I'm in a minivan going home. I doubt Bristol's even thinking about me.

Annie didn't even get to tell Bristol it was a great concert. Lizzy intercepted her on her way backstage to congratulate Bristol. She directed her away from Bristol's dressing room and flippantly offered the opening gig for the next six weeks before giving her instructions for tomorrow. It had happened in such a flash that Annie blinked at Lizzy until the words sank in. Thankfully, Sarah was there to answer for her.

Just look at her Instagram. You're famous, my friend. I'll be there tomorrow night.

Shit. Charley didn't even know about the offer. If she told her now, Charley would call screaming, and waking up Peyton wasn't a good idea. She would tell her tomorrow when she went to get coffee and a doughnut. It seemed so surreal. She was still processing. *Good night. See you tomorrow.*

"Did you tell Charley?"

Annie shook her head. "I need time to let it sink in." Annie looked at her watch. "It was only an hour ago. Weird how life can change so quickly."

"I still can't believe it," Sarah said.

"I know. This is all so fast."

Sarah pulled next to Annie's building and put the car in park.

They hugged longer than usual. "I'm so proud of you, baby sis. Congratulations. Try to get some sleep."

Annie wiped her tears away and laughed. "Thank you. I wouldn't be where I am today if it wasn't for you."

"Stop it. You're going to make me cry, and I don't cry," Sarah said. The last time Annie remembered her sister crying was when their parents died. Even when Peyton was diagnosed, Sarah put all her energy into getting her daughter healthy. Maybe Sarah cried in private, but never around Annie. She was the rock, the foundation of their small family. Annie was the emotional one. She slipped out of the van and quietly closed the door. "I love you."

"I love you more."

❖

"Well, if it isn't Denver's biggest superstar."

Annie braced herself as Charley greeted her with a warm, tight hug. "How do you feel?" She poured Annie a cup of coffee and plopped a cinnamon sugar doughnut on a plate. "Let's go sit. I want to hear about everything." Charley grabbed her own cup of coffee and led Annie to a table. It was after the morning rush, so the place was nearly empty.

"I don't think you're prepared to hear what I have to say," Annie said. Charley reached for her hands. "Honestly, I'm still reeling."

Charley took a deep breath. "Tell me. Oh, my God. Tell me before I lose my shit."

Annie took a sip of her coffee and a bite of her doughnut and laughed when Charley leaned back in her chair and crossed her arms.

"Really?"

She could almost feel Charley's anxiety from across table. "So, after the concert, Lizzy, remember her?"

"Uh, yeah. She was in my office. Of course I remember her."

"Well, she asked me if I would be interested in opening for Bristol for the rest of the tour." Annie stood up and threw her hands up in the air.

"Shut up!" Charley stood and threw her hands up, too. "Holy shit, Annie. Holy shit!"

"I know, right?" Annie prepared herself for another bone-crushing hug. Charley didn't disappoint and twirled her in the process. She begged Charley to stop out of embarrassment at the attention.

"What does this mean? You're going to be on the road with her, with the tour?" Charley asked.

"This means I won't be here for open-mic night," Annie said.

"I'm sure once people find out, they'll be fine. I'll still have it." Charley was all smiles, and it was hard for Annie not to soak in Charley's happiness for her.

"That would be wonderful."

"If you give me your sign-on info, I can step in as hostess. I mean, it won't be the same, but at least locals will still get the online presence."

"That's even better." She texted her login information and promised to check in with Charley.

After two more hugs, Annie left the coffee shop and walked three blocks to her lawyer's office. She'd forwarded the contract the minute she got it. Her lawyer, Dani Grant, had cleared her lunch hour to review the contract and meet with Annie.

"Please have a seat, Annie. I'll let Dani know you're here." The receptionist was attractive and friendly and always kind to Annie. She didn't frequent her lawyer's office, but the administrative assistants always knew her name. "Thank you." She only had to wait a minute before Dani rounded the corner to greet her.

"It's nice to see you, Annie. Come on back."

Dani was stunning. Ice-blond hair and no-nonsense professionalism that Annie admired. She was a nervous talker, whereas Dani seemed to calculate the importance of every word. They never discussed personal lives or made small talk. Time was money, and Dani was entirely too busy for unnecessary words. Annie followed her, eager to find out if the contract was good or if Dani red-marked it. Dani pointed to a small table in her office.

"Have a seat."

Annie obliged. "What do you think of the contract?"

"I had our entertainment lawyer review it, and we think it's solid. We made only one change. The contract says you can't record from stage, but they probably don't realize that you make a living from your online tip jar. Taking that away from you is taking away your livelihood."

"That's weird because I livestreamed last night, and they were okay with it. Actually, they suggested it," Annie said.

"I'm sure it's because this is a standard contract. But just in case, I've made some adjustments. Their on-the-road offer is more than fair, but you still need to maintain your online presence. I gave them two options. Either pay you more per show to offset the income loss generated from your YouTube channel, or let you film from the stage during your set only." She slid a copy of her proposed revisions in front of Annie and pointed at the tabs. "Just page through the changes, and if you're okay, I'll send it back. If they accept, they'll revise on their end and resend. Either way, you still go on tonight. This contract is for the upcoming shows only."

"Do you think they'll rescind the offer? Is this too pushy?" Annie asked.

Dani barked out a noise that wasn't quite a laugh. "This is not pushy at all. They know that what we're asking them to do is perfectly legal and fair. My suggestion is tame. I promise. Plus, if you were able to do these things last night, then it shouldn't be a problem for them to make changes."

Annie took a deep breath. "Okay. What do I need to do?"

"Just sign this form saying you agree to the changes so we have the paperwork here. If they send back a revised contract that isn't what we're asking for, I'll reach out again a bit more firmly."

Annie must have had a look of panic because Dani touched her hand. "Don't worry. They're expecting some sort of pushback. It's a stupid game lawyers play. Just remember to check your emails this afternoon with any revisions." Dani stood, indicating the meeting was over.

"Thank you so much. I would have just signed it without looking it over."

"That's why I'm here. Let me walk you out," Dani said.

Annie looked at her watch. The entire meeting had lasted less than fifteen minutes. "Thank you for meeting me. I really appreciate it."

Dani nodded and signed a piece of paper the receptionist handed her. "Take care, Annie. And good luck. I'm happy for you."

Annie smiled and watched Dani retreat behind glass doors. The law office had a contemporary vibe that was surprisingly light and airy and the exact opposite of what Annie thought a law office should look like.

She was having one of the best weeks of her life. Twenty-four hours ago she had been invited to do two shows that not only paid her well but gave her massive exposure. Now she was getting ready to go on tour with Bristol Baines, and that was going to change her life. Last night onstage she didn't mess up at all. Everything was on the line, even though it was the most frightening and the most exhilarating thing she had ever done.

CHAPTER SIX

I'm glad she had a lawyer look it over. It shows she's smart and doesn't want to get taken advantage of." Bristol handed Lizzy the iPad. "Sign it. Accept the changes. We already told her she could film."

Lizzy nodded and shot off an email to her lawyers. "I'm meeting with her before the set to go over some ground rules for being on the road."

"Do you need me there?" Bristol hoped she didn't sound desperate. Annie was cute and fun, and Bristol missed talking to new people.

"No. You rest up for tonight's concert. We're leaving as soon as possible. We have a long drive ahead of us," Lizzy said.

"Do you ever sleep?"

Lizzy stopped typing and looked at Bristol. "I'll sleep when I'm dead. Right now, I need to make sure you eat, rest, and save your voice for tonight. Another sold-out show ahead."

Bristol hid the disappointment of not being invited but didn't press. She'd have time with Annie over the rest of the tour, and Lizzy always knew what was best. From finding her as a kid to protecting her from slimeball producers like Denny Briggs, Lizzy had never steered her wrong. "Okay. Let me know if anything comes up." Bristol sprawled out on the couch when Lizzy closed the door to her dressing room. She needed comfort so did the one thing she did when the world got heavy. She FaceTimed her mom.

"Hi, Mom." Seeing her mom's face on her screen melted away the stress.

"Hey, baby girl. How are you? Where are you?"

"We're in Denver again tonight. We have tomorrow off, then New Mexico and Arizona for a few shows."

"Are you resting enough?"

"It's hard to sleep when the schedule is so grueling. I can't wait until Labor Day. Then I'll be home for good."

"I can't wait to see you. We'll be at your concert here. And Reece is already making plans for the last one."

"I got out for a bit yesterday. Lizzy found a new opening act since Ali had to bolt," Bristol said.

"What happened to Ali?" Concern pinched her mother's features. She'd met Ali several times over the years and even shared family recipes.

"Bethany went into labor early. She's fine. Ali sent a message and a photo of the baby. She's beautiful. Remind me to send it to you." Bristol's stomach dropped when she thought how perfect the Harts were. Ali had everything. A music career, a beautiful wife, and three daughters. She could walk down the street without people rushing her to get a photo or a piece of her clothing. She must have frowned.

"Honey, I know it's been a long tour."

Bristol rubbed her face. "I feel like I've aged so much the last eighteen months."

"It'll be over soon. Now tell me about your outing. It sounds like it went well."

"Lizzy went to the hospital to get a hydration IV and somehow started talking to a nurse from the children's wing whose sister was there performing for sick kids."

"Well, that's a coincidence."

"Get this. She was playing one of my songs."

"Stop it. Really?"

"Yeah, so Lizzy recorded it, showed me, and the rest is history. She's really good. You should look her up. Her name is Annie Foster."

"Oh, is she the one you did a duet with last night? I saw something on Instagram, but it was only a flash. I'll look her up now. Meanwhile, try to get some rest before you go onstage. You look really tired, baby."

Bristol knew that when her mother told her she looked tired, she was being kind. Annette, her makeup artist, would have her hands full tonight getting her ready for the show. At least she could sleep on the bus tomorrow. This was routine for her. She'd push herself hard until she hit a wall and then slept for twelve hours straight. "I promise to rest after tonight."

"Be safe, and we'll see you soon. Just be strong and know that you'll be done soon, and then you can take off as much time as you want."

Bristol had it in her mind that this was the last tour but hadn't shared that idea with anybody other than Lizzy. She also knew that she talked a lot of shit when she was burned out, but this was different. She felt like she was drowning, and it wasn't getting any better. "Thanks, Mom. I'll see you soon."

"Let me know if you need me. I'll be on the first plane out."

"I love you."

"I love you, too."

Talking to her mother always got her in a good mood. Her father wasn't as soft as her mother and couldn't understand why Bristol wasted her time on pop music and love songs. He called her a sellout but didn't say no when she offered to buy him a loft in downtown Los Angeles with her pop-star money. He refused to see that his artwork was selling only because he was Bristol Baines's father. Nobody had cared about his overpriced abstract paintings before she made it big.

They never had a normal father-daughter conversation, and Bristol craved it. She just wanted her father to ask how she was doing and be invested in the conversation. Thinking about him was exhausting. She curled up on the couch, slipped her AirPods in, and meditated enough to relax. She fell into a deep sleep for about an hour and woke with a start when somebody knocked on the door.

"Bristol. Annie's taking the stage in about ten minutes. Your duet will be in about thirty," Lizzy called through the door.

Bristol sat up fast, completely confused by her rapid heartbeat when Lizzy mentioned Annie's name. Maybe the knocking had startled her, and her heart was catching up. "Okay. I'll be out in fifteen." She switched her yoga pants for torn-up jeans and grabbed a black V-neck to throw on over her cami. She had a minimal amount of makeup on, knowing full well that Annette was going to do magical things with her brushes and pencils in about an hour. She was hungry and grabbed a few carrot sticks from the tray. Another knock. This time Bristol opened the door. "I'm starving."

"I thought you might be." Lizzy held a bag up under her nose.

"Butternut squash with fried sage and steamed vegetables. All vegetarian. It's from a restaurant Annie recommended."

Okay, this time the kick-start she felt in her chest when Lizzy said Annie's name couldn't have been a coincidence. There was something about her. "Yum. Do I have enough time to eat it now?"

"No. You don't want to sing with this stuff in your throat. Eat more vegetables. I'll keep this warm until the set with Annie is over."

"It smells delicious." The thought of food made her smile. The fact that it was Annie's recommendation made it special.

"Since we're leaving tonight, there's a twenty-four-hour diner just outside of Denver that we might be able to commandeer for a bit," Lizzy said.

Bristol had to remind herself that Lizzy was trying to make things easier on her. Maybe this time she could sit in a booth somewhere and eat a meal with people who didn't know who she was. At least in the winter she could hide under puffy coats and beanies. It was harder in the summer, especially when three giant tour buses and several SUVs pulled into a parking lot. They drew a lot of attention.

"We can try that. Or do a drive-through somewhere in one of the cars." Grabbing a fat cucumber slice and a bottle of water, Bristol followed Lizzy out of the dressing room. Her security detail fell into place and escorted her backstage. Annie had switched up her set and added a faster song to her lineup.

"Maybe you've heard this song before, and maybe you were here last night. This is my last song. Fast Cars is up next. I'm Annie Foster, and thank you for being so welcoming. I love my hometown of Denver!"

Annie started strumming, and Bristol walked onstage with only a microphone. She touched Annie's lower back and smiled at her before jumping in on the chorus. They had great musical chemistry and harmonized better than any singer Bristol had sung with before. Annie's comfort level singing in front of thousands of people made Bristol proud of her for some unknown reason. More people were in their seats during Annie's set than last night. Maybe word had gotten out about Annie and how talented she was, or that Bristol joined her on the last song and they were hoping for that little extra concert experience. They finished to whistles and loud applause. Bristol waved as she left the stage for Annie to say good-bye to the crowd and end her livestream.

Her entourage of personal security, Lizzy, the assistants, and her stylist walked with her back to her dressing room. Lizzy warmed the dish and handed it to Bristol. She was used to eating while Phoebe worked on her hair. Makeup would happen after she brushed her teeth and gargled to clear her throat.

"Don't eat too much. You're going to be moving a lot onstage," she said.

It was a catch-22. She needed the carbs for energy, but performing with a full stomach wasn't smart. She had a team of eight dancers that jumped out onstage during six songs. She mixed up her lineup so she could rest between intense dancing.

"I'm getting too old for this," Bristol said. It was a lie. She was in the best shape possible. She should have said she was getting bored with this. She could power through the twenty remaining shows, especially with Annie in the mix.

"Look at these photos." Dom, Bristol's social media manager, was a part of Bristol's entourage. She didn't post a single thing unless Bristol approved.

Bristol scrolled through the eight photos, smiled at the clever caption, nodded, and handed the phone back to Dom. "Thank you."

She sat up straight and allowed everyone who hustled and bustled around her to get their job done. Since the venue was outdoors, Bristol decided on a yellow summer dress with a slight flare at the waist to start the concert. Halfway through, when it changed to the devil portion of the show, she would slip into a high-waist, textured plum skirt, black camisole, and a silver and purple jacket with black swirls. The outfit was flashy but fun.

The first song of the concert was always a fast one to get people excited. Then she slowed it down and played most of her love songs like "My Dreams" and "The Open Road" and "Red Heart." Half of her Grammy wins were sweet love songs that had hope and positive messages.

The second half of her concert was a whole different vibe. Bristol got to show her sexy side. She played faster songs that were about bad breakups, strong women, and finding your true self. She angrily sang the songs when she thought of the injustice that queer people faced daily. She ended it with her song "Forever" a cappella style again. She walked offstage after saying "good night" and waited. The crowd was deafening. Lizzy gave her the thumbs-up from the other side of the stage. Waiting this long was a gamble, but one Bristol knew would pay off. She would end the encore with a rousing rendition of her party anthem "Turn It Up," but right now she wanted to soak up the reaction. She drank water and waited until her band nodded, and they all took the stage together. Two more songs and then she could rest on the bus.

"We love you, Bristol!" a group of fans near the front yelled in the slip of time before she started the final song. It made her smile.

"I love you all, too!" She meant it. It wasn't like her to be overly emotional, but lately the shouts from the crowd were settling heavily on her heart. Maybe because she knew this was her last tour or maybe because she was stretched too thin and her emotions were struggling to stay firm on the taut line of her existence. She finished her final song. "Thank you, Denver, for being one of my favorite places!" She didn't think about what she said. She just blurted it out. "And you gave us one of your own, Annie Foster, who's going to be on the road with us for the remainder of the Angel/Devil Tour. Good night and stay safe!"

Lizzy hugged her on her way offstage. "Brilliant as always."

"It felt good."

"It showed. Now, let's get on the bus and get out of here," Lizzy said.

Bristol knew it would be at least an hour before they left. As much as she enjoyed plush five-star-hotel life, her tour bus was her haven. It was big enough for Lizzy and others to gather and brainstorm about the business, and for Bristol to slip away and get much needed sleep.

Security waited for her to gather the personal items she wanted for the bus and escorted her to the back, where they were parked. She saw the signs her fans held up from behind the barricades and waved to them, but she didn't stop to sign autographs or take selfies. A lot of her signed memorabilia wound up on eBay, and she didn't like that. She dropped her bag and fell on her bed, relieved the concert was over.

❖

"This is the diner?" Bristol split the closed blinds with two fingers to look at the restaurant off I-25. The red neon lights that spelled Betty's Diner reflected brightly against the pale building. It was almost three a.m., and the parking lot was empty. Bristol saw two waitresses and a cook leaning against the counter laughing at something one of them said. She envied the organic exchange. They straightened when they noticed the caravan pulling into the parking lot. "Do you think they'll know me?"

"Well, the buses certainly got their attention," Lizzy said. They watched as security from one of the SUVs jumped out to survey the diner. One of the men spoke into his walkie, and within ten seconds, one of Lizzy's assistants was knocking on the bus door.

"Bruce says it's clear."

This didn't happen often. Bristol, Lizzy, and Lizzy's assistants were ushered into the diner and sat near the back and away from windows. The waitress who took their order didn't appear to know who Bristol was but could tell they were somebody important.

"I'm Suzy. What can I get you all to drink?"

"Waters and coffee," Lizzy said.

"I'll have an orange juice," Bristol said. After a brief glance at the large, laminated menu, she decided on the oatmeal. That would help her sleep until they got to Santa Fe. One night there and one night in Albuquerque. Then a day off until the Salt Lake City concerts.

"Where are y'all from?"

Suzy returned with a steaming pot of coffee and a large orange juice. She poured four black coffees effortlessly.

"California," Bristol said.

"Those are big buses out front. Are you with a politician?"

Bristol bit her lip to keep from laughing out loud. *That's her first thought? A politician?* She kept her head down as Lizzy took charge.

"Something like that. I think we're ready to order now." Lizzy didn't give Suzy time to ask any more questions. Bristol watched as she scribbled down everyone's order, asking the bare minimum and nodding the entire time.

"Toast or biscuit? Side of bacon or sausage?"

"Toast, no butter, and I'll pass on the side," Bristol said.

"It comes with it."

"I'm fine." She handed Suzy the colorful oversize menu and waited while everyone else ordered. Security in the booth diagonally across from them ordered black coffees. Bristol listened to the table discuss the concert and what they were looking forward to the most on the tour. She tuned them out. While she appreciated Lizzy's attempt at providing for her a normal environment, it was hard to ignore the booth of four men dressed in black saying very little to one another or how Suzy and the other waitress spoke in low volumes. Even the rest of the crew outside was wandering aimlessly but close enough to swoop in and get everyone back on the road.

Lizzy held up her hand. "Please don't take our picture," she said to the other waitress, who was cleaning an already immaculate counter across from the booth. Bristol had never seen color explode on someone's face before that quickly. Red blotches fanned out across her cheeks and crept up from the collar of her shirt. The waitress mumbled something and turned on her heel, obviously desperate to be anywhere but here.

"Sorry about that. We don't get a lot of famous folks in our diner," Suzy said as she swooped to the booth with everyone's order. She set Lizzy's plate in front of her and quickly dealt the remaining plates stacked across her outstretched arm. It was an impressive talent. "Let's see. You'll need maple syrup. What else?"

"Extra napkins," Lizzy said.

Bristol ate a few bites of her steel-cut oats and a piece of dry toast. It didn't take long for people outside of their circle to starting filing in and giving them curious looks. "It's starting to get crowded." Several people were taking photos of the buses and of them.

"At least you got a little taste of the normal world." Lizzy linked her arm with Bristol's and escorted her out the back door while one of the assistants paid the bill.

Bristol gave her a weak smile. "Thanks for trying."

Lizzy didn't understand. She tried to, but she couldn't see past the money they were making when they toured. It was a grueling twenty-four-hour seven-days-a-week job, and they were all getting paid very well.

"Go to sleep." Lizzy patted her arm. "I'll wake you up when we're checked into the hotel."

The adrenaline rush from the concert and the warm food in her belly made every part of her feel heavy. She crawled onto her bed in the back of her bus and fell asleep without even pulling up the covers.

CHAPTER SEVEN

B aby, I'm going to miss the shit out of you. Please behave."
Annie slung Raven over her shoulder and leaned her head against Raven's purring chest. She would miss their snuggle sessions and knew her rescue cat would be lost without her, but Sarah and Peyton promised to visit every day and help fill the void. "Auntie Sarah and Peyton will play with you and love on you. I'll be back after Labor Day, okay?"

Raven purred louder. Annie did a quick check around the apartment and reviewed the list she left for Sarah. Water the plants, pick up the mail, and take all perishable items home with her. It was Thursday, and her Lyft driver would be here any minute. Her sister couldn't take her to the airport because work was stacking up and she couldn't get away, but she promised to stop by every day.

"I've managed to raise a child and run a hospital. I'm sure I can handle my fur-ball niece." Sarah's voice dripped with sarcasm.

Annie smiled. "You're right. And you raised me, so I guess you've got the whole cat-sitting thing." She hated leaving Peyton during treatments, but Sarah promised updates daily and would show the kids Annie's shows from the stage. She reviewed her flight schedule that Vaughn sent. After a message popped up on her phone that her driver was downstairs, Annie took a final look around the apartment. She would miss her space but was excited to be on the road touring. She had done only day trips around Denver, and when her channel gained popularity, she worked on that instead of being on the road. She still had bills to pay, and while the tip jar felt slightly like begging, it covered her expenses.

"We're here. United Airlines." The Lyft driver slid into a tight spot behind a bus. Annie coughed at the exhaust and moved away while the driver got her bags from the trunk. "Have a good flight."

Annie nodded thanks and rolled into Denver International Airport with two bags, a guitar, and solid determination to make the most of this opportunity. She marched up to the ticket counter and gave her information to the agent.

"Feel free to wait for your flight in the United Club lounge located upstairs after security, Ms. Foster."

Annie raised her eyebrows at the mention of the first-class lounge. She thanked the agent, slid her bags onto the belt, but kept her guitar case close. No way was she going to check it. Too much risk.

A server wearing a black vest, black slacks, and a white shirt greeted her at the lounge door. "Can I get you a beverage?"

"A water would be great."

"Sparkling?"

"That's fine."

"Coming right up. Feel free to sit anywhere."

There was a low hum inside the lounge, but it was a lot quieter than outside at the gate. Annie sat in a plush recliner that overlooked the Rocky Mountains. She loved Denver and couldn't imagine living anywhere else. Where did Bristol live? Somebody that rich and famous probably had a half a dozen places around the world. Bristol was so admirable. She was everything Annie aspired to be. Annie had seen videos of people crying because she talked to them or took photographs with them. Maybe that was a bit much, but with success came sacrifice, and millions of dollars to live alone in a large mansion didn't sound half bad. She would set up a whole wing in her make-believe mansion for her jam room and invite musicians she met along the way to come over and jam with her. She was Annie Foster, after all. Nobody would turn her down.

"Boarding for Flight 568 nonstop to Salt Lake City will begin shortly."

The announcement pushed Annie out of her fantasy. She grabbed her messenger bag and guitar and made her way down the lounge stairs and to the gate. Being first in line was nice. She asked one of the flight attendants if she could store her guitar in the upright closet behind the pilots. The flight attendant acted perturbed, so she named-dropped. "I'm opening for Bristol Baines in Salt Lake City tonight, and as much as I trust the airline, I couldn't check my baby." She patted her hard case lovingly. Surprise registered on the attendant's face, and she immediately opened the closet and allowed Annie to slide her case under the pilots' jackets.

"Thank you. I'm Annie Foster, by the way."

"I'm Irene. If you need anything, please let me know."

Irene returned with a Coke and a Clif bar, per Annie's request. She wasn't hungry but knew that protein bar would come in handy being on the road and slipped it into her bag. She put in her AirPods and scrolled through Instagram. It was time for a social media update. She quickly looked around for privacy and recorded a ten-second video to post.

"It's Annie Foster. I'm on a plane getting ready to join Bristol Baines on her Angel/Devil Tour. I'm so excited. Check out her tour dates, and I'll see you on the road." She finished just as the passenger next to her put her bag in the overhead and plopped down on the seat. Annie gave her a smile and shuffled so she was closer to the window. The woman's musky perfume overpowered their small space and was starting to give Annie a headache. This was going to be the longest ninety minutes of her life.

❖

She walked over to the man holding an iPad with her name displayed. "Hi. I'm Annie."

"Right this way, Ms. Foster."

He grabbed her bags and held the door of the limo open. Somebody guided her guitar into the seat. She looked inside and gasped. Bristol motioned for her to come inside.

"Hi." Bristol leaned forward to greet Annie.

Annie was more than surprised. She put her hand over her heart and crawled next to Bristol. "What a massive surprise! Hi!" Limos were big, but being inside one with Bristol Baines made the space small. She wanted to know where Lizzy and the assistants were but liked that it was just the two of them.

"I've already practiced this morning. Since I'm not flying through the air on wires this tour, there's not much to do other than show up and sing."

"I'm so happy you're here." Annie wanted to reach out and fix Bristol's crooked collar but didn't dare touch her. They were already in one another's personal space, and while Annie didn't mind the closeness, she was worried about Bristol. They barely knew each other. Bristol seemed shy and reserved and not at all like the person who danced onstage almost every night.

"How was your flight?"

"It was great. Thank you for the first-class ticket. I felt famous and important."

"You are famous and important," Bristol said.

Annie shrugged. "Not yet, but I did get several thousand more subscribers to my channel, and that's amazing."

"You're very good. I'm glad Lizzy found you."

"Thank you for this opportunity. I know you could've chosen anyone, so thank you from the bottom of my heart." Annie tried to sound as serious and grateful as she could without breaking down and crying at her fortune. Her heart skipped when Bristol touched her wrist.

"It's okay. I like helping artists out."

"I love that you do that. Ali Hart, Willow McAdams, Natasha Breeze, and me." Annie noticed that the corners of Bristol's mouth turned down when she mentioned Natasha's name. After landing the gig, Annie did a lot of internet searches about Bristol but didn't know what to believe. It wasn't her business anyway. She was sure somebody like Bristol had somebody waiting for her, even after an eighteen-month tour. It sounded like she'd had two really bad breakups. One with Natasha and one with the daughter of the president of Top Shelf. The internet was pretty sure Bristol exclusively dated women, but she'd never publicly said so. Maybe she didn't care about labels.

"I haven't been wrong yet," Bristol said.

Annie crossed her fingers. "And I hope you're not wrong with me either."

"I'm never wrong." Bristol's voice was low, and Annie shivered at the quiet confidence. "As much as I love us covering 'Brass in Pocket,' maybe you can just sing one of your originals, and I can sing with you."

"Wait, what? You want to sing one of my songs?"

Bristol nodded. "I think it would be better for you if we sang one of your songs instead. I'm a quick study."

"That would be amazing." Annie swallowed hard as she thought about everything she'd ever written and if it was even good enough for Bristol to sing. "There are two on my EP that might work."

"Which ones are you thinking? We would sound great together on the first and the fourth song."

Annie tried to hide her surprise that Bristol knew her music. She kept her voice casual. "You've listened to my EP?"

"Of course. What song are you considering?" Bristol typed on her phone. "I'm going to pull up the lyrics."

Annie froze. All her songs felt elementary and unoriginal. "'In the Light' might be a good one." She'd written it after a breakup. "No. Wait. This is a sad one. Let me find one that isn't so dark."

"Break-up song?" Bristol asked.

"Yeah. Pretty obvious, huh?" Annie asked.

"I have a lot of those, too. It seems like most of us like to pour our emotions out on the page when we hurt," Bristol said.

"Speaking from experience?" Annie's question was bold, but something about their private space made her feel like this alone time was precious and Bristol needed to talk.

"I can't tell you how hard it is to date somebody who isn't in it for my fame. I can't even make friends, really." Bristol's shoulders sank at her confession.

Annie wanted to pull her into her arms and hug her. A part of her felt guilty because she was using her, too. What good was Annie bringing to the tour? She wasn't giving Bristol any new fans, but Annie was raking new ones in daily. "I hope you know that I really appreciate what you're doing for me. And people who've used you are just…" She paused to search for the perfect word. "Assholes. Even in the dating realm."

"Are you dating anyone?" Bristol asked.

Annie shook her head. "No. I've been focusing on my music. My ex called it a hobby and never supported me, so I dumped her."

"I have the opposite problem."

Annie felt heat at Bristol's stare. Intense wasn't the best word to describe Bristol, but it came close. "Well, here's to both of us not falling for the wrong people again." She pursed her lips and paused. "Pull up 'Waiting All Day.' That has a sweet message, and it's fast and will get them out of their seats. Well, the ones who show up at the start." Annie watched Bristol's lips move as she read the lyrics to herself.

"Oh, this is the fourth song. I definitely like the message. It is sweet."

Annie took a deep breath and started playing the song on her phone. Never had she ever lost her train of thought. Staring and singing at Bristol was unnerving, but she trusted herself and sang softly.

"Play the part right up to the chorus again," Bristol said. She sang the entire chorus with Annie and faded out when Annie went into the next verse. It was perfect.

"Wow. That was incredible," Annie said when they were done. Her mouth felt dry. Bristol had the most beautiful brown eyes, and sitting so close without any distractions made Annie's pulse quicken. Her hair was loose and hung in gentle waves down her back.

"I like your song a lot. Actually, I like your whole EP a lot," Bristol said. She looked out the window when the limo stopped. "How are we here already? That was the fastest trip."

"Wow, okay. So, do we need to practice it again?"

Bristol nodded. "We can practice at the venue. We'll head over in about an hour. That gives you enough time to freshen up."

"Thank you, Bristol. The song change is a great idea." Annie slid out of the car but kept the door open. "Are you coming?"

Bristol leaned back into the limo. "No. I use a different entrance. I'll see you later."

Annie waved and quickly shut the door to keep others from seeing Bristol. She was still reeling from being alone and having a heartfelt conversation with her. The more she got to know Bristol, the more she felt a little sorry for her. How awful it would be to never know if somebody wanted to be close to you because of you or because of your success.

Annie followed the instructions Vaughn had sent to register in her hotel room and access her eKey. She got on the elevator with two teenagers who were visibly excited. They whispered before one spoke up nervously.

"Um…hi. Are you touring with Bristol Baines?"

"Yes. I'm Annie Foster. I'll be opening for her tonight. Are you going to the concert?"

They nodded in unison. "My dad got us tickets. He works at Top Shelf Records."

"That's pretty cool. You probably get to see a lot of fun concerts then."

The bubbly brunette who couldn't have been more than fourteen shrugged. "My dad is one of the marketing managers, so we don't always get tickets to the concerts we want, but we did to this one. We're so excited we even made posters." They unrolled two large yellow posters with red letters that read, "We love you, Bristol!" The pink glitter was a lot but gave it a touch of innocent adolescence. Annie smiled at the glitter that had drifted to the elevator floor that was sure to turn up in several hotel rooms as people shuffled in and out of the elevator before the cleaning staff could contain it.

"We're in row Q on the floor."

Annie almost groaned. They wouldn't be able to see much from there. Their row sounded close, but after the VIP and the double-letter rows, they would probably be thirty rows back. And they weren't taller than her so they would be struggling to see the stage. She shot Lizzy a quick text, knowing somebody would get back to her within seconds. "Are you going by yourselves?" Annie asked. She was concerned for their safety but also wanted to know how many tickets she needed to give them. Lizzy's text back said she could have four VIP tickets.

"My mom is going with us." The blonde rolled her eyes as though it was a massive inconvenience for them to have her mother tag along. Annie would have given all of this up for one night with her mother.

"I think that's sweet." When the elevator stopped, Annie held out her phone so they could scan the QR code for VIP passes. "Wait. Scan this. I hope it helps you have a better time."

"Oh, my God! Are you for real? Are you serious?" She and her friend screamed and jumped up and down when the reality hit that they were going to meet Bristol. The blonde threw her arms around Annie, surprising her. "Thank you so much. Gosh. I didn't mean to get into your personal space. I'm just so happy. I can't wait to tell my mom."

"I have to go now, but I hope you have a great time tonight," Annie said.

"Thank you, Annie Foster. You rock!"

She waved at them and followed the arrows down the different hallways to her hotel room. She felt giddy knowing she'd just made their night. Two down, thirty thousand to go.

CHAPTER EIGHT

What was it about her? Bristol ignored the rapid flutter in her chest and the lightness in her heart as she watched Annie perform. Something was different about Annie tonight. Maybe it was her confidence or that she was finally embracing the opportunity, but whatever it was, it was sexy. They had barely gotten to practice, but Bristol assured her she would be ready to sing her song. She'd learned it this afternoon. Music was a part of who she was, and learning a few verses was easy.

"It's like she's a whole new person up there," Lizzy said.

When it was her time to sneak onstage, Bristol grabbed the microphone from a roadie's hand and started humming while Annie was singing. When the fans recognized her slowly making her way to Annie, they screamed with excitement. Bristol started singing softly, careful not to upstage her. She looked into Annie's bright-blue, expressive eyes and saw happiness and pride. Annie was having the time of her life. For the first time in ten years, Bristol forgot the words to a song.

Instead of getting upset, Annie threw her head back and laughed. She kept strumming. "It's okay. We can make up the words as we go."

Bristol covered her face with her hand. "I'm so embarrassed." She leaned closer to Annie. "I'm so sorry. I thought I knew this song forward and backward." She didn't tell her that being this close to her was unnerving. When was the last time she'd felt the little kick in her heart or wanted to stand this close to somebody?

Annie kept strumming and reminded Bristol of the words. Their fans were eating up their exchange. It was flirty, fun, and showed the world that Bristol Baines wasn't as cold as the tabloids indicated.

She took a deep breath and looked Annie directly in the eyes. "Just a little bit longer, my heart grows stronger and stronger." She found the beat again and finished the song. When she was done, she hugged Annie, waved to the crowd, and bounced offstage. She liked surprising the crowd. She liked singing with Annie. It felt good. When was the last time she felt so complete?

"You were seventeen the last time you froze onstage. What happened?" Lizzy and security flanked her on her way to her dressing room.

"I don't know. Maybe I'm tired."

"Or maybe somebody's baby blues got you all messed up." Lizzy smiled.

Enough time had passed since her last relationship that the ribbing didn't sting. She thought about denying Lizzy's remark, but what was the point? "She is attractive, isn't she?" Bristol kept the excitement out of her voice to convey a more laid-back response.

"I should've asked her sister if she's dating anyone," Lizzy said.

"I'm not interested in anything at the moment," Bristol said. She wasn't sure why she added "at the moment." Maybe she was ready, but hooking up with one of the performers or somebody on the tour made for a sticky situation if the relationship went south. She'd made that mistake once and wasn't going to do it again.

Bristol pushed open the door to her dressing room. Annette and Phoebe were in the room standing by to fix her hair and makeup. Her stylist had picked out the two outfits for tonight. As much as she liked summer dresses and light makeup, she loved the turning point in the concert when things got a little grittier and darker. It was almost as if she was playing a part in a movie or play. Breaking out of the squeaky clean good-girl image was tough, but this concert was proving she could be sexy yet still sweet.

"Let's finish the tour first. It feels like a lifetime away."

"The time will go by faster than you think," Lizzy said. She got out of Annette's way and thumbed through the clothing options on racks, even though outfits had been already picked out. She held up a pink shirt and a fun light-gray skirt. "What about this combo? Then you can wear sandals instead of heels. I can't imagine the pain you endure nightly in those death heels."

Bristol snorted. "Three-inch heels aren't bad, but I do love to wear the boots."

Lizzy held up a pair of soft-toe military boots that Bristol had broken in years ago. "Maybe you should think about another pair?"

"Those are my favorite." Bristol frowned as Lizzy laughed and dropped them back in their place.

"They've seen better days," she said.

"We all have." Bristol's voice dripped with sarcasm.

"Touché." She picked up another pair and held them up. "What about these?"

"Those give me blisters."

"Why do you still have them?" Lizzy asked.

"Because they're awesome and give me height."

Lizzy gave up trying to change Bristol's footwear. She scrolled on her phone, making faces and smiling at whatever was on the screen. "Dom is doing a great job promoting the concert. And Annie's getting great press on your page. Even Fast Cars is blowing up. This has been a stellar tour."

Talking about the business side of things in front of the staff was a no-no, but sometimes Lizzy forgot her environment. "Let's focus on tonight. Can you grab me something to drink? Like a flavored water? Thanks." Bristol gave Lizzy a smile and blinked hard twice. It was her signal to Lizzy to stop the discussion. Money didn't matter at this point. Bristol could lock herself into one of her houses for the rest of her life and live off the money she made from this tour alone, but that didn't mean they should discuss it in front of the crew.

She couldn't wait to be done. She wanted to let her guard down. She wanted to walk around town and grab a coffee or pick up dry cleaning or wash her car in the driveway without twenty paparazzi trying to take her picture and printing false headlines. *Bristol Baines spent all her money—has to wash her own car.* Or *Bristol Baines gets own dry cleaning because entire staff quit. Claims she's the devil.*

"You're done here. Off to wardrobe," Annette said.

Bristol was so engulfed in her thoughts she didn't realize her hair was pulled up and curled and her makeup applied. She stepped out of her clothes and slipped into her first outfit. She had exactly ninety seconds for the wardrobe change halfway through. She twirled in front of the mirror. She was wearing a pink skirt and a white sleeveless top. It was a bit too wholesome, but it served its purpose for the angel half. She had faux leather pants and a black shirt picked out for the devil half.

Lizzy pressed her fingers to her ear. "Fast Cars just finished the set. You're up in fifteen."

Bristol took a deep breath. Her confidence was the wobbliest right before going onstage. Once she started singing, she was okay. Getting there, all eyes on her, was unnerving. "Okay. Thanks." Lizzy knew not to bother her right before the show. She put her AirPods in, cleared her mind, and practiced breathing until Lizzy tapped her leg.

"It's go time."

Bristol gave a final deep breath and nodded. "Let's go."

❖

It was just a quick get-together with Annie to review the song, but Bristol was pacing. She'd spent a lot of time in the mirror trying to look casual and adorable. Black leggings, T-shirt with a repetitive small heart pattern, and her hair back in a ponytail. It was almost two in the morning, but Bristol wouldn't fall asleep for another few hours. She jumped when she heard the soft rap of Annie's knuckles on the door.

"Hi. Come on in."

"Thanks." Annie walked only a few steps in and waited for Bristol to shut the door. "I know it's late, but I'm not even tired. Tonight was amazing."

Bristol snorted. "Except for the part where I ruined your song."

Annie touched her arm. "It was perfect. It shows that you're human. Most people think you're a goddess, and your little slip made you seem more accessible."

Bristol was having a hard time looking away from Annie's eyes. They were so blue. There wasn't a speck of any other color but blue. "I'm just a regular person."

"That everybody wants to be like," Annie said.

She hoped that wasn't true. She wanted Annie to be a regular person and treat her like a regular person. "Let's get started. The conference room isn't above any bedrooms, so let's go there. Nobody will hear us."

Annie handed her a printout of the song lyrics. "Just in case you need them." Naughtiness perched at the corners of her mouth. Annie was teasing her, and Bristol couldn't help but laugh.

"Things I'll never live down. Have a seat." Bristol pointed to an empty chair across from the one she sat in.

"Are you sure we won't wake anyone?"

"I'm sure. The advantage of the penthouse suite is privacy. Play away."

Annie strummed until she got the right pitch. "Ready?" At Bristol's nod, she began singing.

Bristol liked her voice so much that she didn't jump in when she was supposed to. It was nice to hear somebody with true talent sing. Annie had control of her voice and knew how to project it so it didn't sound breathy or ragged.

"Are you going to join me?" Annie stopped playing.

"I wanted to hear it all the way through and pick the places where I should start harmonizing." That was only a small lie. She wanted to hear it, but she was caught up in sitting so close to Annie. Lizzy wasn't around. Her security was on the other side of the door. When was the last time she'd been alone with somebody?

"That makes sense. How about here, here, and maybe here?" Annie pointed to the piece of paper Bristol was holding. She was only inches away. Could Annie hear how fast and hard Bristol's heart was thumping? Did she know that Bristol thought about her more than she should? Annie smelled like daisies and fresh clothes. Her hair was damp from a recent shower, and she wasn't wearing makeup. She was lovely, and Bristol wished this moment would last forever.

"That looks good. I promise not to screw it up again."

"It's okay. Like I said before, it shows your human side." She winked at Bristol and started playing the song. Bristol nodded to the beat and jumped in where they agreed. She used the sheet only twice—once to learn the spots and the second time to break eye contact with Annie.

"That sounded so good. Let's do it one more time, and then I'll get out of here and let you sleep," she said.

Bristol didn't want her to go. She wanted Annie to stay and get to know her better. "Can I get you something to drink? I know I'm not drinking enough."

Annie sat back and loosened her grip on the guitar. "Water sounds great. Thanks. I'm going to have to work to stay hydrated and eat more to keep up with the energy of this tour."

Bristol handed her a glass of iced water and put a plate of vegetables and dip between them. "Just in case you're hungry."

"How can you stay so healthy on tour? My willpower is lost, and I just want to eat everything. The muffins and doughnut spread at the arena today was unbearable. I mean, of course I ate one or two, but if I did it every day, I wouldn't have the energy for a show every night."

"You're doing great. I do that so the crew and everyone on the tour can snack while they're working. You'd be amazed at how many people work on putting the stage together. But I hear you. The lull of junk food is so easy when you can't just cook something for yourself."

"Although your suite has a full kitchen. Do you like to cook?"

Bristol thought about what she did on her downtime, but it had been so long she couldn't remember if she really enjoyed cooking or did it because it was her only option when not on tour. "It's hard to cook for just me, but I usually enjoy it. It's better when the family comes over and we grill out."

"Do you live close to your family?" Annie wasn't fishing for information. She was genuinely curious.

"My mom and brother live in my neighborhood in LA. I also have a cabin in Vermont and an apartment in Madrid. When I stay there, they usually come visit."

"As in Madrid, Spain?" Annie's mouth dropped open.

Bristol wrinkled her nose. "Yes. That sounds excessive, doesn't it?"

"Good for you. You're living the dream, and if you can afford it, I say why not? I would love to travel. I've only been to Mexico."

"I've toured everywhere, but I haven't really seen the world. We tried to do better on this tour by spreading it out so we weren't so rushed, but that just made it drag out. I can't tell you how happy I am that we're in the homestretch."

"It has to be so hard to be away from your family and friends that long," Annie said.

"I miss my mom a lot. I'm sure you already understand that. You're really close to your sister and niece. And you have some really great friends." Bristol was thinking of Charley and how protective she was of Annie.

"I already miss them like crazy. My sister raised me, so even though the rest of the tour is only six weeks, this is probably the longest we've been apart."

"Your sister raised you?" Bristol didn't want to ask the obvious. If Annie wanted to tell her what happened there, she would.

Annie slid the guitar off her lap and placed it gently against the table. "My parents died in a boating accident when I was thirteen. Sarah was twenty then and became my legal guardian. She sacrificed so much for me. And now she's dealing with Peyton's illness. She needs a break."

"I'm so sorry that happened to you," Bristol said. She remembered being thirteen, trying to figure out who she was and tripping over her emotions. It was a pivotal moment in her life. She couldn't imagine losing her parents then. "I like your sister. She seems nice." She remembered the eye patch Peyton wore while they were backstage and was curious about it, but didn't want to pry. "You don't have to tell me, but what illness does your niece have?"

"It's a condition called retinoblastoma, which is a form of eye cancer."

Bristol gasped. "Is she going to be okay?"

Annie smiled and nodded. "She is. She's a fighter. She's so tough, and I'm so proud of her. I know she's confused about it because none of her friends at preschool have medical conditions, but she's getting to know the kids where Sarah works, so that makes it easier. She says she's special, and she most certainly is."

"Sounds like the Fosters are a strong family."

"We have to be. All families have their problems, but we'll get through them. Tell me about yours."

Bristol knew people only in the entertainment industry, and they were horribly selfish and greedy. Annie was so genuine. She was a breath of fresh air. "I'm close with my mother. My teenage brother is a pain in the ass, but he has a good heart. My dad's an artist and thinks I'm wasting my talent just to get famous." She gave Annie an eye roll for effect. "We argue about everything, so I'm not really close to him."

"I'm sorry to hear that. The fact that he's an artist is pretty cool, though. What about your mom?"

"My mom runs one of my charities. She never remarried after the divorce. My dad's on marriage number three. The latest wife is maybe two years older than me."

"That's awkward. Tell me about your brother. What's the age gap?"

"He's eleven years younger. I call him my oops brother. He doesn't like that so much."

"He's probably really proud of you. I bet your entire family is. How could they not be?" Annie asked.

Just when she was going to tell Annie things she'd never told anyone except for Lizzy, her phone alarm went off. "Where did the time go? It's already four."

Annie jumped up. "Oh, my gosh. You need sleep. I need sleep. We need sleep."

Bristol just now noticed how Annie's bright eyes were a little droopy. "I'm so sorry I kept you. Thank you for the chat. I needed it more than you know."

Annie hugged her, and while Bristol was completely taken aback by the gesture, she leaned into Annie for strength. She wasn't used to people touching her without her permission. She wasn't offended. It was just foreign to her.

"Sleep well, and I promise to get the words right," Bristol said.

Annie grabbed her guitar case and walked to the door. "I'm not even worried. I think tonight was a bigger success than any other night we've had so far. Thank you again for the opportunity, Bristol Baines."

"Have a good night, Annie Foster." Bristol locked the door and slid under the blankets. When was the last time she'd climbed into bed smiling?

CHAPTER NINE

"Viva Las Vegas!" Annie greeted Charley at the airport with a bottle of champagne. Charley landed at noon, and even though Annie hadn't slept much, she wanted to be at the airport to greet her best friend.

"My famous friend!" Charley made a big production of running up to her and squeezing her so tightly she grunted.

"Ow. Don't kill me before I get to stardom," she said. She leaned back to get a good look at Charley. "It's been less than two weeks, but I missed your face."

"I can't believe I'm here. I can't believe this is happening." Charley grabbed her bag from the belt and followed Annie outside to a waiting limo. "Really? A limo?"

Annie threw her hands up. "Bristol insisted."

Charley cocked her eyebrow. "Bristol now? Just Bristol?"

Annie rolled her eyes. "What else am I supposed to call her?"

"Oh, how I love all of this. You look amazing. Touring suits you."

"Thank you. I feel amazing. Tired, but still amazing." Annie held Charley's hand. "How are you? Was it hard to get away?"

"Nope. I wouldn't have missed this for the world. Vegas and my best friend. Are you nervous about playing here?"

Annie thought about it. The Colosseum at Caesars Palace held only about four thousand spectators. It was an incredibly small venue for somebody as big as Bristol. Both shows were sold out. Tickets on the street were going for over a thousand dollars each. "I don't know why we're playing to such a small audience, but I think it'll have an intimacy that's missing with the stadium tours. I'm kind of excited."

Charley shook her head as her eyes welled with tears. She looked up at the ceiling. So did Annie. "I can't believe any of this. It's so amazing, and I can't think of a more deserving person than you. You've earned it."

Annie brushed away an errant tear. "Nah. I was simply in the right place at the right time. I'm learning that this business is about who you know and luck." She hugged Charley. "Now, we're finally in Vegas. Whatever shall we do?"

"I'm going to gamble, watch my best friend take the stage, gamble some more, drink, sleep, gamble, and watch my best friend take the stage."

"Are you sure you don't mind rooming with me? I figure we won't be in the room a lot." The rooms were cheap, but Annie needed Charley close. She was homesick, and Charley was a large chunk of home.

"I wouldn't have it any other way." Charley checked her watch. "What time do you need to be at rehearsal?"

"Not until five thirty, and since we're staying in the same place, there's no set-up time or anything. I just show up and play. Do you want to grab food?"

"I can wear this, right?" Charley was wearing tight jeans, Converse high-tops, a Night Owl T-shirt, and a black jacket with the sleeves rolled up. Her hair was freshly cut and styled. The ninety-minute flight didn't wrinkle her at all.

"You look great." Annie couldn't help but squeeze Charley's hand.

"Tell me everything. I know we talked on the phone the other night, but tell me how things are going. Like are they footing the bill for everything? Is Bristol nice or icy? What's it like singing onstage with her?"

Annie couldn't help but laugh at Charley's enthusiasm. "It's been the best time of my life. My popularity is growing. I have over a hundred and twenty thousand followers on YouTube now, and all my social media accounts have blown up. I can't keep up with it. I get why Bristol has an assistant for just her social media accounts."

"Are you broadcasting live tonight? Because the venue looks amazing. Oh. What are you wearing?"

They were trying to cram two weeks of information into a ten-minute limo drive. "I need to check with Caesars, but if I can livestream, I will. As far as what I'm wearing, I'm going with a little black dress I found this morning. It's gorgeous and fits me like a glove."

"I'm sure you're going to be a knockout. I can't wait to hear you. I can't wait to see you and Bristol together. The posts online have been so amazing. You both sound great."

"We really do, and I'm not just saying that. It's nice onstage chemistry."

Charley elbowed her playfully. "Oh yeah? Chemistry?"

Annie couldn't stop the blush that feathered across her cheeks. "I mean, she's perfect. She's talented, smart, funny, but she's also kind of sad."

"What do you mean? She seems like she has her shit together. She has the world at her fingertips."

"I think that's the problem." Annie didn't want to gossip about Bristol. She was getting to know her more and more day by day. Their relationship was so fragile, and Annie didn't want to soil it by talking about her. "Anyway. We're here. You're going to love it."

"I haven't been to Vegas in years."

Charley's excitement was infectious. Annie gave her a keycard. "We're on the tenth floor, and it's a million miles away. Be prepared for some serious walking." They entered the casino, and before Annie had a chance to hit the elevator call button, three young girls approached her.

"Are you Annie Foster?"

Annie smiled. "I am." She waited patiently for them to find their words.

They clutched one another and giggled. "We love your music. I subscribed to your channel and know most of your songs by heart." The girl couldn't have been older than twelve.

"Are you going to the concert tonight?"

All three nodded.

"Did you come into town just to see the concert?"

"Yes, and we're so excited. We're here because my mom likes to gamble and my dad is here on business."

"Perfect timing. Are you all being careful?" The idea of three almost teenagers alone in Vegas made her nervous.

All three nodded. "We're not allowed to leave the hotel or each other."

"That's smart. What are your names?"

"I'm Kenzie. This is Celeste and Mattie. Can we get a picture with you?"

Annie tried to hide her surprise. "Of course." Charley reached for Kenzie's phone and told them to pose. She snapped several photos. "What's your favorite song of mine?"

"Oh, we love them all, but probably 'Waiting All Day,'" Kenzie said.

"Great. I'll be sure to say hi tonight. Be safe," Annie said. She turned to Charley and lifted her eyebrow in surprise. They watched them giggle and run off. "That was incredible."

"I just witnessed the first of many cool things," Charley said.

"Come on. Let's go before my head gets any bigger," Annie said. They dropped off Charley's luggage, but before they left the room, Annie's phone rang. She held up her wait-a-minute finger to Charley, who was standing in the doorway waiting.

"Hello?"

"Hello. This is Deandra Fletcher with Four Twelve Entertainment. I'd like to speak with Annie Foster."

"This is her." Annie waited for more information before hanging up. She was on the no-call list, so most people who had her number had it for a reason. She'd never heard of Deandra Fletcher though.

"Hi, Annie. We've been paying attention to you the last few weeks and wanted to know if you have representation."

Annie gripped the phone and waved Charley over to her. "No. I don't have a manager yet."

"That's great news. I'll be at the concert tonight. Can we get together and talk?"

"I'm glad you'll be able to see me perform. I'm interested in hearing what you have to say, but I'm afraid I don't have any time to meet with you at the moment." Annie was excited, but she knew better than to set up a meeting before knowing who she was meeting with.

"I'm not surprised. We can Zoom anytime you have a free moment. I don't know if you know anything about Four Twelve, but we rep Rodeo Bandits, J Kay, and Three Times Wrong. We're always looking for fresh, diverse musicians, and you are exactly what we are looking for."

Annie squeezed Charley's arm and mouthed "oh my God." "I'm not performing next Saturday. We can talk then."

"That's great. I'll shoot you an email with details and more about our company. I look forward to talking in the very near future."

Annie gave Deandra her email address and squealed when she hung up the phone. "Somebody wants to rep me."

"Yes! Who are they? What did they say?" Charley asked.

"Not much. I'll chat with them next week. That'll give me time to research the company, but I recognized everyone she told me they rep."

Charley grabbed her hand. "This is the first of many calls. I can just tell."

Smiling at Charley's words, Annie tamped down the need to shout out her good fortune. She was afraid to embrace it because it could disappear. What if the crowd wanted somebody else? She was already sitting out of six upcoming concerts because of previously scheduled openers. What if they liked that band or singer more?

Charley waved her forefinger at Annie. "Quit overthinking this. I can practically see your doubt. Once you get a manager, they can do all the worrying for you," Charley said.

"What if I pick a bad company?"

"Ask Bristol. Or Lizzy. She's Bristol's manager, right? Maybe she'll offer to rep you, too."

Annie wanted to pace, but they were walking through a casino, which wasn't great for pacing. Her anxiety was ramping up at the thought of her career blowing up. She understood how musicians got overwhelmed. "Can we talk about something else? I need normalcy right now. How's the business? How was the last open-mic night?"

That was enough to get Charley talking. "It was a good turnout. Lots of queer babies were there hoping to get a glimpse of you. Some people didn't know you were out on tour, but when they found out, they were super excited." She kept talking as they sat and only paused to give the waiter their order.

"All that's for you?" Annie asked after hearing everything Charley ordered.

"I'm hungry, and I'm in Vegas to indulge. Oh. Peyton and Sarah stopped by the open mic. They come in on a regular basis after checking on Raven."

"As much as this saddens me, my cat doesn't miss me," Annie said. Sarah had sent photos of Peyton and Raven and a few selfies of her close-up, with Raven off in the distance. They made Annie smile, because Raven really hated everyone except for Peyton.

"Raven totally misses you. You haven't spent this much time apart ever. Peyton is a nice distraction for her. Come on. Eat your lunch. I want to go shopping for an outfit for tonight. I mean, I'm going to be sharing space with up-and-coming musician Annie Foster and her best friend Bristol Baines. I have to look stunning."

"Maybe I should find something new, too. I don't want to recycle outfits when I'm playing only fourteen more shows," Annie said. She always tried to look good, but Vegas had an energy that made Annie want to not just look good, but look her best.

❖

Charley gave her a low whistle when she walked out of the bathroom. Annie did a slow turn and struck a pose. "What do you think?"

"I think you're stunning. That dress is amazing." Charley twirled her slowly and clapped. "Gorgeous girl, are you going to be able to play the guitar in that?"

"I hope so. Bristol mentioned something about hitting the high-stakes room after the concert, and I don't want to have to come back up here to change. You know I hate to miss anything. Also, you look dapper. Sexy." Annie straightened Charley's tie even though it was already straight.

"I never get to wear this." Charley opened the suit jacket and spun. "Plus, it has real pockets. If you need me to hold anything for you tonight, let me know. I've got tons of space."

Annie gave Charley her phone and a compact.

"This is it?" Charley held the small stack and flipped it over.

"My ID and credit card are in the case with the phone. I don't want to worry about a clutch because the minute I drink, I'll forget it at a table or in the bathroom."

"I get it. Are you ready?"

Annie nodded. The energy around her gave her a rush of excitement she'd never felt before. The tiny hairs on her arms rose as goose bumps tingled up and down her. The wave of them scattered over her skin, causing her to shiver. Maybe it was because they were in Vegas, or maybe it was because they were hanging out with Bristol later, but either way, she knew she was in for the night of her life.

CHAPTER TEN

It was hard not to stare. A form-fitting dress that landed mid-thigh on a figure like Annie's was going to draw attention. It certainly caught Bristol's eye as she watched from behind the curtain. Annie's voice was perfect for a smaller venue. It was rich and smooth and reminded Bristol of a warm summer sunset. By now, everybody knew to expect Bristol to join Annie onstage for her last song. Their excitement was palpable and made Bristol smile. She wished she'd had worn nicer clothes for their song or tried harder with her hair.

"This is my last song. Thank you all for coming out tonight. A special shout-out to my new friends Kenzie, Celeste, and Mattie. What a beautiful venue and such an honor to play here," Annie said. She strummed the first few notes of the song, and people started cheering. That was Bristol's cue. She grabbed the live microphone and strolled toward Annie. "Bristol Baines!"

The smile that Annie shot her was pure sexiness. It was brief, but it was there, and Bristol's veins throbbed in response. Tonight, she wasn't going to slip up. She dialed up the charm and stared Annie right in the eyes as she sang her song. She was surprised when Annie didn't back down but embraced the new onstage teasing. When Bristol leaned forward and used Annie's microphone with her, neither one of them missed a beat in the song.

"That's it for me tonight! Up next is Fast Cars. Let's give it up for the star of the night. Bristol Baines."

Bristol waved to the crowd on her way backstage and even bent down to slap the hands of several people who wanted that contact. She never did that. She played to the crowd, but never in a physical way.

She waited while Annie waved good-bye. Watching her interact and give the fans what they wanted made her weirdly proud. Like she was somehow responsible for Annie's success when it was all Annie's talent that got her on that stage. "That was great," she said when Annie joined her twenty seconds later.

"Thanks for always coming out onstage with me."

When Annie threw her arms around her, Bristol stepped into the hug and held her a few seconds longer than normal. Annie didn't seem to mind. "It's been a lot of fun. You've made touring exciting again." Bristol looked up and saw Charley standing a few steps behind Annie. "Hi, Charley. Thanks for coming out for the show."

"That was amazing. Both of you!" Charley squeezed Annie's hand. "The crowd knows your music already. They were singing your songs. How incredible is that?"

Bristol couldn't help herself. She longed to be a part of their camaraderie. She missed having a friend that wasn't part of the tour. "I'm singing her songs, too. How incredible is that?" Bristol winced because that sounded arrogant. Before she had a chance to soften that declaration, Annie clapped.

"It's the highlight of every night."

Bristol smiled. "I'm just playing along. Your music is great, and I'm happy that people get to hear it." Before she said something else stupid and insensitive, she bowed out. "I'm going to go get ready, but don't forget we're going gambling after the show. Stay close if you want to join us."

"Definitely," Charley said.

Bristol rushed to her dressing room. Lizzy was going to be pissed. They needed a solid hour to get her ready, and talking with Annie and Charley had shaved a precious ten minutes off the time.

"Your fans are going to be upset if you're late," Lizzy said the second security led her into the room.

"I know, I know. I got carried away," Bristol said. She sat in the chair and let the team fuss over her. It amazed her how efficiently the crew buzzed around her as though she was the queen bee. Her job was to sit still for the next forty-five minutes and let everyone else take over. "Time?"

"Fast Cars just left the stage. That gives us fifteen minutes," Lizzy said.

A collective gasp from the worker bees as the buzz around her grew frantic. Somebody tripped over a cord, and there was a moment of pause before the burst of activity ramped up. Bristol could feel the energy stir inside and knew that by the time she took the stage, that energy would explode into something that would carry her through the next two hours. Or maybe it was the excitement of the fun planned after the concert that made Bristol giddy. She loathed VIP treatment anywhere but Vegas. Usually, she was stuck in a booth in a club and couldn't partake in any of the festivities because too many eyes were on her.

"Are you ready?" Lizzy stood in front of her.

"Do I look ready?" Bristol asked. She held hands with Lizzy as they took several deep breaths together. Nobody bothered them during this unusual routine they had before each show. They weren't praying, just clearing their minds and ensuring the nerves had worked their way out of Bristol's body so she could start each show clean. Most of the worker bees hovered as though afraid leaving would affect their ritual.

"You're going to slay it tonight," Lizzy said.

Bristol felt stronger emotionally than she had in a long time. "It's going to be a good one."

"Vegas is magical like that," Lizzy said. She wagged her eyebrows. "Let's go."

❖

The best thing about the concert was seeing Annie and Charley in the front row dancing. The whole crowd was, but Bristol felt a connection with Annie that gave her energy to do better. To perform for her. Her routine had to be altered because the stage was smaller, but that didn't deter her from giving her fans what they wanted. She sang her sweet music and played guitar, but when the lights flickered and went dark halfway into the set, she slipped offstage.

She quickly stripped off her little white dress and stepped into black leather pants and tucked in a tight black sleeveless shirt that showed off her toned arms. The crowd chanted "Bristol" repeatedly. She pulled her hair out of the sexy librarian bun and let it flow down her back. In less than ninety seconds, she was back onstage.

A single spotlight shone on her as she sang the first song of her second set a cappella. Bristol's band joined in as she slid into the next song. It was an upbeat fun song, and for the rest of the show, Bristol's eyes kept wandering to Annie. There was an unmistakable attraction between them, and even though Bristol knew better than to act on her impulses, something inside made her want to flirt with Annie. It was all in fun, right?

The rest of the concert was her dancing across the stage, leaning over and singing to the crowd. She was torn when the set was over. She loved the attention, loved that Annie was watching her, but was excited to see how the rest of the night unfolded.

"That's it for me, Vegas! Have a great rest of the night!" Bristol waved to the crowd when the lights dimmed, giving herself and the band a moment to rest before the encore. She had a new song that she wanted to sing, but she hadn't practiced it yet. "Hey, listen. Let's play 'Now or Never,' and then I'm going to play my new song, just me and the guitar." She wasn't asking for permission. She was informing them. They nodded at the change and jogged back onstage.

Lizzy wasn't going to be happy. She liked Bristol to have a track available for purchase on iTunes before she sang it, knowing if fans couldn't find it immediately, they would download it for free off some pirated site. Bristol didn't care. She had enough money, and so did Lizzy.

She turned to one of her roadies. "Get the Martin ready." He sped off as Bristol walked back onstage to music her band had started. "This is one of my favorite songs. Who wants to sing it with me?"

She held the microphone out to the audience to capture their loud voices. She sang the verses but held the microphone out for the audience to sing the chorus. When the song ended and the band waved good-bye again, the same roadie ran out her Martin guitar.

"I'm giving you a sneak peak of a song I just wrote." She pointed behind her to the empty instruments. "It's so new that even my band doesn't know it. Let's just keep it between us, okay?" At the audience's laughter, she continued. "I wrote this a few weeks ago. There's not a lot to do on the road except be alone with your thoughts. So, I write new stuff, and sometimes I record it, and sometimes I play it for my fans first."

She strummed a few chords, and when the crowd settled, she started singing. It was a song about hope. It wasn't as if she wrote it about Annie, but more about what she represented to Bristol. She didn't dare look at Annie for fear that she would know. Instead, she focused on the fans in the upper deck and the teenagers to the left of the stage, who held a glittered sign.

"Thank you for spending your evening here with us." Bristol's voice was low as she said her final good-bye. She waved on her way backstage. A roadie was waiting to take her guitar.

"What the hell was that?" Lizzy asked. Her hands were on her hips, and the look she gave Bristol wasn't a happy one.

"A new song I wanted to try out." Bristol dried off the back of her neck with a towel one of Lizzy's assistants handed her. "I think they liked it."

"You know it's never a good idea to do something like that. Then you'll get a ton of people who will pirate your songs, and the legal battle isn't worth it."

"Maybe it'll just be a freebie. Come on. Let's get ready for tonight. I desperately need a shower."

Her security escorted her to the private elevators in Caesars, where she was rushed up to her penthouse for a quick shower and wardrobe change. They had plans. When did she ever have plans?

"Where are we going first?" she asked Lizzy.

"Did you want to gamble? Or would you rather dance?"

"I think I'd like to gamble. Oh. Did you grab Annie and Charley? We should ask them too." She tried to sound nonchalant.

"They're in the living room."

Bristol felt a flutter in her chest. Annie was here. Just on the other side of the door. The penthouse was grotesquely large, but Caesars comped her the room, as well as several suites for the crew. Pampering her staff was important, and what better place than in Vegas? "I'll be quick."

"Don't worry about it. We've got champagne flowing and appetizers galore. You take your time," Lizzy said.

Bristol washed the sweat away, and as much as she wanted to just stay under the perfectly pressured stream of hot water, the thrill of hanging out with normal people got her out of the shower in ten minutes. Phoebe was waiting.

"How do you want to wear your hair tonight?"

"Just down is fine."

"Easy enough," Phoebe and her assistants had Bristol ready in no time. Bristol's stylist picked dark skinny jeans, ankle boots, an oversized cream-colored shirt, and a field jacket she would wear only if the casino was cool.

"Hi." Bristol kept the greeting simple when she walked into the living room. Annie and Charley were holding champagne flutes and looking out at the flashing lights of the Strip. The rest of her entourage were huddled together laughing at something somebody said, completely ignoring not only the spectacular view, but her invited guests. Annie turned and smiled beautifully at Bristol.

"Thank you so much for inviting us. This is amazing." Annie waved her hand over the penthouse and windows. "I don't think I'll sleep tonight."

"Yes. Thank you. This is incredible," Charley said.

Bristol grabbed a water from the coffee table. "How do you feel about gambling?" She looked at the thin Cartier watch face that rested against the inside of her wrist.

"I'm down to learn." She stifled a yawn. "I feel like I've been up for days," Annie said.

Bristol took a step back. "Oh, if you want to go to sleep, don't worry about me." Annie's fingers on her wrist stopped her. She bit the inside of her cheek to keep from smiling.

"Who can sleep here? This is even more exciting than New York City. I'm okay to gamble."

Charley piped up. "I'm not great either, but I'm excited about it."

Their attention turned to Lizzy, whose voice was suddenly raised above normal conversation level. "I don't care what you think, Bruce. I need six guards. Wake them up if you have to. We need them tonight. Your job is to provide round-the-clock security. That means twenty-four hours a day, which, if I'm not mistaken, includes the night." There was a slight pause in their conversation. "I realize the casino will provide security as well, but their job is the casino, and yours is Bristol. I'll see six of you in five minutes."

Annie looked shocked at Lizzy's outburst. Bristol grabbed a flute of champagne to bring the attention back to them. She tapped her glass against theirs. "Let's go have fun. I think we all deserve a night like no other."

CHAPTER ELEVEN

Annie shivered when she felt Bristol's breath on her hand. She watched Bristol's lips pucker and felt the warmth feather across her fingertips. How was she here tonight, next to Bristol, in Las Vegas, at the high-limits table rolling the dice at a craps table?

"For good luck," Bristol said.

She shot Annie a warm look that caused liquid fire to spread to all Annie's important parts and ignite them to an uncomfortable level. She told herself that Bristol was somebody who really needed a friend and not another person with a crush on her. Besides, she was Bristol Baines, who could have her pick of anyone in the entire world. Annie wasn't the kind of person she would date.

"You've got this," Bristol said.

Annie vaguely remembered Charley, on the other side of her, cheering her on. How she started rolling was all a blur. Somebody told her the rules, and after Bristol's run of bad luck, she was standing with dice in her hand and about eight people shouting numbers they wanted her to roll. She had three good rolls, and suddenly all eyes were on her.

Annie turned to Bristol. "I don't even know what I'm doing."

"You're winning," Bristol said.

Annie licked her lips when she saw how close Bristol was. She could smell the orange blossom of Bristol's shampoo and the sweet amaretto on her breath.

"Roll the dice, Annie," Bristol said.

Was the alcohol getting to her? Was it stronger in Vegas? She'd had only a few sips of champagne and one amaretto sour in the span of three hours. Why did everyone else seem to fade away when she looked deep into Bristol's eyes that were so dark, they reminded Annie of molasses? "What?"

"You need to roll the dice, or you're going to upset a lot of people," Bristol said.

Annie looked back at the table. "Oh. Oh! Okay. Here we go." She threw the dice on the table and held her breath.

"Eleven!" the dealer yelled.

The table erupted with shouts and high-fives. Bristol pulled Annie into a hug and squeezed her. The entire night had felt like this. Spending time with Bristol was as amazing as she thought it would be. She was winning on the table and winning in life. Bristol was friendly, fun, and Annie hadn't stopped smiling since they got to the table.

"You won! You won!"

Annie leaned into Bristol. "I won! How much did I win?" She watched as the dealer counted the chips and pushed the giant pile toward her. "I don't want to play anymore. I feel like we should stop."

"You're on a roll. Keep going," somebody said.

"No. I think I'm done here," Annie said.

"We're going to cash out." Bristol pointed to the chips, and the dealer nodded.

"How much money is there?" Annie didn't realize she was squeezing Bristol's hand.

"A lot." Charley leaned in closer to glance at the stacks. "I'm guessing like seven or eight thousand."

"No!" Annie was shocked.

Bristol picked up the sleeve, and before she handed it to the concierge assigned to her, she checked one last time with Annie. "Are you sure you want to cash in?"

"It's your money. I don't want to lose it." Annie waved her hands in front of the chips.

"It's our money. You won it. We'll split it. Maybe there's something else here you want to play," Bristol said.

Annie didn't want to be reckless, especially with money, even though it was Vegas. It was almost three in the morning. "Everything seems so complicated." Bristol's laugh was throaty and sexy, and Annie wanted to hear it again.

"We could hit the VIP bar upstairs if you want." Bristol sounded up for it, but she looked tired.

"It's getting kind of late. Maybe we should just call it a night," Annie said. As much as she wanted to get cozy in a VIP booth with Bristol, that wasn't what a friend would do. Bristol needed a friend, not someone getting lost in her eyes.

Charley bumped her shoulder. "Really? You're ready to throw in the towel now?" She stared at her incredulously.

"We still have tomorrow night. You said we could hit the club downstairs, right?" Annie asked. She looked at Bristol. "Or are we headed out right after the show?"

Bristol leaned back. "We are definitely hitting the club tomorrow. I know today was busy. And it's after three. I've made spa appointments tomorrow at one. For all of us," she quickly added.

Annie smiled because Bristol remembered to include Charley. "Really? That's so sweet."

"I'm just happy to have someone other than Lizzy and her entourage to go to the spa with."

"That sounds lovely. Thank you," Annie said.

"Let's call it a night," Bristol said.

Annie searched Bristol's face for disappointment but saw only happiness. Genuine happiness. Being Bristol's new friend was important to Annie. Bristol was tender, and it took a lot for her to trust people.

Bristol pointed behind her to Bruce and five other beefy dudes. "I'm going up to my room a different way, but don't forget. One o'clock at the spa. Booked under Lizzy Parr." She gave Charley a quick hug, then Annie a longer one.

Annie smiled at the sensation of Bristol's arms around her. "Sleep well."

"Thank you again for an incredible night. I'm looking forward to tomorrow," Bristol said.

Annie watched as six guards surrounded Bristol and walked her through a back exit. Charley linked her arm with Annie's. "If I didn't know any better, I'd say that Bristol Baines is into you."

Annie scowled at Charley. "Not at all. She's just happy she has a new friend. She told me once it was hard to trust people. This is just her way of being friendly. I think she's really lonely."

"Isn't Lizzy her best friend?"

Annie didn't answer until the other people in the elevator got off.

"I get a weird feeling about Lizzy. Like I know they're friends, but she's forever keeping Bristol on task. It's all business when we're in the arenas and theaters. She's professional with me, but she doesn't have to be so controlling or so mean to her staff."

"Like when she yelled at Bruce earlier?" Charley gave her a look that conveyed exactly how Annie felt.

"Right? Maybe that's normal, but it made me feel uncomfortable."

"I guess she sees it as part of her job. Maybe they've had issues in the past with subpar security. It is her job to protect Bristol."

"Lizzy's more than just overly protective. You'll see it when we're at the spa." Annie unlocked the door.

"Bristol and Lizzy seemed tight at The Night Owl. They were really excited that you signed on."

"Yeah. That's the part that throws me. At first, Lizzy seemed like my biggest cheerleader. Now she treats me as though I'm supposed to bow down to her or something." Annie kicked off her shoes. Trying to look sexy and fresh for hours was hard. Her feet were sore, and she was exhausted.

Charley pulled Annie's phone and compact out and put them on the nightstand between them. "Don't let her get you down. Nobody cares about what Lizzy thinks."

"I'll try not to overthink it. We should probably get some sleep. I want tomorrow's concert to be the best one ever." Annie stretched and grabbed her pajamas.

"It's going to be hard beating the one you just did. Both of you were on fire."

Annie leaned against the doorframe to the bathroom. "It was pretty magical."

It wasn't as if Annie was afraid to undress in front of other women, but when the salon coordinator, Becca, issued the seven of them robes and sent them to the dressing room, the butterflies in her stomach released. She pictured square metal lockers and wooden benches, but forgot the salon was upscale and not a gym. They all had private dressing rooms, and since Bristol rented out the entire spa, they had the place to themselves. Her security detail remained outside the glass doors.

"We're going to split you up. Half of you can go for mani-pedis, while the other half can go for massages," Becca said.

Annie cinched the belt of her robe tighter, anxious to see how they would be divided. She wasn't about to start making demands but took one tiny step closer to Bristol.

"How about me, Annie, and Charley hit the massage tables first." Bristol looked at Lizzy, who reluctantly nodded.

"Okay. We'll just be on the other side of the wall." Lizzy pointed and left the three of them to be led down the hall by Becca.

"I have you scheduled for hour-long massages. We have hot stone, aromatherapy, deep tissue, reflexology, and a few others. Your masseuse will give you all the options."

Annie's personal masseuse, Jessie, a bright and cheerful woman around her age, opened a door and issued her inside. Charley was across the hall with Justin, the only male on staff. It was a surprisingly large room. After a few minutes of wincing at Jessie's deep-tissue massage, she finally got used to the pressure and relaxed. Her limbs were jelly by the time Jessie was through with her. She tucked the corner of the towel above the soft swell of her breasts and followed Jessie down the hall to the sauna.

"Just relax for a bit. If it's too hot, feel free to wait in the relaxation room. Be sure to stay hydrated." Jessie handed her an ice water.

"Thank you," Annie said. She pushed the door open and gasped. Bristol was sitting on a bench with her hair pulled up and glistening sweat rolling down her body.

"Come on in. It's hot, but it feels so good," Bristol said.

Annie felt self-conscious but also sexy. She cleared her throat and sat next to Bristol, leaving enough space between them, but close enough to have a quiet conversation. "Are we the only ones here?"

"That's okay, right?" Bristol sat up straighter, as though it never occurred to her that being alone with her would be a problem.

Annie touched her arm. "It's totally okay." She smiled. "How was your massage?"

"It was exactly what I needed," she said.

"Thank you again for such a wonderful treat. It's very generous of you." It was hard for Annie not to notice Bristol's toned legs or the way the towel crept higher on her thigh every time she wiped the sweat from her brow. Bristol was taller, and her towel had to cover more real estate than Annie's.

"It's important to remember self-care when we tour. It's a lot of wear and tear on our bodies."

A comfortable silence settled between them. Annie wanted to be a woman talking to another woman, developing a relationship. She wasn't sure how to come across that way and wasn't even sure Bristol knew how to accept such an attempt. "What do you do after a massive tour like this?"

"I hide. I head to my house and hide for about three months."

"I feel like your answer should be you head to a resort in the Bahamas or you hike and camp for days so you can be away from people," Annie said. Getting information out of Bristol was hard, even though she understood Bristol's hesitancy. "Or fly to Paris to shop. I mean, I always imagined a lot of famous people walking around carefree in Paris."

Bristol shrugged. "It's not fun to go alone. I don't have anybody to go with."

Annie wanted to blurt out that she would, but she stopped herself. "What about Lizzy?"

Bristol threw her head back and laughed. "Lizzy is like an annoying big sister. And after a tour, we always need to take a break from each other. Day in and day out with the same person who is simultaneously your friend and manager is exhausting. I never know if my friend or my manager is standing in front of me."

"Why can't she be both?"

"Because it can be a conflict of interest. My friend needs to encourage me to sneak away and do risky things, but my manager will lock me up behind hotel doors to keep me safe. I don't blame her. We've had some close calls." Bristol pursed her lips, and Annie noticed a shift in her mood. Those close calls must have been awful.

"What about your family? I know you miss them."

A smile brushed across Bristol's lips. "I do, but my mom fusses over me, and then it's not relaxing."

Annie caught herself from reaching out and grabbing Bristol's hand as a comforting gesture. She touched her arm instead. "I'm sorry success has gotten in the way of living. There have to be places where people won't bother you. I know a lot of famous people vacation in Vail, and from what I understand, most of the locals leave them alone."

"Do you ever go to Vail?" Bristol asked.

"I've been there a few times. It's gorgeous, even in the summer."

"Is it safe to hike?"

"Yes, but you might run into a not-so-friendly animal."

"Like a bear?" Bristol asked.

Annie nodded. "Like a bear or a bobcat or wolf or a moose."

"Nope. No. No way." Bristol waved her hands back and forth in front of her.

When the door flung open, Annie slid away from Bristol as though they were guilty of something for just sitting on the same bench. Charley barreled in, bringing in a swirl of cooler air that provided a moment of relief.

"My masseuse was amazing. Like I can barely walk. Thank you so much for the pampering." Charley slouched across from them. She pushed her sweaty hair back and leaned against the slick wall. "It's so hot. How long have you been in?"

Annie cleared her throat. "Not very long. I just got here. Bristol's been here for a bit."

"Speaking of which, I'm going to shower before our mani-pedis." Bristol stood and walked gingerly to the door. "I'll see you in a bit."

"Please tell me you get this kind of treatment the entire tour." Charley waved her hand in front of her face, trying to drum up a draft.

"This is new to me, so I don't know if this is normal."

Charley sat where Bristol did. "She was looking pretty hot in that not-so-giant towel."

"She looks pretty hot in anything," Annie said. She had reached her limit of hot steam. "I'm going to shower, too. Don't stay in here too long. You look like mush already." Annie opened the door and shivered when the rush of ambient air greeted her.

"Five minutes." Becca swooped in and escorted her back to her private dressing room, where she showered and slipped back into the robe. They were only halfway done with the pampering, and while Annie's body was completely relaxed, her blood was racing. She wanted to get back to Bristol. She could tell Bristol was starting to trust her, and that meant everything.

"Hi." Bristol looked up from the magazine draped across her lap. She looked beautiful. Her damp hair fanned over her shoulders, and her cheeks were flushed. Were her eyes always so bright and happy?

"Hi. What are you reading?"

Bristol lifted a shoulder. "Gossip rag."

Annie plucked it gingerly from her lap. "It's probably nothing you need to read. Let's talk about why you don't want to go hiking with me in Colorado."

"I didn't realize you were offering."

Bristol's playful smile made Annie's stomach flop. "I mean, you're always welcome, and I'll do my best to protect you from any threatening wildlife," Annie said. Her heart sank when the nail techs entered and interrupted them.

"I'll keep that in mind," Bristol said.

Annie saw the moment Bristol's walls went up and couldn't blame her. Would the nail techs sell their conversation to a tabloid? She was starting to understand why Bristol clammed up around people. The magazine she'd pulled off Bristol's lap had an article and photo of Bristol. Annie didn't know what it was about, but she knew it wasn't good or true. They picked similar nail polish colors and sat next to each other.

Charley slipped into the room, clearly refreshed from her shower. "Hello, ladies."

"You're just in time. We picked our colors. The blacks and blues are on the other rack."

"Ha ha." Charley looked over the pink and red hues and turned back to Annie. "You're not wrong." She picked a dark sapphire and slipped her feet into the soaker tub. "What are we talking about?"

"Absolutely nothing. Just relaxing and enjoying the pampering."

Annie widened her eyes and looked at the nail techs, who were busy sorting through their equipment. Charley winked with understanding. They kept their conversation light and sporadic. When they were done, Annie and Charley thanked Bristol and hugged her good-bye.

"I can't wait until tonight," Annie said.

"We're going to rock the place," Bristol replied.

CHAPTER TWELVE

Their second night was better than their first. Even though the venue held the same number of people as the night before, their applause and screams were deafening. In a surprising turn of events, Bristol not only sang during Annie's set, but she also pulled Annie onstage for one of her own songs. It changed the dynamic of the show.

"Thank you, Las Vegas, for reminding me why I love to sing so much."

The buses were rolling out at five in the morning to put them in Los Angeles at the arena before noon. That gave her and Annie four hours in the club's VIP section. When was the last time she let loose and danced her ass off? When was the last time she wanted to? The plan was to meet in Bristol's penthouse at one. That gave her time to shower and change into appropriate clubbing clothes. What she had on was great but covered in sweat, and tonight she wanted to be fresh and flirtatious. She was certain she had chemistry with Annie, and hopefully tonight she could test out that theory.

"Great job. I really felt the energy," Lizzy said. She handed Bristol the usual—towel, cold water, and her phone. "You should check out what Dom posted. You were on fire. I bet you're ready to chill."

"Actually, I'm ready to hit the club."

"I thought we agreed you should take it easy tonight."

Bristol did her best not to snap at Lizzy. "You suggested it. I've decided I want to dance."

Lizzy looked shocked. "I don't have security in place."

Bristol looked at the time on her phone. "It'll take me an hour to get ready. I imagine that's plenty of time for Bruce to prep the guys." At Lizzy's worried look, Bristol lightened her words. "It'll be fine. They can just do a repeat of last night. I feel great, Lizzy. Let me." She kissed Lizzy's cheek. "I'm going to get ready, so I'll see you later."

Bristol turned and stepped into line between her security. She ignored the giggles and gasps as she made her way to the private elevators. A part of her wanted to smile at the fans, but her joy was quickly replaced with sadness laced with fear. People didn't want her. They only wanted to be next to someone, anyone, who could get them more likes on social media.

Phoebe, Annette, and Harper, her stylist, were waiting for her the minute she entered the penthouse. "I was thinking the black pants, boots, and green button-down. You know the one with the shimmer to it. You'll look hot and be able to dance," Harper said as Bristol walked to the bathroom.

"It sounds perfect," Bristol said. She closed the door and stripped off her wet clothes. The water was cooler than she liked, but she wanted to be alert and awake tonight. The massage invigorated her, or maybe it was the time spent with Annie, but either way she was ready for more. She dried off, slipped on a robe, and waited for Phoebe. She looked at herself in the mirror. When was the last time she did something without any help?

"Are you ready?" Phoebe asked.

She sat back and allowed her staff to take over. They had her primped and ready within the hour. Lizzy popped her head in.

"Annie and Charley are here. Security is in place," she said.

Bristol knew Lizzy was pissed. "Hey. Why don't you just stay home tonight? I'll be with security and Annie and Charley. You need a night off." For a moment, Bristol thought Lizzy would take the bait.

"No. Somebody needs to watch out for you."

"Look, I love you, but I don't need a babysitter. Nobody's going to kill me or kidnap me. If they tried, security would take them out. And I'm not going to do anything to get me arrested. I'm going to have a drink or two and dance." She stood and grabbed Lizzy's hands. "Let me have tonight, okay?"

"Is it because you need it, or you need time with Annie?"

Bristol gritted her teeth but kept the smile on her face. "Does it matter? I won't be a prisoner here, Lizzy. Tonight, I'm going out, and that's the end of it."

Lizzy took a step back and nodded. "Okay. Be careful."

Bristol watched her walk out of the room. It was the second time she'd had to remind Lizzy that she was still in charge of things. She appreciated Lizzy's concern most days, but she had a life, too. There weren't any skeevy producers or predatory record executives here.

"Who's ready to keep the fun going?" Even though Annie and Charley stood side by side, Bristol only had eyes for Annie. She was wearing a little black dress, like last night, only this one was shorter and had long sleeves. "You look amazing." She gave Annie a solid up and down and then turned to Charley. "So do you." Bristol appreciated Charley's attempt not to burst out laughing at her redirect.

"Thank you," Annie said.

"No purse?" Bristol asked.

Annie patted Charley's jacket. "She's holding all the valuables. I don't have any pockets, and I don't want to stress about where my things are."

"I understand. How about we find out what Caesars means when they say VIP?"

"Just the three of us?"

Bristol nodded. "And security."

"We're ready," Annie said.

It took a solid ten minutes of walking through the casino to get to the elevators that would take them up to the club. Bristol's blood was pumping along with the beat when the doors to the club opened. They were immediately whisked away to the VIP section. She grabbed Annie's hand as the crowd thickened around them. VIP was up the stairs and overlooked the dance floor. The decor, the booze, and the wait staff were top-notch, but they were still detached from the fun. Once they sat and placed drink orders, Bristol leaned over to whisper in Annie's ear. "Somehow we are going to sneak away and get down on that dance floor."

Annie turned so that her mouth was inches from Bristol's. "We'll need a distraction."

"You're distraction enough," Bristol said. She wasn't sure Annie heard her until she saw Annie's eyes widen in surprise and narrow with something else. Desire? Lust? Whatever it was, it made Bristol's heart swell.

"Now you're just flirting," Annie said.

"I was flirting days ago. This is something else." Bristol was surprised at her own confidence.

"I can have Charley provide a distraction," Annie said.

"What am I doing?" Charley leaned into the conversation after hearing her name.

"We need a distraction so that we can go out on the dance floor." Bristol pointed to the first floor.

"You're Bristol fucking Baines. If you want to dance, you just stand up and tell them, 'Hey, I'm going to dance, and everyone can just watch from a distance.'"

"Charley makes sense. Let's do these shots and head out there," Annie said.

Bristol handed Charley and Annie a shot and tapped her glass against theirs. "Thank you for humoring me tonight."

"I wouldn't miss this for the world," Annie said.

Bristol stood and waved Bruce over. "We're going to the dance floor. You can watch from a distance, but I won't need you out there with us."

He stared at her for the longest five seconds of her life. "Okay. I'll have people posted around. Just signal if you need help."

Bristol bit her cheeks from smiling. "Thanks, Bruce." She grabbed Annie and Charley's hands and quickly walked to the stairs before Bruce could decide it was a bad idea.

"It's so dark in here, nobody's going to know who you are. Besides, you have us as your bodyguards. Don't let my thin arms fool you. I'm pretty scrappy," Annie said.

"I believe you," Bristol said.

"I'm going to grab a drink. You two dance," Charley said. She moved her fingers in a circle motion, indicating they should get started without her. "I'll find you." Bristol didn't miss the wink that Charley gave Annie before she headed to the bar.

Nobody recognized her in the darkness and flashing lights. She pulled Annie close to her and started moving. She loved to dance. Onstage dancing was different than fun, club dancing. Here she could let go. Onstage, everything was choreographed and in sync with several other dancers. Here she could let her hair down and just have a good time. Bristol put her hands on Annie's hips as she swayed. Annie covered Bristol's hands with her own.

"Is this okay?" she whispered in Annie's ear. She couldn't hear Annie's words but felt her nod. They moved slower than the music. Annie's body molded against Bristol's almost wickedly. Annie pushed herself against Bristol. The music was too fast for Bristol to put her arms around Annie, but they moved together until Charley showed up with drinks, breaking their moment.

"Rum and Coke. I'm sorry, Bristol. I don't know what you drink, so I just got you what Annie and I drink."

They moved off the dance floor. Bristol took a sip. It was too bland for her, but she smiled at Charley and took another sip. "Thanks. I appreciate it." She fanned herself with her free hand and watched the people around her move. Nobody acted any different around her. She felt normal. She felt alive.

"You're not the only famous person here," Annie said, but not maliciously.

Bristol smiled. As nice as this was, she knew her life couldn't be clubs and late-night shenanigans forever. "Are you ready to get back out there?"

"Listen. You two do your thing out there, and I'm going to gamble. I hope that's okay? I'm hearing the call of the roulette table," Charley said.

Bristol knew it was a ploy so that she and Annie could be alone. Well, as alone as two people on a crammed club floor could be. "That's great. I promise to keep an eye out for her and not get us into any trouble."

Charley hugged Annie and whispered something in her ear that made her smile and reach for Bristol. They watched as she faded off into the throngs of people. Bristol turned to Annie. "Do you want to go back to VIP? Maybe we can actually have a conversation."

"Sure. I could use the chance to cool down."

Bristol grabbed Annie's hand and climbed the stairs to VIP. They returned to their table, sitting closer this time. Without question, Annie was into her, and it made her feel invincible. She ignored her phone buzzing in her pocket. It was probably Lizzy checking in, and Bristol wanted the night off.

"Do you know those people?" Annie pointed to three women who were talking to one of Bruce's henchmen and pointing at them.

Bristol squinted in the dark room and felt a chill overtake the heat that Annie had put in her heart. "Shit."

"Shit?" Annie looked at Bristol and back to the women, who were now approaching them.

"Sterling. Top Shelf executive and my very ex-girlfriend." Bristol gritted her teeth and pasted on a fake smile. Her entire body was tense as she leaned forward in the booth. "Hello, Sterling."

"BeeBee. It's so good to see you." Sterling leaned forward and kissed Bristol's cheek, then held out her hand to Annie. "Annie Foster. I'm a big fan. I'm Sterling Mayfield."

She slid into the booth without being asked. Her friends pulled up chairs without being asked, too. Bristol leaned back and crossed her arms. Sterling was here for a reason, and Bristol knew better than to ask but couldn't help herself. The sooner they knew why she was here, the sooner she and her primped and pampered posse would leave. "What are you doing here, Sterling?"

"Looking for you, of course. Unfortunately, we missed your show. We just arrived about an hour ago."

"This is kind of a private party," Bristol said.

Sterling looked offended, even though Bristol knew she wasn't. "Oh. I didn't mean to interrupt, but I know you're leaving in just a few short hours." She looked at Annie. "I'm here on official Top Shelf Records business."

The chill in her bones exploded into a thick, icy mixture that stole her breath. "Oh? What could that be?" Bristol asked.

"We have an interest in signing Annie. She's been great on the tour, and if we don't make a move now, I'm afraid somebody else will gobble her up."

"Wait. What?" Annie asked.

"Yes, the same label that reps Bristol wants to rep you. How does that sound?" Sterling's nasal voice sounded as annoying as somebody shredding Styrofoam, and Bristol tried hard to show zero emotion. She could hear Lizzy's voice in her head telling her that Top Shelf was a reputable company, and just because it wasn't working out for her didn't mean that it wasn't good for somebody like Annie. She could also be a sounding board for important decisions if Annie signed with them.

"Oh, my God. That's amazing," Annie said.

Bristol could feel Annie's excitement. She wanted to be happy for her, but trying to smile while Sterling was wolfishly cornering Annie wasn't possible. She hoped Annie would see Sterling for the snake she really was.

"What do you think, Bristol?" Annie asked.

Bristol forced a smile. "I'm not surprised. You're very talented."

"She is. That's why I'm here." Sterling brushed her fingertips over the back of Annie's hand. Annie slowly pulled away and reached for her water but didn't take a drink.

"I'd love to hear what you have to say. Honestly. I don't even have a manager yet," Annie said.

Sterling waved her hand. "Oh, you don't need a manager. You'll make more money without one."

"You most definitely need one." Bristol had to speak up. Even if Annie didn't go with Top Shelf Records, she needed somebody who would fight for her. She turned to Annie. "If there's one piece of advice I'm going to give you, it's definitely get a manager if you want to go this route."

Annie cocked her head and, as though picking up on Bristol's hesitancy, leaned back, too. "All of this sounds really nice, but can we talk about it another time?"

"Yes. We literally just got done with a concert, and we're unwinding," Bristol said.

Sterling laughed and touched Bristol's arm. "Lighten up, BeeBee. We've come so far since we were kids. We're both successful and loving life, and I want Annie to have the same success you've had with us." Sterling turned to Annie. "Bristol is still mad at me for breaking her heart when we were teenagers, which was a super long time ago." She pouted her lips dramatically, and her entourage laughed. "Come on. Let's have fun." She waved her hand to the server who was on standby for Bristol's table. "We'll take a bottle of your finest champagne. We're celebrating!"

Bristol clenched her jaw and stared at Sterling, who was busy avoiding eye contact with her. Sterling was slithering into different personas, trying to find the one who appealed to Annie most. The excited agent didn't work, so she quickly slipped into party girl, best friend.

"Let's just have fun tonight, and we can discuss business tomorrow. What's your phone number, Annie? I'll be sure to reach out when you're on the way to Los Angeles. Maybe if you have some time, you can swing by the offices and take a tour of the place. That is, if Bristol gives you time off. I remember her being quite demanding." Sterling winked coyly at Bristol.

"She's great. I've had the best time the last several weeks," Annie said. She handed Sterling her phone so she could input her information.

The move irritated Bristol as she watched her entire night start to unravel. Annie's body language said she was excited about Sterling's unwelcome pop-in. Bristol didn't blame her. Being approached by a record executive was exciting. She was just worried that Annie didn't seem to realize how much Sterling was trying to manipulate her.

"Great. I'll text you later today since it's already almost three." Sterling took the bottle of champagne from the server to pour everyone at the table a glass. "Since we're all here, let's toast to a successful future and many more tours."

Bristol watched Annie's face light up at Sterling's words. Top Shelf was a popular recording company that many stars wanted to sign with, but what they didn't know was that Top Shelf liked to bleed their stars until there was nothing creative left in them. They were bulldogs when it came to business—forgetting that they were dealing with people who had emotions and feelings. It was all about money—who could fill the stands and stadiums and bring them the largest profit?

Bristol wasn't going to sign a new contract with them. With the tour ending soon, she knew Lizzy was fighting to keep them at bay by telling them Bristol was busy writing a new album. She wanted to finish the tour and walk away from music, at least for the next few years. She sighed when she realized she would love Annie's life and Annie would love hers.

"Bristol, when are we going to get new music from you? I heard you dropped a new song for your fans. Daddy wants you to come in after the tour and work out a new contract." Sterling's voice purred, and Bristol bit back the bitter retort that sat at the end of her tongue.

She was working on a new album, but Top Shelf wouldn't get

their greedy little hands on it. Denny would never produce another of her songs. And Sterling wouldn't be able to brag that she landed it. "I know we have a meeting scheduled once the tour ends. We can talk more about it then, not tonight," Bristol said.

"Oh, I know Lizzy doesn't want us discussing business. She thinks it interrupts your process." Sterling rolled her eyes. "We're anxious to get together and discuss your contract. Maybe you should come in with Annie and chat with my father while I give Annie the tour of the place."

Bristol pushed away the glass of celebratory champagne. She wasn't in the mood to deal with Sterling. The happiness that had filled her just minutes ago was replaced with a darkness she had been running from since the tour started.

"I doubt I'll find the time." Bristol made a big production of looking at her watch. It was hard to see the hands, so she guessed. "Well, it's getting late, so I should probably go upstairs and get ready to leave."

"I'll go, too," Annie said.

Sterling put her hand on Annie's. Bristol noticed. The urge to rip Sterling's arm off her body was strong.

"Oh, stay for a bit. We just opened the bottle of champagne," Sterling said.

Annie looked at Bristol. "What do you think?"

Bristol knew their moment was over. She forced a smile. "If you want to stay, go ahead. Just give yourself enough time to get packed and to the bus by five." She kissed Annie on her cheek and whispered, "Don't agree to anything before you get a manager. Sterling is smooth. Be careful."

Annie squeezed her hand and nodded. Disappointment filled Bristol that Annie didn't leave with her. Her security detail picked her up at the stairs. "Bruce, leave somebody here for Annie. I want to make sure she gets out of here without any issues."

"Will do."

By the time Bristol got to the penthouse she was angry. Angry at herself for letting her guard down, pissed at Sterling for ruining her night with Annie, and disappointed in Annie for not sticking by her side. Logically she knew she shouldn't be mad. Annie was an adult and obviously more into a career than a relationship. Even though that statement probably wasn't true, Bristol wanted to wallow in self-pity for a little while longer. When her phone rang again, she looked at the name and answered it. "I know, I know. It's completely my fault."

"I tried to warn you." Lizzy sounded tired. One of the biggest things they had in common was their dislike of Sterling Mayfield. Bristol knew her personal side, and Lizzy knew how she conducted business. Bristol hated that Sterling had been her first girlfriend. It was a long time ago, and those feelings had hardened the older and wiser she'd become, but she still felt tainted. "I know. I could have sneaked out of there had I paid attention."

"I even called Bruce, but he said Sterling was already in the VIP section. From her calling me to finding you took about five minutes."

"She must've picked up my itinerary from her daddy." Bristol hated that her every move was recorded for safety reasons. It was probably more for tracking reasons, but as much as she hated it, it got her out of a few sticky situations.

"It doesn't help that your phone is technically a work phone. Check to see if you're sharing your location with anyone."

Bristol looked and saw that Lizzy was right. Her location was shared with Lizzy, Bruce, her parents, and Top Shelf Records. "Did you know they were tracking me?"

"No, but I'm not surprised."

"Screw that. I'm turning it off." Bristol was so angry her hands were shaking.

"Don't bother. It will only piss them off. Plus, then they will know you figured it out."

"I'm not letting them track me. Can somebody get me my own phone?"

"I'll send someone out right now. You'll have it before we leave Vegas," Lizzy said.

"Thanks. And have them only program people I like in it. It'll be my personal one." There was a small victory in knowing that she would have that control back.

"Did Sterling try to get you to talk about the next album?" Lizzy asked.

"She tried, but I deflected. I told her I was out having a good time and business could wait."

"Did she press you?"

"Not really."

"Did she embarrass you? We know how she is when she's trying to impress somebody new. Everyone else is the butt of the joke."

"She tried. She made it sound like we were childhood sweethearts again, calling me BeeBee. You know, her usual bullshit."

"Well, then why do you still sound angry?" Lizzy asked.

Bristol pinched the bridge of her nose and groaned. "Because the twatwaffle ruined my night by stealing my date!"

Chapter Thirteen

After five minutes alone with Sterling and her friends, Annie knew she'd made a terrible mistake. When Sterling first sat down, Annie thought Bristol was just mad her ex had showed up. After talking for five minutes, she knew it was because Sterling had bad vibes.

Her selfish dream of making it big had outweighed her desire to be with someone wonderful like Bristol. They were getting along so well, too. Annie was sure Bristol was going to kiss her. She could tell by how close Bristol sat and how they held hands, because just friends didn't do that, did they? She was reeling at the realization that her one-sided crush wasn't so one-sided. Bristol was into her, and Annie had just fucked that up by making the wrong choice at the worst time.

"Top Shelf is the company you want to sign with. I mean, you could be as big as Bristol Baines," Sterling said. She leaned closer to Annie. "Bigger than Bristol. You already have such a strong internet presence. I've seen your YouTube channel explode over the last month."

Annie smiled at the compliment. She had worked hard over the last few years, with no breaks except for this one. And she knew she owed it to herself to hear all offers. That's why she was on tour. Exposure and opportunity. Bristol's message came through loud and clear about getting a manager before making any rash decisions. "Thank you. I've worked hard to get where I am."

"And I'm here to make sure you get what you deserve. All the fortune and fame you want."

Annie didn't like the way Sterling pushed, but she knew that was part of her job. She was there to make sure Annie got signed, and as much as Annie wanted to walk the fuck away from this table, she knew it was rude, and she was in no position to burn bridges. While Sterling cooed over Annie's presence onstage, she tuned her out and thought about Bristol. Her stomach was in knots wondering if Bristol was upset or if she understood Annie had to play the game.

"I appreciate the confidence you have in me. I would love a tour of the place. Why don't you text me tomorrow? Like Bristol said, we should pull in about noon." She stretched and yawned. "In the meantime, I should probably get packed up and maybe catch a nap before we head out. Touring is draining."

"It's not that bad," Sterling said. She finished her second glass of champagne and put the glass firmly on the table. "We'll work with you on a tour and make sure it's not a concert every night. Bristol likes to push herself. This wasn't supposed to be an eighteen-month-long tour. It was only supposed to be a year, but she pushed it out."

Annie quirked her head. It didn't sound like something Bristol would do, but she knew all about biting off more than she could chew. "Thanks again. I'll see you tomorrow." She nodded at Sterling's drunk friends. "It was nice to meet you both as well."

Sterling waved her phone at Annie. "I have your number now, and I'm not afraid to use it."

Annie waved and gave a deep sigh of relief when she walked down the VIP stairs. She was greeted by one of Bruce's security guys. His hair wasn't buzzed like the rest of Bristol's security detail. He looked like a dude out in the club, except for the Spaulding Security polo stretched over his muscles. "I'm Cam, and I'm here to make sure you get back to your hotel room safely. Are you headed there now?"

Annie was seriously thinking of heading straight for Bristol's room but wasn't sure what to say. How much time had passed? Bristol had left her thirty minutes ago. "Yes. Thank you, Cam." Showing up this late was in poor taste. She would just explain herself to Bristol when they got to the venue tomorrow.

"If there's anything you need, please don't hesitate to reach out," Cam said as he delivered her to her door.

"Thank you." The suite was quiet, so she shot off a text to Charley.
Hey. I'm up in the room. We're leaving in about an hour. How's

it going on your end? She wasn't worried about Charley's well-being but was afraid she would miss saying good-bye to her. Charley's flight wasn't until tonight, so she had the room until at least eleven.

On my way now. Be there in a few.

Annie didn't want to miss saying good-bye to Charley. She needed her strength and her advice. Vegas had started off with a bang, and then something unsettling had happened when Sterling Mayfield showed up. With a sigh, she scraped up her toiletries, shoved her clothes into her suitcase, and threw everything onto the bed. She decided to send a text to Bristol to let her know she was back at the room in case Bristol thought otherwise.

Thanks for having Cam wait for me. He walked me back to the room. I'm here safe and sound.

She held the phone and waited for three little dots to tell her Bristol at least saw the message and was responding. After five minutes of staring at the screen, she gave up.

Charley burst into the room with her hands raised and both fists fat with stacks of cash. "Guess who got a hand payout?"

"Woohoo! How much did you win?" Annie asked. She smiled when Charley gave her a tight hug.

"Four thousand and change. Are you all packed?"

Annie nodded and pointed at her suitcases. "That's a nice little treat to take home. What time will your flight get in?"

"Around seven tonight." Charley scouted the room for anything Annie might have left behind. "Hopefully, I don't blow all of this."

"Even if you do, it's been a super-fun trip and totally worth it." Annie extended the handle on her luggage and grabbed her messenger bag. "I have to go. I'm sure everyone is downstairs already." Annie checked the time. She still had a few minutes. "Checkout time is eleven, but you can store your bag downstairs."

"Hell. I'll just cart it with me. Maybe I'll check out a few other casinos. Try my luck elsewhere."

She hugged Charley. "Thanks so much for coming. I had the best time with you." She wanted to tell her about her night and the exchange she had with Bristol and Sterling, but it was too fresh, and she was still processing.

"Keep me posted on anything exciting."

"Let me know when you're home safe." Annie waved off Charley's help and grabbed her bags. "I'll let you know when we get to LA." She dreaded the bus ride and hoped for some peace and quiet. She noticed Bristol's bus wasn't in the lot and checked her phone again to see if Bristol sent her a message. Her only notification was breaking news on CNN.

When Annie boarded the bus, Vaughn handed her a blanket. "Try to get some sleep. It'll take a while to reach the arena."

"Thanks, but I doubt I'll be able to sleep."

Vaughn smiled warmly at her. "Long night?"

"Long couple of days." Annie lowered her voice. "I'm still processing everything, but I was approached by two different record labels in Vegas, and I don't know what to do or how to feel about it." She didn't know why she'd told him when she hadn't even told Charley all the details. Maybe he felt safer because he was removed.

"That's amazing," Vaughn whispered. "Who?"

Annie hesitated. Vaughn had been nothing but kind to her, but he was still Lizzy's assistant.

"No. Never mind." He covered his ears playfully. "Don't tell me. If you want to chat, you let me know, okay?"

Annie smiled. "Thanks, Vaughn, for everything. You've been very sweet and nice to me on this tour."

He winked and moved toward the front of the bus to give her privacy.

After the last six hours of swirling emotions kicking at her chest, Annie didn't think she would be able to calm down enough to relax but stretched out on three seats and fell sleep before the bus even moved from the curb. She woke up five hours later as the bus jerked in Los Angeles traffic.

She picked up her phone and sighed. Still nothing from Bristol. Determined not to give up, she typed, *Los Angeles makes Denver look small.* She wanted to keep the message friendly and light. She wanted to follow up with another text but mentally scolded herself. She didn't want to be a pain in the ass. She genuinely liked Bristol and not because she was the most successful pop star in the world, but because she was warm and kind.

When the bus stopped next to the arena, everyone filed out and headed inside. Not really knowing what to do, Annie followed the crowd in. They all had a purpose except for Annie. She walked around, getting to know the layout of the arena, found her dressing room, and headed down to the main floor after seeing people delivering food. She was hungry and couldn't remember when she ate her last meal.

"Lunch is here," Clarissa, one of Lizzy's assistants, announced to the many workers on the stage. Annie wasn't in the mood to eat with anyone, so she politely grabbed a sandwich and sat in the stadium seats. People were moving about doing their jobs efficiently. After a year and a half on the road, the crew knew exactly how to work fast together. When her phone vibrated several minutes later with a message, her heart catapulted into her throat, only to lodge there when she read who it was from. It wasn't Bristol.

If you still want a tour, I'll send a car to collect you in thirty minutes. That'll give you time to tour the studios and still get back in plenty of time to rehearse.—Sterling

Annie took a deep breath and closed her eyes. She had to make a decision that was best for her. Since Bristol was either ignoring her message or busy with something else, she had to decide. *Sounds good. Where should I wait?*

I'll drop you a pin. See you soon! I'm excited.

If Annie was being truthful, she was excited, too. She wasn't going to sign anything until she had a manager, or at least her lawyer, to look over any contract. That gave her an idea. She composed a quick email to Dani and asked if the firm knew any reputable entertainment managers in the Denver area. She popped the last bite of her sandwich into her mouth and made her way to the location on her phone. She showed her pass to the security guards stationed out front as a limo pulled up smoothly next to her. Sterling poked her head out when the driver opened the door.

"Perfect timing. Get in."

Annie slipped in and sat opposite Sterling, who looked fresh and sober even though she and her friends had polished off at least one bottle of champagne and a few rounds of shots last night before Annie excused herself. "How was the rest of your night?"

"Wonderful. Vegas is great. I try to get there as often as I can. Was that your first time?"

"Yes. I loved the venue. Gambling was fun, but I sucked at it."

"It's not for everybody. Did you like the VIP room? Vegas really takes care of Top Shelf Records. Something to think about," Sterling said. She offered Annie a water from the compact refrigerator. Annie found her to be charming and sweet, a complete change from last night. She relaxed and gave Sterling her attention.

"We're one of the largest record companies in the United States and have signed some of the biggest stars, but you already know that. We give our clients everything they could ever want. Signing you would be the biggest thing we've done all year. You would be supported with Top Shelf's time and money. We have the best studios to record in, with some of the best producers."

Annie held up her hand. "I know all about Top Shelf. You've been on my radar for a long time, ever since I picked up a guitar when I was twelve. You don't need to impress me. I'm already impressed."

Sterling leaned forward and touched Annie's knee. "Then tell me what we need to do to sign you?"

Annie felt the jolt in her touch. Not because she was attracted to Sterling, although she was pretty, but because the person who could do the most for her career was offering her everything she'd ever wanted. "Honestly, I want to get through this tour and then do what I can to find a manager before I commit to anything."

"I completely understand." Sterling looked out the window and smiled. "Good news. We're here."

"That was fast," Annie said. She waited until the driver opened the door for them. Annie felt slightly frumpy in her summer dress and flat sandals standing next to Sterling, who was dressed in designer clothing and heels. She followed Sterling into the building.

"We have the entire building, so let's start in the studios. I don't know who's recording today, but we're going to find out."

Annie couldn't help the shiver of excitement at the possibility of seeing one of her favorite artists cutting a new album. Sterling tapped lightly on the first door, even though the light above it was red, indicating that somebody was in the studio and they weren't to be disturbed. A grumpy technical engineer opened the door. When he saw Sterling, he instantly dropped the scowl.

"Who's in there?" Sterling asked.

"Kingston Brock," he said as his gaze moved from Sterling to Annie.

Annie took a small step behind Sterling. Sterling turned to her. "Do you like Kingston?"

She didn't but also didn't want to be rude. "I'm not familiar with their music."

Sterling asked to see the schedule. The engineer quietly closed the door and returned with a tablet that he handed to Sterling.

"Okay. We have four artists recording today who you might know. And a few new ones."

Annie wanted to see the list immediately but waited for Sterling to name off the artists. When she heard Willow McAdams was there, she had to tamp down a squeal. "I know Willow McAdams's music." She hoped her voice was chill. Willow had scored several number-one hits in the last year.

"Let's go say hello," Sterling said.

Annie followed her down the hall and around several corners until they stood in front of studio fourteen. Sterling knocked softly and stood back. The door flew open, and a giant man towered over them. Again, Annie shrank back, but Sterling took a step forward.

"Dez, we're here to see Willow." Immediately, he took a step back and ushered them inside.

"Sorry about the interruption, Willow." Sterling waved through the glass at Willow, who returned the wave.

"It's no problem. What's going on?"

"Just doing a quick tour. I have Annie Foster with me, and she wanted to see the studios."

Willow waved Annie inside. "You're touring with Bristol right now, aren't you? Is the tour over?"

It took all of Annie's mental effort not to jump up and down with excitement. She was meeting Willow McAdams, and Willow knew who she was! "Not yet. We're doing a couple of shows before we head up the West Coast. We'll be done by Labor Day."

"It's so nice to meet you," Willow said.

"It's great to meet you, too. What are you working on?" It was hard to have a conversation with everyone watching you.

"My third studio album, called *Tricks and Treats*."

"So, I'm hearing it first here," Annie said.

Willow nodded. "Did you sign with Top Shelf?"

Annie shook her head. "Not yet. I just pulled into town for a concert, and Sterling asked me to come in for a quick tour." She couldn't help but smile. She was floating at everyone's confidence in her, but was she ready for such a long-term commitment? Peyton seemed to be doing well from the treatments, but seeing her on FaceTime video chats wasn't the same thing as holding her on her lap and smothering her with kisses and hearing her sweet laugh in person. It was also nice to give Sarah and Chase a night off from the pressures of having a sick child. And then there was Raven. What did musicians do with their pets when they traveled for months at a time? Raven would never forgive her. It wasn't as if she could take her along. She was a high-anxiety cat who hated to leave the apartment. Going to the vet required tranquilizers and prayers. Touring with Raven wasn't an option. "How do you cope with pets and family on the road?"

Willow set down her guitar and gave Annie her full attention. "It's not easy. I'm very close with my sisters and my parents. It's within my means to fly them places if they can get away from their lives." She gave Annie an encouraging smile. "I've decided that I'm the artist who can only do short tours. Top Shelf is very supportive of my schedule and what I want to do. How Bristol Baines is doing an eighteen-month tour is beyond my comprehension. She's a beast."

"She's amazing," Annie said without hesitation. She sat up straighter when she heard the click of the microphone right before Sterling interrupted them.

"Sorry, Annie, but we have to go. Willow has a lot to do in a short amount of time."

Willow gave her a quick hug. "Good luck. I hope to see your name around here soon."

Annie finished the studio tour on a high. Sterling was completely chill. Gone was the high-pressure salesperson trying to get her to sign on the dotted line. She chalked it up to alcohol and tension between Bristol and Sterling. They had a past, and it didn't end well, according to what she'd read online. She didn't want to gossip, but maybe she should ask Vaughn about it.

"Not a bad setup, right? I don't mean to cut it short, but I know you have to get back and do a practice run onstage before tonight's concert," Sterling said.

Annie was surprised that it was almost four and still no text from Bristol. "For sure. Top Shelf is an amazing company."

Sterling didn't join her in the limo, citing work, but promised the limo would get her back to the arena in a flash. "Can we have a verbal agreement that you won't sign with another label until you get a manager and sit down with Top Shelf first?"

Annie didn't want to burn her bridges yet, and honestly had it not been for Bristol whispering in her ear last night, she would have eagerly signed with them today. She shook Sterling's hand. "Once I'm done with the tour, I'll get a manager, and we'll reach out to you first."

Sterling dropped the sexiest smile that did nothing for Annie. She wasn't interested in her that way. "I will hold you to it. See you later tonight."

Annie was surprised. "Oh. You'll be at the show?"

"I wouldn't miss it. Maybe if you're up for it, we can go out after the show. I might not be Bristol Baines, but I can still get us into the best clubs in the city," Sterling said.

Her smile was so sincere that Annie had a hard time saying no. "I'm leaning toward yes, but let's see how I feel after the show. I'm still exhausted from Vegas."

Sterling held her hands up and backed away from the limo. "Go. I'll see you later. We can plan something if you're feeling up to it. Break a leg, and rock the crap out of that arena."

Annie laughed when the driver closed the door. Where was this charmer last night? Sterling Mayfield had turned out to be more than Annie gave her credit for. She ended up being nice and professional while still having a personal touch that made Annie feel like more than a number for Top Shelf Records.

CHAPTER FOURTEEN

I saw her getting into a limo a few hours ago."

Dom pointed to an exit behind them. Lizzy growled and looked at her watch. Bristol put her hands on her hips and turned to face the stage. "Hopefully, she'll show up soon." She knew Sterling had given Annie the studio tour. While Top Shelf was impressive on the outside, Bristol hoped that Annie took her advice and didn't do anything stupid like sign with them without an agent.

"I'm sorry I'm late." Annie jogged up behind them carrying her guitar on her back. "Traffic to get here was awful."

"That leaves you fifteen minutes of practice time. I'd hustle up there if I were you," Lizzy said.

Bristol didn't like the tone Lizzy took with Annie, even though she wasn't happy with Annie's whereabouts today. "I can shave off a few minutes of my practice," Bristol said. She finally met Annie's eyes. "Make sure you're comfortable up there and the sound techs get it right. Don't rush. Lizzy gets anxious when we play a large crowd."

Annie's cheeks flushed with embarrassment. "Thank you. I won't take a long time up there." She swung her guitar to her front and made her way onstage.

Bristol turned to Lizzy. "Let's not make her feel like shit before a show, okay? Can we do that?"

Lizzy squared her shoulders and faced Bristol. "You lost sleep because of her."

Bristol regretted confiding in Lizzy. "That's still not a reason to make her feel bad. I can't blame her for looking out for herself. I'd do the same. And don't forget, you were her biggest cheerleader in Denver." Bristol turned and marched back to her dressing room. She was so conflicted. Her heart was angry, but her head understood what Annie was doing. They'd only known each other for what? A few weeks? That wasn't enough for any loyalty regardless of whatever sparks were happening between them. It wasn't like Bristol had confided any of her feelings about Top Shelf with Annie. She didn't even know that talking to Sterling was pissing Bristol off.

"Okay. We won't talk about Annie." Lizzy followed Bristol back to the suite.

Trying to keep her voice as casual as possible, Bristol asked the question Lizzy wasn't going to. "I wonder how the tour at Top Shelf went?" Bristol shrugged as though it wasn't a big deal. "Did she text anything?"

Lizzy was monitoring Bristol's Top Shelf phone. Half an hour after she and Lizzy had hung up the night before, Clarissa had shown up with a new phone. She'd already set it up and entered the contact numbers Lizzy had given her. Lizzy hadn't included Annie's number.

"I left your phone on the bus, but there wasn't anything an hour ago," Lizzy said.

That didn't sound like Annie. Bristol had gotten used to her sending little texts at the end of the night and looked forward to them more than she realized. Maybe Lizzy was lying. Maybe she wanted Bristol to focus solely on the tour and not on the cute musician. It was hard enough to keep up the pretense of working on an album when there were so many moles on tour with them. Lizzy probably didn't want to deal with another Natasha Breeze on top of that. "I can just talk to her backstage tonight. I'm sure she'll tell me," Bristol said.

"You look tired. Why don't you try to get some rest?"

Bristol couldn't remember the last time she'd slept. She was too amped up to sleep from Vegas to Los Angeles. Too many thoughts were spinning in her head, and she couldn't just focus on one thing, so she gave up and let her mind wander for five hours. Most of her happy thoughts led her back to Annie, but some of the bitter ones did, too. She should have elaborated more about her relationship with Sterling to Annie. She didn't hate Sterling because she broke her heart. It was because she preyed on people. She took advantage of Bristol and so many others.

Tyson Mayfield didn't care. He encouraged his daughter's shady tactics. He was a numbers guy who wanted a fat wallet and bragging rights. He had plenty of both. When Bristol worked up enough nerve to tell him she didn't want to work with Denny Briggs, Tyson promised she wouldn't have to, but the exact opposite happened. Denny ended up producing her next two albums. If it wasn't for Lizzy sitting in on every session, Bristol didn't want to think what Denny would have tried to do to her. Actually, she knew exactly what he would have done. The same thing he did to Ruby Delgado. Sterling knew exactly what was happening to Ruby and did nothing to prevent it. She and Tyson were disgusting. Bristol couldn't wait to finish the tour and shove any contract they tried baiting her with right in their faces.

Bristol felt a wave of gratitude for Lizzy. "You know you're the best, right?"

Lizzy looked concerned but masked it with a smile. "We're almost done. What's the countdown now?"

"Eleven. Only eleven more shows."

"That's less than three weeks." Lizzy held her hands up for Bristol to slap. Bristol smacked them with enough force they both shook their hands from the sting. "Top Shelf has been asking about signing a contract for that fake album I told them you've been working on all tour. I have a feeling they're going to hold us hostage on the last concert."

"Good luck. Too many people are going to be around," Bristol said. She was ending their tour with the proverbial bang with three other well-known artists. When news had spread that the final concert was star-studded, secondhand-ticket-outlet prices skyrocketed. General admission seats were selling for at least five hundred dollars. VIP were going for at least two thousand. The concert started at five and ended at midnight. Logistics were going to be a bitch, and Lizzy was beyond stressed working with the arena on the details.

"Are you really just going to run away from all this? Can you do it?"

Bristol shrugged. "Ask me in six months."

"Will do. Now, go relax. I'll get you for Annie's set, if you still want to do it."

Bristol frowned. "Of course I do."

"Then I'll get you in an hour."

When Lizzy closed the door, Bristol flopped onto the couch. She was tired—physically, mentally, and emotionally. She plugged her ears and covered up with a blanket that Lizzy delivered from the bus. Trying to tune out the background noises was easy. Ignoring her loud thoughts proved to be more difficult and shaved valuable time off her nap.

❖

Annie was smiling when Bristol showed up onstage next to her at the end of her set, but her eyes were guarded. Maybe she thought Bristol was mad at her for going on the tour or coming back late from it. She sang Annie's song and, in a move that surprised them both, kissed her cheek before she skipped offstage.

"What was that all about?" Lizzy asked while half jogging just to keep up with Bristol's pace.

"Just keeping the peace." She was greeted by a flurry of activity as her stylists buzzed around her to get her wardrobe ready. Phoebe patted the chair to get started on her hair. Bristol was getting tired of coming up with new looks. It was easy to let her hair down and wear something sexy and black, but the wholesome look during the first half was wearing thin. She wasn't feeling it today and agreed on a pair of ankle jeans, a cute white sleeveless shirt with a Peter Pan collar, and designer sneakers made just for her. She needed solid but fashionable shoes for the dance routine.

"Fast Cars just got off. You're up in fifteen," Lizzy said.

The buzz around her became feverish even though she was ready. She closed her eyes right before more hairspray was spritzed on her updo.

"Ready?"

She opened her eyes when she felt Lizzy's hands on hers. They did their breathing exercises, and when it was time to go, Bristol felt calm and collected. She stood in the wings, waiting until the lights went out and the crowd screamed with delight. It was hard not to smile. The rush of endorphins exploded throughout her and pushed her onstage to her mark. Tonight, she was starting the concert a cappella just to mix things up. Her eyes were closed when the spotlight hit her. She waited a solid twenty seconds for the crowd to settle. When it was obvious they weren't going to, she started singing, knowing they would quiet down. She sang the words clearly, loudly, and by the end, her voice was just a whisper. They ate it up and begged for more. The band ran onstage, and a roadie quickly delivered her favorite guitar. She slipped the strap around her neck and started strumming the second song. When the stage lit up, Bristol could see rows of smiling faces. Some were singing with her word for word, and some were just nodding to the beat. What she wasn't expecting to see was Sterling and Annie. She quickly focused on other fans in the first few rows and kept her glances to them minimal. Sterling was having the time of her life, beer in hand, while Annie only smiled when Bristol caught her eye. Annie swayed her hips to the rhythm and drank what looked like ice water. Her blond curls bobbed with the beat, and even though Bristol tried to look everywhere but at Annie, those piercing blue eyes kept drawing her back. It was the longest concert. Sterling was ruining everything, but Bristol couldn't do anything about it. They were smack dab in the middle of the front row. They were hard to miss.

"LA is my home," Bristol yelled to fifty thousand fans, who screamed back how they loved her, how they missed her, and how happy they were she was home. "I always forget how good it feels to be back." This was the part of the show where Bristol took a quick break before dancing with eight professionals in the background. She chatted with the crowd as though she was very interested in their lives but was really taking a breather. She hated choreography, but dancing enhanced the show, and the fans loved it. With the price tag of a ticket so steep, she had to keep up with the trendy concerts other artists offered. She drew the line at swinging on circles high above the stage. She didn't mind rising from below the stage but refused to be elevated for any reason. Bristol wasn't a fan of heights.

She switched her guitar for a headset microphone and quickly but carefully clipped it against her ear. It amazed her that something so tiny could produce such a loud sound. She gave the signal to her band to start the next song and got into position. The dance was sweet but turned flirty at the end. She was ramping the fans up for the devil part of her concert. Tonight, she wasn't going to pull Annie onstage. She wasn't feeling it. She focused on her footwork. The words flowed effortlessly from her lips. Her music was in her soul. That wasn't the hard part. Keeping up with her dancers on very little sleep or food was hard.

Lizzy was waiting when Bristol came offstage. "Listen to how much they love you," she yelled. She handed Bristol a cold water and a towel.

Bristol nodded. She was saving her voice for the encore. She had two songs left, and her throat was feeling scratchy.

Lizzy always knew the signs. "I'll have a hot tea waiting for you in your dressing room. Save some of that for tomorrow."

Bristol saluted her and jaunted up the steps back onstage. Her band members were close on her heels. They finished the set quickly, and Bristol wished everyone a safe night. She marched back to her suite and peeled off her drenched clothes. A shower would have to wait. Tonight, she was going to her house. It was an hour drive, but she needed to feel something comforting. She wanted to wake up in her own bed and know that at any moment her mother would pop in. Her family would be at the concert tomorrow night. Her brother was getting home from his internship tonight. She slipped into workout pants and a T-shirt. Security was there to get her to the limo, where two security cars would escort her away from the venue.

"Bristol! Bristol, wait!"

She heard Sterling's voice but pretended not to. Her detail put space between them and got her safely into the limo. She didn't see Annie, but everything was a blur. Fans who managed to slip through unsecured areas were pressed flat against the limo banging on the windows. Bristol shrank back in her seat.

"We'll be out of here in a minute, Ms. Baines," Willie, a regular driver for Bristol when she was home, said. Normally they waited until most of the crowd had left, but tonight Bristol just wanted to get home. She relaxed when the arena was a disappearing dot behind her.

"Let me know if you need anything."

"Thank you, Willie." She waited until he raised the privacy glass between them and pulled out her phone. She wanted to text Annie, but she still didn't have her number. She pulled up Instagram and smiled. Dom was great at her job. All platforms were full of tour photos, videos, and quotes. She made a mental note to give Dom a raise. She busied herself by watching TikTok videos, and in no time, they were pulling up to her gated community. Willie gave identification to the security post, and Bristol rolled down the window to prove it was her.

"Ms. Baines. Are you back from your tour?" Mac asked. Bristol always liked Mac. He was courteous and professional with her and the other celebrities who lived in this neighborhood.

"Only back for the night, but my tour will be over in two weeks." She trusted him not to sell her information to the press and tipped him well every year at the holidays to ensure her privacy.

"It'll be nice to have you back when you're done. I'm sure you miss being home," he said. He punched in the code that opened the tall, wrought-iron gate.

She nodded to him and told him to have a good night before she raised the window. She brushed away a few tears that fell when her estate came into view. Seeing the world was great, but there was nothing like the comfort of coming home, even if it was just for a few short hours.

CHAPTER FIFTEEN

Delilah's was a popular club with tons of celebrities, but all Annie could think about was getting back to the hotel and sleeping for at least ten hours. It was after midnight, and she was dragging. How Sterling did it continuously was beyond her comprehension.

"You were so great onstage," Sterling said.

Annie was impressed with how Sterling managed to use large hand motions and not spill her wine. "Thank you again for this opportunity. I'm having so much fun."

Sterling cocked her head and pursed her lips but didn't say anything. She slightly shook her head as though erasing a thought and held her wine glass against Annie's. "That's what we do. Enough about that. Tell me about your life back in Denver. You do music for your day job, right?"

How did she know that? "Yes. I'm a contract jingle writer, but I took the last month off to do this tour." She glanced at the time again. It was almost twelve thirty.

"You keep looking at the time, and I'm starting to get a complex," Sterling said.

"I'm sorry." Annie automatically put her hand on Sterling's. It was more of a reaction to calm her, but within seconds, Sterling had intertwined their fingers. Now they were holding hands, and as much as Annie wanted to pull away, she didn't want to offend her either. "I have a lot going on tomorrow. I also haven't slept the greatest in days."

Sterling nodded sympathetically. "How about we watch the rest of the concert tomorrow from the company suite? We can have dinner and a nice conversation. You can meet my dad and a few of the executives. There won't be pressure to sign with us. It'll be a good time." As she spoke, she rubbed her thumb across Annie's fingers.

Annie hated every second of contact between their joined hands. Maybe it was because she knew Sterling would be her boss if she signed with Top Shelf, or maybe it was because she was attracted to Bristol and not Sterling. Either way, she wanted out of this situation. Sterling's idea had merit, and agreeing would give her an out for the rest of the evening. "That sounds like a nice plan. I really should go now though."

Sterling let go of Annie's hand and grabbed her phone. "I'll have the driver meet us out front. He can take you back. Come on. I'll walk you out."

"Thank you. That's very nice." Annie followed her to the front of the bar. It took a solid ten minutes to get to the door because of all the people who stopped Sterling to say hello. She made sure to introduce Annie to every single person. She met two blockbuster movie stars, a top model, a morning talk show personality who used to host a reality show, and tons of musicians, some she recognized and some she didn't. When they finally made it outside, the limo was there waiting. "Thanks again for tonight. I had a great time."

"It was my pleasure," Sterling said.

Before Annie had a chance to react, Sterling pulled her close and kissed her. Annie stumbled back and held her hands up. "Hold on. I don't want there to be any misunderstanding."

Sterling held a perfectly manicured hand to her chest as though shocked. Annie wasn't sure if it was because she got turned down or if she was playing it up.

"I'm sorry. I guess I read you wrong. I didn't mean to make you uncomfortable. This is entirely my mistake," Sterling said.

"I'm fine. I just don't think this is a good idea, especially if you want me to sign with Top Shelf. Let's keep this professional." She tried hard to keep the anxiety out of her voice, but Sterling's move really threw her off.

Sterling nodded. "I understand. Have a good night, Annie. I'll see you tomorrow."

As poised as she could manage, she crawled into the limo and started breathing again when they pulled away from the curb. LA was tough and the women were intense. The ride to the hotel took twenty minutes. Sitting alone in the limo made her realize how tense and tired she was. Annie had never been so excited to get back to a hotel room in her entire life.

❖

Her phone's vibration was loud on the glass nightstand. She reached for it and swiped it on. "Sarah? Is everything okay?"

"Everything's fine. You told me to call you on my lunch break."

Annie looked around the dark room. "What time is it?"

"One. So eleven your time."

Annie rubbed her face with her free hand and stretched. "Sorry. I'm exhausted. As much as I'm loving this life, I can't wait to get home. I don't know how people do this every night."

"Do what?" Sarah asked.

"Stay out all night, every night." She pushed the covers off and turned on the small lamp on the nightstand. She winced at the bright light and wiggled her way into a sitting position. "How's Peyton?"

"So far, everything is good. She's responded well to the treatments. She wanted me to tell you that she's taking excellent care of Raven, and she's organized your mail by color," Sarah said.

Annie chuckled. "I'm sure Raven's kicked it around by now. She hates piles. Thank you again for taking care of her. I know she's difficult."

"It's a good thing she loves Peyton so much because she despises me."

"She does not," Annie said, but they both knew she was lying. "Tell me about life."

"I'm pretty sure you need to tell me about what's going on in yours. How's the tour? How's Bristol?"

"Touring is so much fun, but only because I'm touring with somebody big. I'm sure if I was the headliner, we'd be staying at two-star hotels, not four-star."

"How was Vegas? Charley said it was amazing, but she was too busy to give me details."

Annie couldn't believe she'd left Vegas yesterday. It felt like a lifetime ago. "We had so much fun. VIP is awesome. I felt like royalty everywhere. Bristol even assigned a security guard to me one night when I stayed out later than she did."

Sarah laughed. "I'm so jealous. We're going next time I catch a break."

Annie's heart fell just a little bit. Her sister had so much on her plate, with no real break in sight. "When I get back, we'll go somewhere fun. And it can just be us girls." It wasn't that she didn't love Chase, because she did, but she and Sarah were so close that sometimes it was just awkward with him there. "Peyton included."

"I'm going to hold you to that," Sarah said. "Tell me about what's been going on with you. The concert isn't for another hour, so we have time to catch up."

Fuck. Annie had forgotten she was doing a virtual concert for the kids today. She scrambled out of bed and pulled clothes out of her suitcase. She had fallen face-first on the mattress last night. Her smudged makeup was going to take forever to scrub off. At least her guitar was in the room, so she didn't have to scramble to get that off the tour bus. "So much has happened, I don't even know where to begin." Annie couldn't have spoken the truth more. "Four Twelve Entertainment wants to sign me. They rep Three Times Wrong."

"Oh, I love them. That's amazing."

"It gets better. Top Shelf wants to sign me too, but everyone I trust is telling me to get a manager."

"Oh, my God! That's even better news. It's your dream come true."

"Yes, but touring is grueling, and they are known for throwing their artists out on the road after each album."

"But isn't that the business?" Sarah asked.

"Yeah, maybe when we were kids. Music is different because of social media and all the available platforms artists have. Concerts are one thing, but there's so much more available." Annie thought about her words and found them to be true. The industry had changed so much. She remembered her parents telling them stories of standing in line at the venue for concert tickets when they were teenagers.

As if reading her thoughts, Sarah said, "You know I'm super proud of you. I always knew you could hit it big. Mom and Dad would be at every one of your performances if they could."

"I was just thinking about them. Remember how Dad used to tell us about the lines they had to physically stand in to buy concert tickets? I can't even imagine," Annie said.

"I can't imagine a world without the internet. How was life even possible? What was social media back then? Friday night at the roller-skating rink?" Sarah laughed. "Remember the mix tapes they made? I think I still have Mom's from when she was in college."

"I have some of her letters she wrote to her friends. On paper." Annie laughed with Sarah. As much as they teased their parents, they both missed them terribly.

"Listen, lunch is almost over, and I have some paperwork before the concert, so I'll let you go. Give me thirty minutes."

"Sounds great. I'll see you soon." Annie disconnected the call and jumped into the shower. It didn't matter what she looked like for the kids. She could just throw her wet hair up in a bun. She still needed to wash all the ickiness of the twenty-four hours off. She had everything ready to go for the concert with only a minute to spare.

"Welcome, Annie Foster," Sarah said.

Annie waved. "Hi, kids. How are you?" A chorus of "fine" and "good" answered her. "Do we have any requests today, or should I just wing it?" Annie knew Sarah would have to pull requests from the kids, as most of them were quiet and shy.

"How about something you're playing on tour right now. What's your favorite song to sing?" Sarah asked to spark interest.

Annie thought for a moment and decided on the song she sang with Bristol. "I bet everyone here knows this song." She strummed and started singing. By the end of it, half the kids were singing, and Sarah was dancing down the aisle, making the kids laugh. She wasn't a great dancer but also wasn't trying very hard. The goal was to make the kids have fun. A few nurses popped in to check on machines and IVs and danced with Sarah. The concert was over too quickly, and Annie didn't want to say good-bye.

"Thank you for letting me play my guitar for you." Annie waved to the children and smiled as they waved back.

"See you later, sis," Sarah said before ending the Zoom call.

The concert invigorated Annie. She wanted to get out and see a little bit of Los Angeles before she was expected at the arena. The rumbling in her stomach motivated her to get up and out in search for food. She slipped into shorts, a T-shirt, and sandals. Nobody would recognize her. She found a coffee shop and ordered a latte and a slice of lemon pound cake. She sat at an empty table near a window, popped a piece of cake into her mouth, and almost choked when she opened her Twitter feed and read what was trending. "Oh, fuck."

CHAPTER SIXTEEN

"Where's my child?"

Bristol stretched and peeked her head out from beneath her thick comforter. Sleeping in her own bed was therapeutic and much needed after so many months away. She opened one eye. "Tell me you have doughnuts."

"Primo's doughnuts and their world-famous coffee. Do I know my daughter or what?"

Bristol reached out and Vanessa hugged her. "Thanks, Mom."

Vanessa sat on the edge of Bristol's mattress and handed her a steaming cup and a glazed doughnut. "You deserve a sugar reward for being on the road for so long. It always takes a toll on you."

Bristol knew that was her mother's way of telling her she looked rough. Subconsciously, she patted down her hair and tried to wake up. "I haven't been sleeping the best. And we just got done with Vegas. You know how I never sleep there." She took a bite of the sweet pastry and expressed her appreciation with a loud moan. "These are the best. I can't wait until I'm home and can have these every weekend. Tell me what I've missed."

Vanessa moved the plate with the doughnut from her lap onto the nightstand and tucked her hair behind her ears. She curled both hands around the eco-friendly disposable cup. She was always so gentle. It was one of the things Bristol loved about her mother. Show business was hard, but her mother was always ready to hold her if she needed strength. Her mother was her hero. She taught Bristol how to play the piano, how to braid her hair a million different ways, and how to stand up for herself.

"Your brother got home about midnight. He's still sleeping."

Bristol waved her hand as though it didn't matter that her little brother didn't race over to see her even though it had been almost nine months. It stung. "He's living his life. Plus, I'll be home in two weeks."

"He's very excited about your final concert. He wants eight VIP tickets. Do you think you can swing it?"

"Ha! The answer is no because even I can't get that many, but he can ask me himself. He knows how to text." She knew her reaction was childish, but it bothered her that he wasn't here.

"He'll stop by before you head to the arena. What time are you leaving?"

Bristol looked at the clock. It was almost noon. She'd need at least an hour onstage before sound checks for Annie and Fast Cars. "I should probably leave by two."

Vanessa cupped Bristol's face. "I can't wait to have my daughter home. It's been lonely without you."

"It's been pretty lonely on the road, too. Next time I go anywhere you'll have to travel with me. Reece is old enough to be left alone." Bristol laughed at the absurdity of that statement. He was the most immature teenager she ever knew. Her mother didn't pick up that she didn't say the word tour again.

"I'll have him stay with his father and put the alarm on so if he tries to sneak in, security will be here in no time. That'll teach him," Vanessa said.

"Will it, though? He probably won't grow up until he's thirty. Perhaps giving him everything was a mistake." Bristol knew spoiling her baby brother wasn't the best thing to do, but it felt good to be able to make him happy with large gifts, and he was appreciative. All the attention had been on her for so long that when Reece came along, her parents were hyperfocused on her career, and her little brother fell into the background. Indulging him alleviated her guilt.

"He's a good kid. That's what I'm focusing on." Vanessa shrugged.

"He really is," Bristol said.

"So, tell me about this Annie Foster woman."

She wanted to pretend she didn't know what her mother meant but couldn't help her automatic smile when she heard Annie's name now. "Lizzy found her in Denver when she went to get hydration therapy. She's really good."

Vanessa put her hand on Bristol's knee and gave it a gentle squeeze. "You look like you're having a good time with her."

Bristol felt the blush spread over her skin. "You know, I like her. She's fun, honest, nice, and doesn't care that I'm this superstar. She treats me like a person."

"And she's very pretty."

"And she's very pretty." Bristol laughed and echoed her mother.

"What's the problem?"

Bristol leaned back against her pillow and sighed. "Professionally, we're in different places. I know my attitude about the business would kill the relationship before it even started."

"Aw, baby. You're too hard on yourself." She pulled Bristol into a hug and rubbed her shoulder. "Once you're done with this tour, you'll spend some time regrouping. You just need time. Your attitude will change. Music is in your soul. Even if you don't stay with Top Shelf, you can go somewhere else where you aren't doing as much."

"Mom, it's not just that. I can't go anywhere or do anything without getting mobbed. Lizzy has me locked down for my own safety most of the time. I love singing and performing, but I wish nobody knew me." She took a bite of her doughnut and wiped the crumbs off her lap.

"Look at how many lives you've touched in such a positive way. Your music has reached people on the other side of the world. You have made a difference. I couldn't be prouder of you. You took on a lot of responsibility at such a young age. But maybe we pushed you too hard."

Bristol grabbed her mom's hand. "No. This is one hundred percent me. I wanted to be the famous rock star. I wanted this lifestyle."

Vanessa kissed the top of Bristol's head. "I'm sorry it's so hard for you. That's why I'm hoping Annie or somebody like her could ground you."

Bristol couldn't remember ever bringing anyone home to meet the family. She even kept her relationship with Sterling a secret because of their age difference. She had yet to feel a spark with anyone, the one that made her forget the pressure of her life. It seemed pointless to bring home someone she had no real connection to. Annie was the first person to make her take pause.

"Mom, Top Shelf is heavily pursuing her, and like I told Lizzy, what's not great for me now might be great for her. Not every musician has my history with them. That's what she wants, and I don't blame her. She's really good. She deserves a chance."

"That's why I love you so much. You're selfless. How about we eat these in the kitchen? You know how I feel about crumbs in the bed." Vanessa stood and grabbed the box.

"I need to get up anyway. But this was exactly what I wanted. I wanted my mother to be here first thing when I woke up." When the doorbell rang several times in a row, they both smiled.

"Do I have to give him tickets?"

"You can always give him backstage."

Bristol groaned and held her head in her hands. "Oh, God, no. I can't even imagine."

"You'll be in a million TikTok videos and Instagram posts," Vanessa said.

Her brother added knocking to the incessant doorbell ringing.

"I'm coming, you little asshole," Bristol said and cinched the tie on her robe tighter before throwing the door open.

He had grown a few inches but was still her lanky kid brother with thick, wavy hair and long eyelashes. He propped his shoulder against the door frame and gave her a single nod.

"Hey. What's up?"

She shook her head and pulled him inside and into a hug. "Get in here, you jerk. How are you? Why are you so tall now?"

"I got all the good genes. You got the talent, but I got the good looks." He struck several model poses that only made Bristol roll her eyes. He wasn't wrong. Once he stopped growing and filled out more, he could model.

"Okay, Zoolander. Mom got us doughnuts. Come in and tell me about your internship."

He linked his arm with Bristol's and escorted her to the kitchen.

"Did you get some sleep?" Vanessa asked while hugging him.

"I'll take a nap later. I wanted to spend some time with Bristol before things got crazy. How's the tour going?"

"It sucks, and I can't wait to be home. Where are you planning to go to college?"

"It's between Vanderbilt and UCLA. They're the ones after me." He tore a glazed doughnut and shoved half into his mouth.

"You know you can go anywhere, right?" Bristol asked. She had set aside college money when Reece was twelve. He could go anywhere in the world, but Bristol hoped he'd stay close for her mother's sake.

"They are the best baseball schools. Who knows? Maybe I can play for the majors."

"Great idea, but how about get an education, too. And have fun," Bristol said. She was envious of her brother's life. He had a great junior prom, tons of friends, and was getting ready to start his senior year.

"Oh, I plan to reinvent the word fun wherever I go."

"Just be responsible and respectful." Vanessa ruffled his hair.

He leaned back. "Mom, not the hair. It's my moneymaker."

Bristol cleared her throat. "I'm the moneymaker, you jerk. Sold-out concerts, remember?" Bristol said. She almost saw the light turn on when she said concert.

"Hey, sis, do you think I could get seven extra tickets for the final show? I mean, you're great and all that, but X-Treem will be there, and so will DJ Spinz Madness and Willow McAdams. Maybe she'll be the future Mrs. Baines."

"Yes. Your future sister-in-law," Bristol said.

"You'll never settle down. I'll be married and have kids way before you will," Reece said.

His words stung, and Bristol took a sip of coffee to hide her reaction. She knew he was kidding, but at the rate she was going, he wasn't wrong.

"Willow is closer to my age. You might be almost eighteen, but your maturity level is about a solid fifteen."

Reece looked at Vanessa for support. Vanessa shrugged. "She's not wrong. Shall I remind you what happened at the beginning of summer?"

"Wait. What happened?" Bristol asked. She looked back and forth at them, waiting for one of them to explain.

Reece ran his hand up and down his face and shook his head. "It wasn't my fault."

"Judging by mom's face, I'm thinking it was. What happened?"

"Illegal fireworks and a carbeque."

Bristol groaned. "What car?"

Vanessa pointed to herself. "The Porsche, but I have a replacement on order."

The Porsche was the first car Bristol had purchased for her mother after the divorce. It was sporty but not too over the top. Even though her mother didn't drive a lot, it was time for a new one, but not because it burned up. "How long do you have to wait?"

"It should be here within the month."

Bristol turned to her brother and threw her hands up. "Why?"

Reece hung his head. "It wasn't my fault. Evan lit a firework that hit Mom's car. We thought it had burned out, but it hit something underneath. By the time we put it out, Mom's car was toast. Literally. Charred and scarred."

"Not funny, bro. Was anybody hurt?"

"No. Evan brought the fireworks. I tried to stop him, but things just kind of got out of hand. Don't worry. I got into trouble, too. Mom took my phone away for a week and gave me chores. Chores!"

Bristol looked at her mom. "Why didn't you tell me?"

Vanessa waved her off and busied herself with cleaning the counter, which was already pristine. Bristol had a cleaning service every week, even when she was on tour. "You need to stay focused when you're on tour. Anyway, what time do you want us to be there?"

"I'll send a car to get you at four. It'll take forever in traffic. Who are you bringing?" Bristol asked Reece.

"Lu, Tam, and Carter. That's cool, right?"

It was hard to stay mad at Reece with his sheepish grin and charming demeanor. And Bristol thought his girlfriend Lucy was okay. She'd known his best friend Carter since he was ten, and he was still extremely nervous around her. "Yeah. That's cool. I need to get ready. Thanks for breakfast, Mom." She kissed her mother on the cheek and high-fived Reece on her way back to her room.

"Hey, can we do a TikTok real quick?" Reece pulled out his phone.

"Maybe tonight at the show." Bristol made a circle motion in front of her face. "Not before this is made up."

"Come on. We share the same DNA. You're cute enough."

"Bye, troll." Bristol stuck out her tongue before turning on her heel to get ready for another grueling night.

❖

Bristol had just finished warming up with her dancers and was sprawled on her dressing-room couch when Lizzy looked up from her phone, her brow furrowed and her mouth pressed into a straight line. "I guess we know what her answer is."

Bristol grabbed Lizzy's phone and stared at the screen. The headline *Top Shelf Wooing New Talent?* was accompanied by photos of Annie and Sterling holding hands and kissing.

An unwelcomed heat feathered across her cheeks and down her neck. The photo of them kissing infuriated her. "I hope she knows what she's doing."

She handed Lizzy the phone back as calmly as possible. Why was she putting so much stock in Annie? There was nothing wrong with what Annie was doing. Except Bristol knew the journey ahead was brutal and Top Shelf was a company that cared about their artists only when they were making money. She knew because Tyson was blowing up her phone. Lizzy was keeping him at bay by telling him Bristol was trying to write songs for a new album, and he was destroying her focus. Lizzy was spreading the same rumor to everyone else connected to Top Shelf.

Bristol resented Top Shelf for taking away her passion. For a blip of a moment, Annie gave her back the passion, but they were on different paths, and she knew the difference would be too much to bear. Even though they had a spark, Bristol couldn't pursue it after this very public display on her screen with such a terrible person.

"What are people saying about the concert?"

Lizzy could respect when Bristol wanted to change the subject, so she pulled up reviews. "Bristol Baines Is Still Banging."

"Shut up. You're making that up."

Lizzy snorted. "They're all good. Nothing out of the ordinary."

"Good." Bristol couldn't get the photos out of her head. She was disappointed in herself. She'd missed her opportunity with Annie even though she'd been trying to convince herself that it wasn't the right thing for either of them.

"Bristol?"

She looked up at Lizzy. "What?"

"I asked how your night was? Did you get to see your mom?"

Bristol's heart filled with warmth. "She greeted me with Primo's coffee and doughnuts this morning. I had a half hour with her before Reece showed up. Get this. He barbecued my mother's Porsche over the summer."

"What? And here I thought he was straightening up. Isn't he touring colleges?"

"Yes, but he's hesitant to make a decision. I think he's waiting to find out where Lucy's going to school."

"Aw. Young love," Lizzy said. She put her finger in her mouth as though gagging. It made Bristol laugh, which was exactly what she needed. Release. She was drowning in too many emotions—this close to the end of the tour and this close to home.

"It's the only time he's not being an ass."

"I can't wait to see him. It's been a long time."

"You'll be surprised," Bristol said. She dragged herself up and looked at the time. "I need to get ready."

"Annie takes the stage in forty-five minutes. You have about an hour before we need you up there."

"I'll be out in a few. Get the team together." She watched as Lizzy slipped on the headset and flipped into manager mode.

CHAPTER SEVENTEEN

Is Bristol in? I really want to talk to her." Once Annie saw the photos of her and Sterling on several websites, she knew she had to talk to Bristol. It looked bad, but nothing had happened, and it was important that Bristol knew the truth. They'd had a special moment in Vegas, and Annie didn't want to lose that fragile connection over a misunderstanding. She'd texted, but the messages went unread.

"She's busy but will see you onstage shortly," Lizzy said. She folded her arms, letting Annie know she wasn't getting past her.

"It'll just take a moment. I promise."

"I'm sorry, but you'll just have to wait."

Annie heard voices inside and tried to look over Lizzy's shoulder. She saw everyone except Bristol. "I'll just text her again."

Lizzy pulled a phone out of her pocket. "I have her phone. She won't look at it until after the concert."

Annie let her shoulders slump. "Okay. I'll just see her later, I guess." She turned but stopped when she heard Bristol's voice.

"Let her in."

Lizzy said something low to Bristol but stepped aside when Bristol nodded.

"Thank you. I wanted to talk to you." Annie looked at all the people buzzing about. "Alone, if at all possible."

Bristol stared at her and showed no emotion. She wasn't even smiling. "Can we please have the room for five minutes?"

Annie stepped aside as stylists and assistants immediately stopped and left the room.

"Five minutes," Lizzy said and shut the door behind her.

"I'm not going to pretend that you didn't see the photos of me and Sterling, but I wanted to explain what you saw." Annie knew the smile pasted on Bristol's lips wasn't genuine. She had seen and felt a pure Bristol Baines smile, and this wasn't it.

"You don't have to explain yourself. What you do on your time is your business," Bristol said. She continued towel-drying her hair as though Annie was another assistant ready to help her with her wardrobe or makeup. There was distance in the way she looked at her. The warmth was gone.

"I want you to know that those pictures weren't a depiction of what happened. She kissed me without my consent, and I told her that wasn't cool." Annie balled her hands in frustration. When Bristol stopped combing her damn hair and stared at her, Annie knew she finally had her attention. "We went out to talk about the company, and she hit on me, and I turned her down. I was caught off guard in both those pictures. I didn't want her to touch me or kiss me. I'm not a willing participant in either photo."

Bristol's demeanor cracked. "Are you okay?" She reached out but pulled her hand back before she touched Annie.

Annie took a step closer. "I'm fine. It wasn't a big deal, and I made sure she understood that I wasn't interested. Because I'm not."

"Good, because she's not a good person," Bristol said.

"I know you used to date a long time ago and she probably broke your heart, because she seems like the type."

Bristol sighed. "It wasn't just that. I was a young sixteen, and she was a very advanced nineteen-year-old. She dated me to get me to do everything her father wanted. Once more contracts were signed and tours were mapped out, she dumped me. Annie, she preys on people. I know you can make your own decisions, but you need to know that about her. I don't think she's changed. I think she's gotten bolder."

Annie took a step closer. "I appreciate your advice about Sterling, and I believe you, but I'm also an adult. I won't sign anything unless I'm absolutely sure. Also, I have a pretty good lawyer who won't steer me wrong." She took another step closer. If she wanted to, she could reach out and gently pull Bristol closer, but she didn't. "I came here because I want you to know that I have no desire to start a personal relationship with her, contrary to the stupid tabloids. The hand-holding thing was dumb, and I couldn't pull away fast enough." She put her hands on her chest to emphasize her words. "I wanted you to know because you understand better than anyone that people are quick to assume things on social media and tabloids." Annie saw Bristol's shoulders relax as the truth sank in. The sense of relief almost made her cry. For some reason, having Bristol on her side meant more to her than impressing a major record label. "The kiss was a complete surprise. I told her that I didn't want her to get the wrong impression."

"Thank you for telling me."

Annie wanted to rant about how unfair it was and how social media was having a field day with it, but her relationship with Bristol was new, and Bristol was still skittish. "But I also want you to know that she invited me to Top Shelf's suite to watch the rest of the concert and meet some people tonight." Bristol stiffened but nodded.

"I get it. It's important to at least hear them out," Bristol said.

Annie put her hand on Bristol's arm. "Thank you for understanding. Record business aside, Sterling isn't my type."

"Oh?"

"No. I prefer women who are sweet and honest." Annie took Bristol's hand and was struck by how much different touching her felt than touching Sterling. Bristol was warm, and her fingers were strong from playing instruments for years. She felt safe holding Bristol's hand. Sterling had thin, bony fingers that were cold and uncomfortable to hold.

"How do you know Sterling's not sweet and honest?"

"Because you don't like her. And you're always truthful," Annie said.

Bristol leaned closer. Annie licked her lips, hoping that Bristol would press her full lips against hers. They were finally going to kiss. Her heart jumped in anticipation.

The door opened and Lizzy called, "We've got to start getting you ready, Bristol."

Bristol stepped back and gave Annie a soft smile that didn't reach her eyes. "Of course."

"Will I see you up there?" Annie hoped she didn't sound as desperate as she felt.

"Yep."

It wasn't a resounding "I can't wait," but it was affirmation, and

Annie knew Bristol was true to her word. She reached for the doorknob as the door was opening. "I'll see you up there."

Lizzy pushed her way inside. "You need to be onstage now." She pointed to Bristol. "And you need to get ready. Big night tonight."

"I'll see you later." Annie found herself in the middle of Bristol's entourage of stylists as she made her way through the doorway. Her own dressing room was the size of a large closet, and probably was, but she quickly checked her makeup and grabbed her guitar. Security escorted her to the stage. She stood on the top step, waiting for her cue to head to the microphone already in place. The stadium was full. People were in their seats. For the first time, she felt a few flutters of panic. She took several deep breaths, and when the stage manager tapped her shoulder, she marched out onto the massive stage and waved to the crowd.

"Hello, Los Angeles! I'm Annie Foster, and I'm going to play a few songs for you." She quickly plugged in and sang her first song. She was happy Sterling wasn't in the front row, but someone who looked like an older version of Bristol was. Impulsively, she waved. "Hi, Bristol's mom." Instantly she regretted doing it. She shouldn't have outed her like that. She knew that Bristol valued privacy, but the woman just smiled and waved back. So did the teenage boy standing next to her. Probably Reece, her younger brother.

She belted out her second song and loved that most people were singing along. By the third one, the stadium was up dancing and singing with her. She turned to her phone, which was livestreaming, and focused on it for about ten seconds. She yelled, "Hello!" and waved before turning back to the crowd in the stands.

By the time Bristol joined her onstage, the crowd was deafening. Annie laughed and shrugged at Bristol. They picked up the song from the beginning, and when it was over, Bristol blew her mother a kiss. Annie blinked back tears. "Bristol Baines!" She waited until the cheers softened before she introduced herself again. "And I'm Annie Foster. Thank you for such a warm welcome!" It took all her control not to skip offstage. Her skirt was somewhat restrictive, and the last thing she wanted was to fall after such an uplifting performance.

"That was great!" One of the guitarists from Fast Cars high-fived her on the way offstage. It felt good. She thought about sticking around for their performance, but it wasn't for another fifteen minutes.

"Ms. Foster?"

Annie turned to find a young man dressed in a blue suit and a black button-down shirt flagging her down. "Yes?"

"Hello. I'm Kimball. I'm with Top Shelf Records. Sterling Mayfield asked that I escort you to the private suite."

Since security didn't stop him, she figured he was legit. Her heart fell. She was on such a high, and the last thing she wanted was to spend the evening with Sterling. She'd agreed last night to appease her but seriously regretted it. "Sure." Several people along the way yelled out "great set" and "incredible job." Her heart soared at their kind remarks.

Sterling swooped into Annie's personal space and grabbed her hand the moment Kimball opened the suite door. "Annie! You made it. Come in here. I want you to meet my father, Tyson Mayfield." Annie gritted her teeth at Sterling's touch, knowing full well they'd just had a conversation about consent earlier. Not wanting to make a scene, Annie went along with it and broke free from Sterling's grasp to shake Tyson's hand. "It's nice to meet you. Thank you for the invitation."

His teeth gleamed when his lips spread into a smile. Annie wanted to shrink back at the smarmy vibes that rolled off him. His dark hair was slicked, and the cologne he wore was so strong that she almost recoiled at its potency.

"Annie Foster. That was quite a show you just put on for us. I'm looking forward to working with you at Top Shelf. We have big plans for you." Tyson cupped her hand between his.

Annie hated when people shook her hand with both of theirs. It was awkward to pull away, but she did while keeping the smile on her face. "Well, I haven't made a decision, but I'm excited to hear what Top Shelf can do for me."

He faked a shocked look and turned to his daughter. "Sterling? You haven't signed Annie yet? Give this girl everything she wants."

Sterling stepped into her father's embrace. "I'm trying. And you know I always get what I want."

Annie smiled uncomfortably. "Thank you. Do you mind if I head to the bar for a water? I'm pretty thirsty from the performance."

"Where are my manners?" Once again, Sterling grabbed her arm and steered her to the bar.

Annie ordered a water and looked at the appetizers in the suite.

She was hungry, and even though it was buffet style, the food looked untouched.

"Help yourself to the food. The plates are on that counter," the bartender said. He pointed behind his shoulder.

Annie wasn't sure if eating in front of people was rude or not, but she was hungry, and it gave her time away from Sterling. She grabbed fruit, vegetables, hummus, and pita bread and slid to the front of the suite to watch Fast Cars finish their performance. They were good, and Annie hoped that by being on this tour, they, too, would get their big break. What she wanted was two minutes to herself, but what she got was Sterling gliding into the seat next to her.

"What will it take for you to sign with us?"

Of course, Sterling would strike up a conversation right as Annie took a hefty bite of food. It was going to take some time to chew it, so she held up her finger for Sterling to wait. Covering her mouth she said, "Tell me what a typical new-artist offer is?"

"I'm sure at this point you can write your own contract."

Annie smiled because it was starting to sink in. She had a future in music, and it would be lucrative. "Give me some examples."

"Most new artists get a three-record contract with all the perks."

"What are the perks?"

"A tour, radio shows, television talk shows. We get them out in front of the world the best we can."

Annie nodded politely. "Time off?"

"What do you mean?"

"Like between recording albums and touring. Is there any time off?"

"Of course. We'll give you a set amount of time off after each completed tour and before you go to the studio to record."

"Days? Weeks? Months?"

"Honestly, a few weeks usually? It's whatever you want."

"How much time does Bristol take off?" Hopefully, she wasn't prying.

Sterling waved her off. "Oh, Bristol is a machine. She hops from tour to studio to tour to studio. Falling out of the limelight happens quickly so she knows the best thing to do is keep writing, recording, and singing to fans to stay on top."

That didn't really answer her question. Sterling made it sound like it was Bristol's choice. "The Angel/Devil Tour is almost over. Is she taking any time off before heading to the studio?"

Sterling moved around in her chair as though uncomfortable or nervous. "She is. Once she's done, we're going to meet with her and Lizzy to discuss what's up next for her. I can't really go into specifics because of confidentiality stuff." She put her hand on Annie's arm, almost causing her to dump her plate onto her lap. "Oops. Sorry about that. Let's focus on you. What perks interest you? A new car? Use of Top Shelf's condos around the world? I mean, all of that can happen."

Annie sighed. Sterling was going to have to learn to keep her hands to herself. When Sterling said "car," Annie immediately remembered the promise she'd made her sister. "I appreciate your vote of confidence in me and my success. I'm working on getting a manager, and as soon as I do, I'll have them reach out."

Sterling laughed. "You really don't need one. You can trust me."

Annie again almost choked, but this time over her attempt to cover up a snort of disbelief. She patted her chest. "Oh, that dip was a bit spicier than I was expecting." Even though she was still hungry, she put her plate down. "I promise that at the end of the tour, I'll have a manager, and we'll give you a call. I just realized Bristol is about to take the stage, and I wanted to be down there." Annie stood and shook Sterling's hand. "Thank you so much for the invitation. This is a beautiful suite. I will keep in touch."

Behind Sterling's fake smile, Annie could see her grit her teeth. "Have fun down there, and come back up after. We keep the suite open for at least an hour after the show."

"Thank you. I'm sure I will." Annie wasn't sure of their schedule. They were headed to San Francisco tomorrow for two shows there. Annie wasn't opening. Another singer was already booked. She had never been to San Francisco, so she looked forward to the time off to explore. It took a few minutes for her to get out of the suite as people stopped her to congratulate her on a good performance. When she was on the other side of the door, she gave a big sigh of relief.

"Ms. Foster? I'm here to escort you back to the stage or the VIP section. Your choice," Kimball said.

"I'd like to catch the concert from VIP, please." She figured Sterling sent him with her to keep an eye out, but after the third time she was stopped by fans, she realized it was for her own safety. People knew who she was. She posed with fans who wanted selfies and felt so important when people worked up the nerve to stop her, but she understood that people could easily invade her personal space quickly. She felt a few hands brush her arms on her way down the stairs to VIP and was grateful she had the escort. "Thanks, Kimball." He nodded to her and allowed her into the designated VIP section. Annie smiled and waved at the fans who yelled her name.

"Sit with us, Annie." Vanessa waved her over after several people stood and scooted over to make room.

"Hi. I'm Annie Foster. I'm sorry about pointing you out, but I was just so caught up in the moment. You look like you and Bristol could be sisters."

Vanessa squeezed Annie's hand. "It's fine. Most people know I'm from here. I'm Vanessa." She turned to get the attention of the tall teenager beside her. Same brown hair and expressive brown eyes as Bristol. "This is Bristol's baby brother, Reece."

"Nice to meet you." Annie had to raise her voice as the crowd started getting louder, knowing that Bristol was due onstage any moment.

"Your music is great," he said. His arm was draped across the shoulders of the girl next to him, who easily looked twenty-five years old but was probably his age. She was busy scrolling on her phone and talking to a girl on the other side of her.

"Thanks," Annie said.

"How are you liking the tour?" Vanessa asked.

"I can't possibly find the words to tell you how excited I am that Bristol picked me."

"You two are brilliant together. I mean, you're both good, but together you have chemistry onstage."

The heat on Annie's cheeks wasn't because it was a hot California night. She knew they had chemistry, too. "Thank you," she said shyly. "I'm glad you and Bristol were able to see each other today. I know she's been missing you all." Annie wanted to say more but knew it was inappropriate since they'd just met, and she didn't know Bristol enough to speak on her behalf. Or that it was even her business.

The lights cut out, signaling the start of the show, and Annie couldn't hear anything other than screaming fans. She and Vanessa smiled at one another, knowing full well that having a conversation over the next two hours would be impossible. There was a quick burst of quiet activity on the stage as her band slipped on and the roadies slipped off after putting equipment in place. When Bristol ran into the single spotlight, Annie held her breath. She looked so beautiful and serene. Her long hair was pulled back in a fishtail French braid. She was wearing a cream-colored A-line skirt that flared right above her knee and a cold-shoulder blouse that accentuated her curves but covered them modestly. The color of her lipstick matched her blouse. The soft pink made her pouty mouth seem even more kissable. Bristol always fussed about how much makeup her stylists put on her, but seeing it from the crowd's perspective, she looked amazing.

"We love you, Bristol!" the crowd yelled.

Bristol didn't have her guitar with her on the first song. Annie smiled because she loved the new a cappella version of her number-one hit. After the song was done and a roadie ran her guitar out to her, Bristol took the time to chat with the crowd. Annie couldn't believe how calm and confident Bristol was onstage. She had seen this concert several times now and was still in awe every time she watched Bristol perform.

"Good evening, Los Angeles. It's great to be home." Annie could tell by Bristol's wide smile and genuine laughter that she meant it. "I slept in my own bed last night for the first time in almost nine months. It was great. What was even better was that my mother, who's here tonight—hi, Mom!—woke me up with Primo's doughnuts and coffee. I think I cried." The crowd laughed, and several "Hi, Moms" were heard. Bristol plucked a few strings on her guitar. "Who's ready for an amazing concert?" After twenty seconds of fans screaming at the top of their lungs, Bristol said, "We started off strong with Annie Foster. Subscribe to her YouTube channel right now. Go ahead. Pull out your phones. I'll wait." She playfully strummed and added, "And download Fast Cars' latest album *Turbocharged*. It's fantastic." She paused for effect. "Okay. If we're all done, let's get back to some music."

Bristol didn't have to turn to her band to let them know when to start the next song. They just knew. Annie could barely organize a small venue at The Night Owl without tripping over equipment and other performers, but Bristol made it look easy. She was completely in charge, and that made her even more attractive to Annie. The first half of the concert flew by. When one of the band members started the drum solo, everyone knew it was time for the switch. Annie wondered what Bristol was going to wear for the devil portion. Her wardrobe was vast. Colored spotlights spun in circles around the arena like a perfectly timed laser show. It kept the crowd entertained during the ninety seconds Bristol had to change her clothes and let down her hair.

A lone white spotlight found its way to the stage. Bristol slipped into the bright circle wearing a purple butterfly crop top with long sleeves and black pants. Annie couldn't see Bristol's shoes, but it didn't really matter. For the first time all tour, Bristol's midriff was showing. Not only was it more skin than Annie had seen before but it also revealed a very toned and flat stomach. The pants were low on her hips, and the only thing Annie could do was stare. She didn't even try to sing with the crowd. Bristol had rendered her speechless. She swallowed hard when Bristol made her way to the front of the stage and gave her mother and brother a quick wave. Annie felt her heart explode, and a kaleidoscope of emotions twirled through her when Bristol winked at her. Maybe it was for somebody else in the crowd, but until the concert was over, she was going to tell herself that wink was hers.

CHAPTER EIGHTEEN

I'm so happy you're here," Bristol said as she hugged her mom and Reece. She was fresh from the shower, wearing a T-shirt and shorts. She assumed it was only family on the tour bus, but she was delighted to see Annie sitting at the table.

"Honey, you did such a great job. Those fans of yours are so loud," Vanessa said.

Bristol noticed her mother's voice was a bit loud for normal conversation. It would take several hours for the ringing in her ears to subside. She laughed and nodded. "You should have worn your ear plugs."

"I know," Vanessa practically yelled and pulled her into another hug. Bristol sank against her mom and felt tears well up. She needed this—to be around her family. Even her annoying brother was a sight for sore eyes.

"Now can we do a TikTok?"

"I was just thinking that it was great to see you, and then I remembered that you talk," Bristol said. At her brother's shocked look, she caved. "Fine." Bristol rolled her eyes to seem put out, but secretly she loved making her family happy, even if it was doing stupid videos. "What do you want to do?" Her brother explained a new dance trend. She learned the moves in ten minutes. Reece started it, and Bristol jumped in behind him to finish it. It was a thirty-second video that ended with them crashing into one another because the space on the tour bus was too confined. Lucy recorded them and yelled, "It's perfect," then stopped recording.

Bristol untangled herself and helped Reece up. "Are you an influencer now or still just playing around?"

"Playing around. I told you I want to play for the Dodgers. That's more of a career goal."

"Your arm is only going to get you so far," Bristol said. "Let's sit and talk. I'm tired, and we're hitting the road in a few hours." As nonchalantly as she could, she slipped into the round padded bench beside Annie. "Thanks for spending time with my family." Being so close to Annie that she could feel her body heat made Bristol's insides twist with nerves. Annie's eyes were bright and beautiful, and her curly hair was pulled back to offer some relief from the heat of the summer night.

"I'll never get tired of watching you onstage," Annie said.

When Bristol looked at Annie's lips then back up to her eyes, she felt that exciting jolt that had been happening more and more when they shared space. "Thank you. It was a good night, wasn't it?"

"What do you have to eat around here?" And the award for worst timing ever went to Reece. He slid into the booth beside her, bumping her into Annie. He cringed and apologized.

"Sorry about that. Apparently, my body is shutting down because I need food."

Reece faked feeling weak and made a big production of laying his head on the table and pointing to his mouth.

"You're ridiculous. Food will be here in five minutes," Bristol said. She looked at Lucy, Tam, and Carter sitting on the couch across from them. "Why are they shy all of a sudden?"

"I don't know. Lu seems to be all about Instagram and TikTok. At least I can look up from my phone. She doesn't seem to be able to." He motioned for his friends to come over. "Don't be rude."

Bristol blushed but didn't correct him. They were being rude.

"I'm sorry, Bristol." Lucy sat next to Reece. Vanessa sat on the other side of Annie. Reece's friends sat in cushy chairs across from the table. "This is a really posh bus, Bristol. I bet touring is easy in this thing."

Bristol smiled. She was so young and so uninterested. She wondered if Lucy was taking photos and posting them. "Thanks. Also, please don't post any photos of the inside of the bus. For safety reasons, okay?" Bristol bit back her smirk when Lucy's eyes widened with panic.

"Oh, definitely won't," Lucy said.

Bristol watched as Lucy casually hit a few buttons on her phone while trying to make it seem like she wasn't in full panic mode. After a few furious clicks, Lucy's shoulders relaxed, and she put her phone facedown on the table. Carter opened the door when they heard a knock, and someone announcing the catering service was there with food. Reece playfully pushed everyone out of the way and hovered over the staff as they set up the food, plucking warm chicken tenders and a brownie from the serving platters.

"Can you not be such an animal? There are plates and silverware available." Bristol put her hand on her hips and scowled at her brother. She'd picked the menu knowing her brother and his friends would eat things like chicken tenders, French fries, cole slaw, and potato salad, but she also knew that grease made her voice sound froggy, so she added salads and grilled chicken.

"This is a lot of food," Annie said.

"My brother eats like a horse. Trust me. Most of what you see here will be gone in an hour."

"Your family dynamic reminds me of mine. It makes me miss Sarah and Peyton."

Bristol covered Annie's hand with her own. It was warm and soft and fit perfectly. "Less than two weeks." She pulled her hand away and smiled encouragingly at her.

"Hey, Bristol." Reece interrupted them. "You never answered me. Are you going to give me eight tickets to the finale?"

"Do you even know eight people?"

"Ha, ha, ha." He snorted. "I'm auctioning them off on eBay to the highest bidder. I mean I could pay my college tuition."

Bristol bumped her shoulder against his. "You already have a college fund."

"I'm teasing. I want to bring some of the guys from the team. You know, senior year starts next week."

"I'm not letting eight pre-frat guys have the best seats in the house."

"Reece, honey, it's the last concert," Vanessa said.

"Tonight was the concert for that," Bristol said. "I could've easily hooked you up."

"But your final concert is..." Reece paused and put his fingers up to his lips and made a chef's kiss. "It's going to be magnificent."

"I'll give you four tickets. That's it."

"How many are you giving Mom?" he asked.

"Don't worry about it. Top Shelf is limiting comp tickets because it's such a sought-after event. Every person onstage gets a four-pack, so that fills up VIP fast."

"But you're the headliner. You should be able to get more."

"I have more people in my life than just you. Mom wants to bring some friends, too."

He put his arm around Vanessa. "Hey, Mom. Who's your favorite son?"

She pushed his arm away. "You are my favorite son, for sure, but you're not getting my extra tickets."

Reece sighed. "Fine. I'll take the four. Thank you."

There was another knock on the door, and Bristol knew it was Lizzy. It was pushing three in the morning, and they had a long drive up the coast. She wasn't ready for her family to go but never pushed for them to stay. She wanted her mother to know that she could do this, could finish the tour without breaking down. It was only for a few more weeks.

She hugged and kissed them as a few tears fell on her cheeks. "I'll see you soon."

"Stay strong, baby girl. I'll greet you with doughnuts again in bed on the morning you get back."

Bristol nodded and waved as security took them away. It was just her and Annie.

"I should probably go, too. You're probably exhausted," Annie said. She slipped on her shoes that she'd kicked under the bench.

"Family time pepped me up. You can stay if you'd like. We're all going to the same place." Bristol smiled and hoped her desperation didn't come across in her words. She didn't want to be alone, but she also didn't want to be around Lizzy. She wanted to ride the high of being happy and feeling loved and normal for the first time in what felt like forever.

"I mean, sure, if you don't mind. I should probably grab my bag from the other bus. I don't think I want to fall asleep in this." Annie looked down at her stage outfit. She looked up at Bristol. "I mean, if you wanted me to stay the whole way. On this bus. As friends. Ack!" She buried her face with her hands in embarrassment.

Bristol laughed. "There's plenty of room here. We have six bunks. Sometimes the band sleeps here when we're working on songs. Other times Lizzy and her assistants stay here when the regular bus gets noisy. This close to the end, most people just want their own space," Bristol said.

"Do you want your own space? Tonight seemed like a lot for you."

"Tonight was wonderful. I've been emotionally rejuvenated. I'm ready to finish this God-forsaken tour," Bristol said.

"Let me go grab my things. I'll be right back," Annie said.

Annie seemed nervous but also excited. There was nothing for Bristol to do except brush her teeth. She'd already showered and was wearing clean clothes. She pulled up a national news app on her phone and scrolled through the headlines. Being on tour felt like being in a different world. Days rolled together, weeks felt like months, and anything good felt like it was gone in a second.

Annie knocked on the door and peeked in. "I hope you don't mind that I brought my guitar. Just in case you felt like playing something."

"Come on in. Get comfortable. Lizzy said we're taking off soon. It's always best to get out of town when the traffic is light," Bristol said. She felt nervous at how calm Annie looked. She was so quietly confident standing in front of Bristol. "Let me show you where everything is. The bus is divided into three sections. You can have any of these bunks. The band sleeps in the other bus."

"Nobody else stays here? All of this is yours?"

Bristol shrugged. "Sometimes Lizzy and her assistants sleep over, but mostly they pop on after we've all stopped for gas or whatever. They stay up front and plan the day or figure out where I'm supposed to be. Sometimes they have me booked on a radio show or morning talk show."

"It's unbelievable to me how many people are needed to make this tour happen. Like a hundred people, right?"

"Around that. Half is from Top Shelf. Like the roadies and the set crew. Lizzy and her assistants are from her agency. I hire my own security, and I hire the opening act."

"You were serious about that? I thought Top Shelf was paying me. I remember seeing their name on the contract." She was so excited to be offered the job and relied on her lawyer to button things up, she'd never considered the logistics of the contract. Annie stopped, and a flash of irritation crossed her features.

Bristol, confused at Annie's reaction, took a step back. "Technically Lizzy's company pays you on my behalf. Top Shelf provides the stage, so that's why their name was on the paperwork. Is something wrong?"

Annie sat down and sighed. "It's fine. I just assumed Top Shelf hired me through you and through Lizzy's company. They never corrected me when I thanked them for the opportunity."

Bristol tamped down her irritation. "They are somewhat involved since you're technically on their tour with me, but they don't pay you, they don't rep you, market you, or anything until you sign with them." Annie looked at Bristol with such vulnerability. To touch her would be wrong, but she obviously had just found out something unsettling, and Bristol wanted to help. "That's why you need a manager. They'll weed through all of this for you, and if they're good, they'll protect you."

"What do you think about Lizzy as a manager?"

Fourteen years of friendship, partnership, and business flashed in Bristol's mind. Lizzy got her everything, but she also pushed Bristol for more. She never doubted their friendship, but if Lizzy had to choose between Bristol and work, Bristol would have to find a new friend. Bristol wasn't her only client. "Honestly, I'm surprised Lizzy hasn't already approached you." Bristol grabbed her new phone. "That reminds me. I got a new phone, but Lizzy's assistant didn't put your number in."

Annie frowned and typed her number in. "When did you get a new phone?"

"Las Vegas." Bristol looked uncomfortable. "It's not a big deal. I was irritated that Top Shelf had my location, so Lizzy got me a new phone that no one has the number to."

"Except me?"

Bristol smiled. "And Lizzy and my family."

"Why did Top Shelf have your location?" Annie waved her hands in front of her face. "Hold on. Let's not talk about that. We just had an amazing concert, and you got to see your family for the first time in a long time. Tell me what else puts that beautiful smile on Bristol Baines's face?"

"What's on the list now?"

Annie pretended to think hard. "Family, doughnuts, puppies, kittens, children, books, new guitars, old comfortable boots, a crisp fall day, building a snowman outside your niece's window when she can't play in the snow with you, a hot cup of tea with honey, and a crackling fireplace that you fall asleep in front of because it's so comforting."

Bristol pinched her lips together. "Hmm. That sounds suspiciously like your list, but honestly, it's not far off mine. How's Peyton doing?" Bristol took Annie's hand out of comfort but didn't let go when Annie flipped her hand so they could entwine fingers. Bristol's heart vibrated. She was afraid Annie could feel the quickening beat through her fingertips.

"She's such a fighter. She doesn't complain about how unfair life is. She looks forward to going to the hospital to see her friends there so she can make them feel better. I miss her so much."

Bristol smiled. "She sounds amazing. I'm thankful she's going to make a full recovery."

"So am I. She'll have to wear glasses for a while, which I know she's not happy about."

"You have the same color eyes as her, right?" Bristol asked. It gave her the opportunity to stare directly in Annie's eyes without fear of getting caught.

"Hers have a bit of green in them."

"And yours are like a tropical ocean. They're very beautiful." Bristol could feel her confidence blossoming now that nobody was around. It was nice to sit back and flirt with Annie.

When Lou knocked on the door to inform them they were leaving, neither Bristol nor Annie pulled her hand away. While it was nice to hold hands and talk about normal life, Bristol needed to feel Annie's warmth next to her. "Can I get you a drink? We have water, soda, or juice."

"I'll take anything at this point," Annie said.

Bristol pulled herself from Annie's grasp and grabbed two sodas and two waters from the refrigerator. "Oh. We also have lemonade."

"That sounds delicious."

Bristol put all six drinks on the table and sat next to Annie instead of across from her. Her body hummed with excitement at the possibilities. When the bus jerked forward as it pulled away from the curb, Annie touched Bristol's knee, either to keep her from sliding away or falling off the bench. Bristol's excitement grew. "The first jolt is always the worst. The rest of the trip will be smooth sailing." Bristol wasn't sure when it happened, but they were holding hands again and having a nice, easy conversation about family, food, and songs.

"I don't know how you're so graceful between chords. I feel like a clumsy monster when I play. It's the one thing I listen for with other people. You are so incredibly smooth in your transitions," Annie said.

"Grab your guitar, and let's see what you're doing," Bristol said. She'd noticed, but Annie's hesitations were so slight that they didn't bother her like some guitarists' did. She watched Annie as she carefully opened her case and pulled out her guitar.

"It's not top-of-the-line or anything, but I've been playing her for so long I can't retire her," she said.

The guitar had seen better days but still had a beautiful sound. "How long have you had her?"

"About eight years. It was the first major purchase of my life. Who needs a car when you have a beautiful guitar like this?"

"Wait. You don't have a car?"

The sound of Annie's laughter made Bristol's stomach quiver. "I have a car, but she definitely cost less than the guitar."

"Whatever it takes. I think you're doing great," Bristol said. She admired Annie for going about things differently than she did.

Annie blushed. "Thank you."

Bristol liked how she didn't try to compare their levels of success. That was the difference between a fan and a friend. "Now play something." She leaned forward to watch Annie's hands. After several minutes and a few suggestions, Annie was able to improve.

"I can't believe this. I've been playing forever, and you improve me in ten minutes." Annie said.

"Don't take it personally. Remember, I was taking piano, guitar, and voice lessons for years before I even cut an album. I practiced every day for hours with overpaid music teachers. Hey. Let me grab my guitar," Bristol said. She returned with her Preston Thompson acoustic. "Since we're sharing our babies, here's mine." She handed it to Annie.

"Oh, my gosh." Annie leaned the neck of her guitar against the table and stood to wrap the strap of Bristol's around her neck. "She's gorgeous." She ran her hands over the smooth rosewood neck and body. "How many guitars do you have? I don't think I've seen this one before."

"On this tour I have six, but she stays on the bus." Bristol leaned closer to Annie. "I don't trust anyone with her."

Annie was so close and her breath a mere whisper. She widened her eyes playfully. "But you trust me."

Bristol nodded slowly. "I do."

"Can I play your guitar?"

"Why, Miss Foster, that's such a personal question."

"May I?"

"Of course," Bristol said. Her face got really close to Annie's as she maneuvered around her to sit. "Play me something."

Annie thought for a moment and strummed chords until she got comfortable. "She's so smooth. I love her."

"Don't forget what you just learned," Bristol said. She smiled when Annie closed her eyes to concentrate. She was flawless. Her skin was smooth. Slight laugh lines at the corners of her eyes became more pronounced when she smiled as she felt her way across the strings. Bristol wanted to kiss her. When Annie opened her eyes and started singing, Bristol caught herself leaning closer and made herself sit back. Annie was giving her a mini concert. When she finished the song, Bristol applauded.

"You have such a clear voice. It's so impressive."

Annie touched Bristol's arm. "And I would kill for yours. It's so sexy, and your range is incredible."

"So, together we sing perfectly," Bristol said. "The fans think so. The messages Dom weeds through daily are amazing. They want us to sing more." She picked up Annie's guitar, and for the next hour, they played several random songs. It was the best time Bristol had ever had on the tour.

"It's five thirty in the morning. We need to get some rest," Annie said after noticing the time.

Bristol wasn't ready to say good night, even though she knew they both needed sleep. "Let's drop a teaser on social media." She picked up her phone and hit the camera button. "Is a picture okay?"

"Yeah. Totally." Annie moved closer to Bristol to fill in the frame.

"That's fine. We're holding each other's guitars. That should generate talk," Bristol said. She tried not to smile so hard, but she was happy. Snap. They took one photo that looked like two friends playing guitars. Bristol swallowed hard when Annie rested her head against her shoulder. Snap. It was precious, and Bristol's heart sped at feeling any part of Annie pressed up against her. She turned to look at Annie, and they laughed. Snap. Bristol felt like they were in a photo booth. On a whim, Bristol kissed Annie's cheek. Snap.

CHAPTER NINETEEN

When Annie felt Bristol's warm lips against her cheek, she almost melted. If the phone wasn't in Bristol's hand, Annie would have turned her head and kissed Bristol on the mouth. But Annie wasn't sure making a move was the best thing. Plus, this was Bristol Baines, international superstar, and Annie didn't want to fuck things up. No, if Bristol was interested, she would have to make the first move.

"Was that okay?" Bristol asked.

Annie pretended she didn't know what Bristol meant, even though her cheek still throbbed from where Bristol's lips had brushed it. "It was fine."

Bristol handed her the phone. "Scroll through and let me know which ones you're okay with me posting."

Annie felt weak with Bristol so close to her. She stifled a shiver when Bristol's long hair brushed her arm. "I think they all look great." She took a deep breath, knowing she was about to cross a line between them. "We look good together." Her voice was low, and when she turned to face Bristol, Bristol was staring at her mouth.

"I'll post them all. Give them something to talk about. Come on. Let's get you to bed," Bristol said. They both blushed at her innuendo.

"Probably a good idea," Annie said. It wasn't that she wasn't confident around women. She just never knew when to make the first move. Tonight wasn't the night she would try her luck. And five thirty in the morning didn't seem like the best idea either.

"You can leave your guitar here in the closet. Nobody will mess with her." Bristol hid a yawn behind her hand. "You can use the tiny bathroom here, or you can use my bathroom."

"I'll use this one here. Thank you for inviting me. It's been a very fun day. And night. And, well, morning," Annie said.

Bristol pulled her into a soft hug. "Sleep well." Annie felt Bristol's lips on her cheek again and held back a soft moan. Bristol pulled back. "Let me know if you need anything."

"You sleep well, too," Annie said. She waited until Bristol closed the door to the back of the bus and leaned against the bunk. What was wrong with her? Obviously, there was something between them, so why wasn't she acting on it? She softly banged her head on the mattress before digging out a T-shirt and pajama shorts for bed. Why was she so scared? If she made a move and Bristol shot her down, she would only have to feel horribly awkward for like ten days.

She grabbed her toiletries and opened the door to a bathroom that rivaled the size of one on an airplane. It took her a good five minutes to get ready, and by the time she picked a bunk, the sliver of light that peeked out from Bristol's door had gone dark. *Fuck. Way to go, Annie.* She pulled the cool sheet over herself and pouted. What should she have done?

She wanted to call her sister for advice, but she knew Sarah was busy getting the day started. Plus, she didn't want to wake Bristol. She started a breathing exercise to help her relax, and right before sleep took her, she heard Bristol's door open and saw soft light spill out into the aisle. Through the bottom of the privacy curtain, she saw Bristol stop in front of the bunks.

She rolled onto her side and slid the curtain back. "Are you okay?"

Bristol jumped and put her hand on her heart. Annie would have laughed at the startled look on Bristol's face, but the second her eyes landed on what Bristol was wearing to bed, she swallowed hard.

"Yeah. I just wanted to make sure you were good. You surprised me. I thought you'd be on the lower bunk," Bristol said.

"This way I'm actually taller than you. I'm good though. Thank you for checking on me." Why was Bristol here? Ideas—nice, flirty ideas—popped into her head.

"I felt like we weren't finished with things," Bristol said.

Annie leaned forward. "Oh?" She watched Bristol take a step closer.

"It was such a good night, and I ended it too abruptly."

It was as if a lightning bolt struck her right in her heart. Bristol wanted to kiss her. She was standing in front of Annie wearing a tank top and a pair of boy shorts, looking vulnerable and nervous as fuck. Annie threw caution aside and crooked her finger at Bristol. She brushed her lips softly across hers. "Does this help?"

Bristol nodded and stood on her tippy-toes to get closer. "This helps a lot."

Their lips met again, passionately this time, after they'd established consent with the first feathery kiss. Annie broke their connection to slide out of the bunk and stand in front of Bristol. She wasn't going to let this opportunity get away. She hooked her finger in the waistband of Bristol's shorts and pulled her flush against her. The moment their eyes met, their mouths connected. Bristol's lips were full and pressed hungrily against Annie's. Annie felt both weak and strong as Bristol's velvety tongue stroked hers. She moaned with desperation and hunger. When was the last time she'd been kissed so thoroughly? Her knees felt weak, but the fire that ignited and spread throughout her kept her upright and greedy for more. She wrapped her arms around Bristol to keep her close.

"You're shaking," Annie whispered. "Are you cold?"

"I'm definitely not cold," Bristol said.

Annie ran her hand down Bristol's arm and entwined their fingers. "I like holding your hand because I know what you can do with these fingers." After realizing her innuendo, she covered her mouth with her hand and put her forehead against Bristol's. "You know what I mean."

Bristol smiled and swiftly kissed her. Annie knew it wouldn't go beyond what was happening right now. She didn't want that with Bristol. She wanted it this to mean more than a one-night stand or a quick fling on a tour bus.

"I know what you mean," Bristol said.

Annie couldn't help but smile. She'd known they had chemistry, and the last three minutes proved it. "You need to get some sleep so, as much as this pains me, go behind that door and lock it."

Bristol giggled and kissed Annie on the neck. Annie moaned as Bristol's lips and tongue made their way from her neck, up to her jaw, and over to her lips. After another minute of kissing, they broke apart.

"Okay. I'm going." Bristol dropped Annie's hand and took a step back. "I've wanted to kiss you for a long time."

Annie wanted to pull Bristol back into her arms for another kiss, but it was getting late, or early, and that would have been selfish. Bristol had a concert tonight, and Annie didn't want to be the reason she didn't perform at a hundred percent. "What took you so long?"

"I'm really bad at reading people," Bristol said.

Because Bristol looked so vulnerable standing in front of Annie, Annie pulled her into her arms and held her. "You read me right. Now go get some sleep before you don't."

When Bristol closed the door to her bedroom, Annie sank onto the bottom bunk. She didn't have the strength to climb up. What had just happened? She touched her lips and found them tender and still tingling from Bristol's mouth. Holy fuck. She'd just kissed Bristol Baines. No way was she going to sleep now. Her energy level was off the charts, and she had no way to blow it off. She got on her phone to see if Bristol had posted the photos. She had, and so many people were delighted but also supportive. The queer internet was already speculating. There were only a few jealous remarks, and Annie scrolled past them. Nothing could have spoiled her mood. Not even snippy comments on their photos. If they only knew what had just happened here.

❖

Annie heard footsteps and shrank into the bunk when she recognized Lizzy's voice. She checked the time on the phone and was shocked to find that it was almost eleven. Lizzy knocked softly on Bristol's door.

"Bristol? Are you awake? Are you alone?"

Annie didn't like what Lizzy was implying. She pulled back the curtain. "Well, I'm not in there, if that's what you're thinking."

Lizzy looked at her in surprise and completely avoided what Annie had said. "I'm sorry. Did I wake you?"

Annie shrugged her off. "It's time to get up."

"Late night?"

It was Annie's turn to ignore Lizzy's question. It was weird how hot and cold Lizzy was with her. One minute she acted like she liked her and the next looked at her with such disdain. "How much longer until we get to the arena? It seems like we're getting close." Annie could feel the bus idle in traffic.

"We're about five minutes from pulling into the Chase Center. We have rooms at the Rembrandt. I'll have Vaughn email you the room information and key so you can freshen up. I know you're not on tonight, but you'll have access to everything like before."

Annie swore Lizzy's demeanor softened. Maybe she appreciated that she didn't find her in Bristol's bed this morning. "Great. I'll change and get out of everyone's way. I'm sure you have a lot of business to tend to today." She really had no idea but wanted out of the small space she shared with Lizzy. After grabbing her bag, she slipped back into the freakishly small bathroom and got ready for the day. She threw her hair up in a bun because she didn't have the patience to try anything else. She gathered her things and stealthily made her way to the front of the bus. Bristol, Dom, Lizzy, and her assistants stopped and stared. Annie smiled at the attention.

"Good morning, everyone."

"Good morning, Annie," Bristol said.

Annie held her breath when she saw Bristol. She looked amazing. Her hair, still damp from her shower, was braided back and hanging over one shoulder. She was sandwiched between Lizzy and Dom going over whatever was on the iPad.

"Good morning, Bristol." Knowing she was totally interrupting, she sat far away from them. "As soon as we stop, I'll jump off."

"It's no rush. If you want to stay, you can."

Annie smiled. "I've never been to San Francisco, so I might just look around. Do you need me for anything?" she asked. She blushed when she caught Bristol's wink.

"You have a good time. San Francisco is a fun place," Bristol said.

The bus chugged to a stop, and Annie looked out the window. Chase Arena was huge, but she was more excited to see the sights of San Francisco that she'd seen on television and in movies. "I'll take lots of photos and send them to you. Do you mind if I leave my guitar here?"

"That's fine. I'll tell Lou and Dave to give you full access if you return and we're all inside."

"Thank you," Annie said. She exchanged her overnight bag for her backpack, grabbed her sunglasses, and set out to enjoy the hills and hotspots of San Francisco. She FaceTimed Sarah when she reached

Bay Front Park. "Look at where I am." She flipped the view so Sarah could see the ocean.

"That's so beautiful. I'm jealous."

Annie noticed the dark circles under her sister's eyes. "How's life? You seem stressed. Is Peyton good?"

"She's great. It's just work. So many staff members are taking vacations, and it's hard to fill the schedule."

"Play the lottery. Then you can win millions and never have to work again."

"I don't need the lottery when I have you," Sarah said. They made faces at one another. "Did you find a manager? Did you call Dani?"

"Not yet. I don't know what I'm going to do. Top Shelf promised me everything I want, but they seem to be in it for themselves. Does that make sense?"

"No, because I don't understand any of this. Don't sign anything."

Annie shook her head. "I'm not. I told Sterling Mayfield that I promise to hear what Top Shelf had to offer first after the tour and after I find a manager."

"Let's talk about the photos with Sterling," Sarah said.

"Oh, that's not the real story."

"I mean, it sure looked like she was very comfortable with you. What's the real story?"

Annie thought for a moment. What if Sterling had planted people ready to take photos of what had happened that night? Anger flooded her senses the more she thought about it. "I wonder if she planned those photos just to piss Bristol off?"

"Why would Bristol care?"

Annie smiled when Sarah mentioned Bristol. She looked around to ensure privacy and put the phone closer to her face. "Bristol and I hooked up."

Sarah pulled back. "Shut up! Are you kidding me?" She put her hand over her mouth and looked around. "What? Like hooked up, hooked up?"

"We kissed last night, and it was amazing. Like full-body-against-body kiss. Even though we have some off-the-charts chemistry, I wasn't going to let it go further because I don't want to fuck things up."

"What does that mean?"

"I panicked, truthfully."

"Oh, stop! Forget about all that. Is she a good kisser? Who kissed who first? I feel like she kissed you because she comes across as such a strong woman who's kind of a control freak. Tell me I'm wrong."

"I kissed her, and you are totally wrong. It was lovely. She was lovely."

"That's it? That's the story?" Sarah sounded disappointed.

"That's a super-huge story!"

"I'm teasing. It really is. I'm so excited for you. Tell me what happened."

Annie looked around again to make sure nobody could hear her before she told her sister about her and Bristol's sexual tension. Sarah sighed when Annie described how Bristol returned to the bunks and said they had unfinished business between them. She squealed when Annie told her she kissed Bristol first.

"That's so romantic. She seems so nice. I hope there's something there. Bristol couldn't do any better than you."

"I'm still in awe." She noticed her sister's attention was getting pulled in different directions. "Go. I'll send photos and keep you posted about what happens on the rest of the tour. Tell Peyton I love her. Maybe I can FaceTime tonight?"

"Sounds great. Love you. Be safe."

"Love you, too, sis." Annie disconnected the call and smiled. She was on the top of the world. She took a stroll along the footpath until hunger pangs nudged her to find food. She grabbed a Lyft to a casual seafood restaurant with a high rating on Yelp! and ordered a hot crab sandwich and fries.

The waitress slid her plate in front of her and refreshed her iced tea. "Are you Annie Foster?"

More people were starting to recognize her, which warmed Annie's heart. "I am."

"I have tickets to tonight's show. I didn't know you were performing."

"I'm not. Bristol has a local musician scheduled for tonight and tomorrow."

She adjusted her now-empty tray against her hip. "I wish it was you. Oh, do you mind if I get a picture with you?"

Annie swallowed the fry she'd snagged off her plate and wiped her mouth with her napkin. "Of course not." Her waitress squatted beside her and took a photo that she immediately posted on Instagram. "Can I tag you?"

"That's fine."

Annie watched her scurry away and show other waitresses loitering behind the counter her phone. It was still such a high that people recognized her on the street. A month ago, nobody knew who she was. Now she was taking photos with strangers. She dug into her food with gusto and scrolled through neighborhood news back home.

How's your day off?

Her heart skipped several beats when an unknown number popped up on her phone. Immediately, she knew it was Bristol. She debated being flirty but settled on being honest.

It's beautiful by the water. Wish you were here. Sure you can't sneak away? She added a sad face for effect.

I wish. I'm just about ready to Zoom with a local midday news show.

What station? I'll tune in.

Annie slipped in her AirPods and waited for Bristol's answer. She waved over her waitress and asked for the check.

The Bay's Day's News.

That was a horrible name for a show, Annie thought. *Are you on the tour bus?* Annie took a drink of tea right as Bristol sent her a photo. She choked at the unexpected surprise and grabbed her napkin to stop from dribbling all over the table.

"Do you need anything else?" The waitress put Annie's check on the table and waited until Annie gave her a thumbs-up, signaling that she was okay.

"No, thank you." Annie smiled and handed the waitress her credit card. She waited until the waitress ran off to close out her ticket to look at the photo of Bristol closely. With her hair loose around her shoulders and her kind eyes, she was breathtaking. Annie remembered those full lips pressed against hers and on the soft, sensitive spot on her neck. Annie touched the screen and smiled.

Did it come through?

Stop texting me. I'm too busy staring at a beautiful woman on my phone, and your messages are messing up my concentration. She dropped a wink emoji after her text and bit her bottom lip to keep from squealing. Who was she anymore?

Gotta go. We'll chat later.

Annie tipped and signed the receipt. She wanted to get back outside and send Bristol photos of the view and maybe slide in one of herself. It didn't make sense to send her photos of the ocean since Bristol lived near it, so she snapped a photo of the Golden Gate Bridge and a cute puppy with a caption that read *puppies amirite?* And finally one of her with her hair loose and curly around her shoulders. *You can always postpone the concert and hang out in the park with me. I can buy us wigs and hats. Nobody will recognize us.*

Annie sat on a shaded bench and pulled up the website to watch the interview. She missed the introduction but saw the five-minute Zoom chat between her and Michonne Michaels, anchorwoman for *The Bay's Day's News.* She flirted hard with Bristol, who politely smiled and answered her questions professionally. A tinge of jealousy tugged at Annie's heart. Michonne was beautiful and classy. The gorgeous suit she was wearing was nicer than anything Annie had in her closet. It dawned on her that if she started a relationship with Bristol, or if Bristol would even want one, it would be hard to see people falling all over themselves just to be near Bristol. She probably received tons of fan mail and gifts every day. Annie's heart slipped a little bit when she thought about how hard it would be to date somebody as famous as Bristol. Not that one tiny make-out session meant they were an item, but Annie had to think about what that really meant. She was the jealous type, but not one to storm off or slam doors. She believed in communication, but it was a two-way street.

Her phone buzzed with a new message from Bristol. *You have the prettiest eyes in the world.*

And just like that, Annie forgot all the doubts that had flooded her brain a moment ago. *Oh, yeah? Thank you.* She knew her eyes were her best feature, so she wasn't going to play the game of *oh, no, they're just ordinary, you're being too nice.* It had taken her six attempts to get the perfect selfie, and it was all about her eyes. *I just watched your interview. I don't know how you can sleep for only four hours and look so good.*

Bristol sent five laughing emojis with tears. *I have an entourage of makeup artists who are paid a fortune to make me look like I'm well rested and alive.*

That's not true. I just saw you without any makeup on, and you looked incredible. But I do think you need more sleep. Promise me that when the tour is over, you'll stay in bed for like a week, only waking up to eat and drink and shower.

When the phone rang, it startled her, and Annie almost dropped it. It was Bristol. "Hi."

"Hi," Bristol said.

"That was a good interview." Annie wanted to go on about everything she noticed, from her sexy smile to the tiny heart necklace that rested just below the soft spot between her collarbones, but Bristol had to be tired of hearing nothing but compliments everywhere she went.

"Michonne does a great job at making guests feel at ease."

"She was flirting with you." Annie couldn't help but point out the obvious.

"She was, but I'm not interested in her."

"Oh?"

"Nope. Not her."

"Even though she's lives in California and is just a plane ride away?"

"Not even a little bit."

"Oh. That's good to hear," Annie said. She decided she was horrible at flirting and decided to abandon it. "What are you doing the rest of your day? More interviews?" She hated herself for changing the subject, but she was nervous and felt the need to fill the silence.

"The usual. I'll practice with the dancers to make sure I don't forget the routine."

"You're flawless onstage," Annie said.

"Only because I practice so much." Bristol laughed softly. "I mess up a lot."

Annie pressed her lips together tightly as she thought about how hard Bristol was on herself. "You're great. Don't let them get you down. Less than ten performances left." Her voice softened. "You can do that, right?"

"I can and I will. But enough about work. What are you going to do now that you have two nights off?"

"I don't know really. It's kind of fun seeing things that I've only ever seen on television. San Francisco has so many things to do, but I'll definitely be at the concerts."

"I'm excited to see you again. Did Lizzy send you the mobile key for your room?"

"Vaughn did. Thank you. I'm excited to take a hot shower and put on clean clothes." Annie checked her watch. There was still time to shop for an outfit for tonight. By now, she'd recycled her clothes and had yet to see the same thing on Bristol. Not that it was a competition, but she wanted to look better for Bristol. The clothes she had were simple and comfortable, but not sexy. She needed sexy.

"I'm sure you know, but after the concert, we're having a little get-together at the hotel. Please say you'll be there. I'd love to see you again."

Whatever emotion was jackhammering at her heart, Annie took a deep breath and let it in. "I'll be there."

CHAPTER TWENTY

Good night, San Francisco!" Bristol yelled to the crowd, who screamed for her not to go. One encore was enough. She signaled to the stage manager, who slowly turned on the lights, letting concertgoers know the show was over.

She was drenched in sweat and knew she had to eat and drink something before she passed out, but all she could think about was getting back to the hotel and hanging out with Annie. Sure, everyone on the tour would be there, but that wasn't why she was so excited. It was seeing Annie again. Annie gave her something that she hadn't felt in a long time. Hope. It fluttered behind her rib cage and tickled her heart. Maybe it was okay to let her guard down again. It was hard to tell, because right now, Annie was new to the scene and relied somewhat on Bristol's guidance. She knew what would happen the minute Annie got a manager. It would change everything. She should pull back in case feelings got in the way and ruined a blossoming friendship, but she already knew she was in it for more.

"Right this way, Ms. Baines."

Bristol heard Bruce's voice and followed him through the back entrances of the arena to a limo. She wanted out of there fast to get back to the hotel. Even though it was just her own crew, she had to dress the part. Harper had laid out several different outfits for her to choose from. She picked out black leggings, a white V-neck, a muted black shirt she left unbuttoned, and her combat boots. By the time her hair stylist and makeup artist showed up, she was in the chair waiting.

"What look are we going for tonight?" Phoebe asked and circled Bristol as though sizing her up. "Ultra chic? Casual night in?"

"Not as much makeup as I wear onstage. My skin hates me right now."

Annette grabbed moisturizer while Phoebe swooped in to give suggestions about her hair.

"Maybe keep at least half down? I don't want the weight of it to give me a headache." Bristol wavered about what looked best on her.

"How about we straighten it and pull it back in a twisted ponytail?"

It was a look that Bristol liked but could never wear onstage running and dancing around. "I love it. Let's do it."

Annette and Phoebe bobbed and weaved around one another until Bristol was ready to greet her guests. Lizzy peeked in and informed Bristol the alcohol and appetizers were laid out, ready for consumption.

"I love tour family night," Lizzy said. It was good to see Lizzy relaxed and in jeans. Her hair was down, and her clipboard and headset were somewhere else. The only thing in her hand was her phone and a drink that smelled like vodka with a hint of cranberry juice. Since Denver, Lizzy had cut back on drinking, which made Bristol happy, so seeing her with alcohol was unsettling, but Bristol kept her mouth shut.

"We're almost done here," Annette said. She stood back and spritzed Bristol's face so her makeup wouldn't smear. "Perfect as always."

Bristol never knew if Annette was complimenting her own work or Bristol. She leaned forward and nodded. "Perfect as always."

The entire top floor was theirs. Ballrooms A and B were open for their party. Plush couches and wingback chairs were arranged in clusters in the large hallways for people to break off and chat if they didn't want to stay in the ballrooms.

Bristol knew she was good for only a few hours before she had to throw in the towel. Her bandmates could stay up all night and still perform the next day, but not Bristol.

"Let's have fun tonight. No worries, just fun," Lizzy said. She grabbed Bristol's hand and waved at Annette and Phoebe to join them. "Leave your stuff. Let's grab a drink."

Bristol couldn't help but smile at how happy everyone seemed. It was important to let her entire team know that they were important to her. Hanging out with them always boosted morale. She chatted with some of the set builders on her way to grab a glass of wine and thanked them for keeping her safe onstage. Her phone buzzed, and she smiled immediately, knowing only one person would be texting her right now.

I'm here, but I'm not sure where to go.

The entire floor is the party. I'm getting a glass of wine in Ballroom A. Would you like something to drink? Bristol didn't mind waiting in lines, but the moment she did, people scattered out of the way to give her immediate access to the front. That bothered her.

"Great concert tonight," Sondra said. Her voice was low, and she was having a hard time keeping eye contact. Liquid courage in the form of an Anchor Steam rested in her right hand.

"Thanks for all your hard work, Sondra. I know we're demanding with our instruments, but you do such a great job of keeping our equipment straight for each concert."

Sondra looked surprised that Bristol even knew her name. She opened her mouth and closed it several times before nodding quickly and racing off. Bristol sighed. She wished people could be comfortable around her, but she was both the star and the boss, and that was the dynamic no matter how hard she tried. She thanked the hotel bartender for the two glasses of wine and turned right as Annie walked into the room. She was wearing a light blue sundress that Bristol hadn't seen before, and she looked incredible.

"Bristol? Did you forget something?"

Bristol turned to find Clarissa, one of Lizzy's assistants, staring at her with concern. Yes, Bristol thought. I forgot how to breathe. "I'm fine. I just got lost in thought. Thanks for the nudge." She had to slow her steps on her way to Annie. "You made it." Annie looked up at her, and Bristol couldn't tamp down all her strong feelings. She took a sip of her wine and handed Annie the other glass.

"I'm sorry I'm late, but it looks like things are just getting started." Annie took the glass from Bristol and smiled. She was unbelievably sexy. Bristol took another sip of wine.

"You don't really need sleep, do you?" Bristol teased.

"You look wonderful. I'd stay up all night if it meant talking to you longer than twenty minutes," Annie said.

Bristol heard her name a few times as people from different groups were waving her over, but she just wanted to sit and flirt with Annie. "Those twenty minutes might have to wait a few more. I hope you don't mind, but since this gathering is my idea, I need to make a quick round." She felt the heat of Annie's hand on hers.

"Don't worry about me. I'll grab some snacks and hang out with anybody who'll talk to me. See you later."

Bristol smiled, knowing she would thank everyone here and make a beeline for Annie the second she was free. She squeezed Annie's fingers and left her to chat with her dancers. As she moved around the room, she always knew where Annie was. She found her over at the bar talking with some of the stagehands and later laughing it up with Dom at one of the tables as they both scrolled on their phones. When she saw Annie and Lizzy together ten minutes later, she excused herself and joined them. Not that she was worried, but Lizzy was very direct, and if she offered to represent Annie, Bristol wanted to make sure it was a good fit. "Hi, ladies. What's going on here?" She slid into the chair next to Lizzy so she could look directly at Annie.

"Tour talk, mostly. It's been a great experience for everyone," Lizzy said.

"If I'm not interrupting, I'm going to steal Annie away."

Lizzy sat back and threw up her hands. "Go for it. I need another drink anyway. I'll see you both later." She stumbled over a chair and caught herself. "Still upright."

"Ignore her. Want to go somewhere private where we can chat and not have everyone bother us?" Bristol tried to look innocent, but when Annie lifted her eyebrow at her, she laughed and pulled Annie closer so she could whisper in her ear. "Okay. It's a trick to get you alone."

"I've been waiting all night for you to whisk me away," Annie said.

Annie's words sent a shiver along Bristol's spine. "I know the perfect spot." It took them longer than she would have liked to make their way down the long hallway to Bristol's suite, but once they were inside with the door locked, Bristol felt both relief and excitement.

"Are they going to miss you?" Annie sat on the couch. She placed her drink on the coffee table and looked at Bristol expectantly.

"They see enough of me. This is just a little preparty before next week's finale. Top Shelf will throw that down in Los Angeles."

"Tour schedules confuse me. Why not just have three concerts in a row there to end instead of bouncing around state to state, city to city?"

"It's all about space. Trying to map out a tour and find the size arenas we want is difficult. We're up against graduations, sporting events, other concerts, speaking tours. We squeeze in where we can," Bristol handed Annie a water before sitting next to her.

"Planning a tour must be stressful."

"It's one of the things Top Shelf does right. They have a team of schedulers who figure it all out."

"It sounds intricate."

"Can we talk about something else?" The last thing Bristol wanted to discuss was the tour. It already ate up most of her time.

Annie groaned. "I'm so sorry. Lizzy just got me thinking about the whole process."

Bristol reached for Annie's hand. "Let's talk more about you. Tell me about your day today."

"I got to see the ocean for the first time in a long time."

"But the mountains are beautiful where you live."

"I love seeing them every day, that's true," Annie said.

Bristol scooted closer to Annie and touched the hem of her dress. "You went shopping today. I love the color." Bristol took her time appreciating the form-fitting dress and ran her finger along the hemline just above Annie's knee. The energy in the room changed.

Annie leaned into Bristol and kissed her. Bristol wasted no time in responding. She tilted Annie's chin up and pressed her lips against her soft, full mouth. Her tongue brushed across Annie's lips, softly waiting for permission until Annie opened her mouth. Bristol moaned when she felt Annie's tongue against hers. She deepened the kiss until they were both moaning. Annie traced Bristol's face with her fingertips before running them down her side to settle at her waist. Bristol pulled Annie onto her lap. "Is this okay?" She rubbed her thumb on Annie's lower lip and smiled when Annie placed a kiss on it.

"It's perfect," she said.

Bristol's eyes drifted shut when they kissed again. Annie's body was warm, and the deeper they kissed, the more Annie moved against Bristol. Bristol placed her palms on Annie's thighs and stroked until Annie growled in frustration.

"What?" Bristol pulled away, even though she knew exactly what she was doing.

"You're teasing me," Annie said breathlessly.

"Oh? You mean here?" Bristol moved her hands up higher until her fingertips barely touched the line of Annie's panties at the top of her thighs.

Annie's breath quickened, and her bright blue eyes darkened with desire and need. She nodded. Bristol ran her fingers back and forth over the seam. It was almost impossible to tell if the smoothness was Annie's skin or the silk panties. When she felt Annie's hands at the back of her neck pulling her mouth closer, Bristol moved her hands higher, so her thumbs brushed the soft silk right above Annie's mound. It took every bit of self-control not to flip Annie, pull off her dress, and touch her everywhere. A couch wasn't the most romantic place to make love to her, but the bedroom seemed so far away.

Off in the distance, Bristol's rapid pulse throbbed under her skin and boomed in her head. All her senses were hyperfocused on Annie. She leaned forward and tried to shrug out of her shirt. Her body felt like it was on fire. Annie's hands were on her shoulders, helping her, and when they both finally tugged it off, Annie lost her balance but landed safely on the couch. Bristol sat up long enough to throw the shirt down and kick off her boots. She wanted to take Annie into the bedroom, but she didn't want to put any space between them. "Are you okay?"

Annie smiled. "Good thing I landed on something soft." She reached up and cupped Bristol's cheek. "I'm so good."

"Yes, you are." She slipped one thigh between Annie's legs.

"You feel so good," Annie whispered against Bristol's mouth.

"You're so beautiful." Bristol's voice shook. She felt Annie tug at her hips to pull her fully between her legs. When she sank into Annie's softness, they both moaned. Bristol couldn't stop her hips from rotating and pressing into Annie. This wasn't how she'd seen the night going down, but if Annie was in, she was, too.

"I know you can hear me!"

They froze as a heated exchange took place outside Bristol's suite. Bristol looked at her door, expecting somebody to burst through it.

"Bristol! I know you're in there!"

Bristol looked at Annie and swore under her breath. "It's Lizzy."

Annie scrambled to a sitting position and tugged at the hem of her dress. "Is she okay?"

"It sounds like she's drunk. Great." Bristol grabbed her shirt from the floor and slipped it on. She opened the door wide enough to stick her head out. She blocked the opening so that Lizzy couldn't see inside. "What's going on?"

Lizzy had her back against the wall with the beefy security guard standing over her. "Where did you go? The party is just getting started." She pushed the security guard away and stumbled into the suite. Bristol wasn't about to block her. Lizzy wasn't a happy drunk.

"We wanted to get away from the noise, so Annie and I are in here," Bristol said.

Annie looked completely undisturbed and slightly bored holding her drink from earlier. The flush of pink on her skin was the only giveaway that something other than just chatting was going on in the room. Lizzy was thankfully oblivious.

"Good idea. It's so loud out there." Lizzy pointed to the closed door. "Mr. Muscles wouldn't let me in. What are you talking about? If Annie and I are a good fit? She might sign with me."

"No. We weren't talking about music. We were talking about Colorado and what Annie likes to do for fun back home."

Lizzy plopped down on a chair, spilling her drink in the process. Bristol was seething that their night had been ruined. "Will there be a conflict of interest if I rep both of you?"

This wasn't the conversation Bristol wanted to have now, or ever really. "No. How about we pick this up in the morning? Come on. I'll get you back to your room."

Lizzy waved her off. "It's okay. I'll just crash on the couch. Annie? Can you move so I can sleep?"

Annie immediately stood. "You know, maybe I should go. You're going to have your hands full here."

She gave Bristol a weak smile and a shrug. Bristol clenched her fists and mouthed "I'm sorry" to Annie.

"Don't go on my account. I'll chat with you, too," Lizzy said.

"You're almost asleep. Let's put the drink on the table and kick off your shoes. I'm going to walk Annie out. You stay put." Bristol pointed at Lizzy as though she were a child. Bristol grabbed Annie's hand and made a whimpering sound. "I'm so sorry about this. As much as I want to kick her out, I know she needs me."

Annie hugged Bristol. "I understand. Good luck with her." She paused and held Bristol's hands. "This will keep." She placed a swift kiss on Bristol's lips and walked out of the suite.

Bristol took three deep breaths before turning to her drunk friend, who was quickly fading on the couch. She was angry at the lack of privacy with Lizzy around. Another three deep breaths. It wasn't her fault. Lizzy was being herself, and this was what she did. With her hands on her hips, she looked at Lizzy, who was now softly snoring and speaking gibberish. She sighed, pulled off Lizzy's shoes, and covered her with a blanket. She put a glass of water on the coffee table and found a small trash can that fit between the couch and the table if Lizzy got sick in the middle of the night. She grabbed her phone.

I can't even tell you how mad I am right now.

Annie responded immediately. *Don't worry. Take care of her. We can pick up later. Thank you for such a wonderful night. Get some sleep.*

Bristol flopped down on her bed, cooled from Lizzy's interruption, but still on fire. When was the last time she'd made out with anyone or even had sex? She stripped, slipped under the covers, and sulked until she fell into a fitful sleep.

CHAPTER TWENTY-ONE

It had been three days since the party, and Annie and Bristol couldn't find time to be alone. With the tour ending, Bristol's every waking moment was spent giving interviews, meeting charities, even shooting a commercial. Annie couldn't get close to her no matter how hard she tried. She didn't want to seem desperate or, worse, not interested.

Sterling was blowing up her phone, trying to sign her. Dani, her lawyer, sent her two names of entertainment managers that she still had to call. She had gotten an email from Americana Records asking to sit down with her. Americana was a lot smaller than Top Shelf or Four Twelve, but they repped Seth Wylie and Prairie Girls, folk musicians Annie adored. Seth Wylie—with his dreamy curls and poetic lyrics—had inspired her to start writing music as a teenager. Her guitar case still had an "I Heart SW" sticker. She couldn't believe she was on Americana's radar.

Annie was busy, and she was only the opening act. She couldn't imagine how many directions Bristol was getting pulled in. Tonight, they were back onstage together. There were four more concerts left, and even though she was sad that this magical time was coming to an end, she was eager to see what the future held for her.

She smiled when she saw Peyton's face on her phone. "Hey, baby girl. What are you doing?"

"Talking to you. Where are you?"

"I'm in Portland, Oregon. Do you know where that is?" Peyton shrugged one tiny shoulder in the frame of the phone. "It's all the way by the ocean. Very far from Colorado."

"When are you coming home? I start school next week. Like kindergarten, not preschool," Peyton said.

"I can't believe what a big girl you've become. And I love your new glasses." Annie was worried that Peyton would fight having to wear glasses, but Sarah said she liked the attention she was getting from them.

"Look at the ladybugs." Peyton couldn't figure out how to show Annie the sides of her frame, but Annie pretended she saw them.

"Those are so much fun. What are you looking forward to the most when you go to school?"

She rolled her eyes at Annie. Rolled her eyes! When did she grow up?

"I've been going to school."

"Yeah, but that was preschool. Kindergarten is the start of big-kid school. Do you have a new backpack yet?"

Peyton's eyes lit up. "I do. It's red and has ladybugs on it. Want to see it?"

"Of course. Having the right backpack is important. Have you met your teacher yet?"

Peyton nodded. "I like Miss Emily. She knows your music."

"You talked about me to your teacher?"

"Uh-huh. She went to your concert here and said she's been to Charley's."

There was a slight scuffle, a few giggles, and Sarah's face showed up on the screen.

"I can't believe Peyton called you. Are you busy right now?"

Annie looked around the stadium. They were still working on the stage. "No. I'm free for the first time in forever. Peyton picked the best time to call me. What are you up to?"

"School next week. Most of her preschool friends are in her kindergarten class," Sarah said.

Annie watched as Peyton crawled on Sarah's lap to be a part of the conversation. "Peyton said her teacher likes my music. Is she cute?"

"Really? You're dating you-know-who, and you're asking about Peyton's teacher? What has being on the road done to you?" Sarah asked.

Annie laughed. "Trust me, I'm not dating anyone. I was just making conversation with my sweet little niece."

"When are you coming home?" Peyton asked.

Her question tugged at Annie's heart. "Soon. I'll miss your first day of school, but I'll be home next week. Does Raven miss me?"

Peyton shrugged. "I think so."

Sarah kissed the top of Peyton's head and slid her off her lap. "Why don't you put your bag away and grab a snack?" Sarah waited until Peyton was out of the room before she turned her attention back to the phone. "What is going on?"

"What do you mean?"

"I mean with Bristol."

Annie sighed. "We're so busy we can't even find time alone. She gets zero time to herself."

"That's dumb. She's the star. Why can't she just say 'Hey, I want a break. I'm going to go hang out with Annie. Don't interrupt me.' I mean, she gets a say in her daily activities, right?"

Annie didn't know how to answer that question. Maybe she didn't, and Top Shelf and Lizzy were pushing her to the limits. Maybe Bristol didn't know how to say no. "I don't know really. Lizzy pushes her, and sometimes I think she puts too much on Bristol."

"That's sad. Isn't there a rule about trusting your manager with your life? They have to do what's best for you, not what's best for them. It's like an investor. If you do well, they do well."

"That's the idea, I think. I should probably call the two Dani suggested."

"Since you're sitting there doing nothing, why don't you call them? Dani gave you two contacts, right?"

"I really didn't want to deal with this until the tour was over and I had some time to reflect and relax."

"Okay, so call them and make appointments next week or the week after and tell everyone to settle the fuck down. I know you're hot right now, but this is a huge decision. It might even be a good idea to have Dani's team review any contract," Sarah said.

Annie rubbed her face as her anxiety grew. "Why is this so hard? Why can't I make a decision?"

"You should think about that. What's holding you back? You know what it's like on the road. People are starting to recognize you. Your EP is getting tons of downloads on iTunes. Maybe doing what you're doing is working for you. Just don't let anyone pressure you, okay?"

Annie nodded. "I know. Thank you for looking out for me. I owe you big."

"Now get to work so we can see your adorable face in person. We miss you."

Annie felt the tears well and blinked them back. "I miss you all, too. I'll see you soon. I promise." She disconnected the call and decided Sarah was right. It was time to start making decisions. She called the first company on Dani's list. The representative seemed friendly enough, almost too laid back, and she scheduled a sit-down two days after the tour ended. She didn't like the vibe of the second call, so said she would be in touch but knew she wouldn't call them back. She called the local Chevrolet dealer in Denver and asked to speak to the manager of new cars. Twenty minutes well spent. She had time for one more call.

"Where have you been? I haven't heard from you in months!"

Annie laughed at Charley's exaggerated statement. "I called you last week. And we texted three nights ago."

"I know. I just miss you. Open-mic night isn't the same without you. When are you done?" she asked. "And why is there so much banging in the background? Where are you?"

"Portland. The crew is setting up the stage. I can't even begin to tell you how much goes into planning a tour. Things I never thought of just to get in front of people."

"Did you get a manager yet?"

"No, but before you yell at me, just know that I have a sit-down with Mountain Entertainment in Denver. I called both recommendations and felt the most comfortable with this one."

"Shit. I wish I knew the first thing about managing," Charley said.

"You don't want this job," Annie said. She saw how hard Lizzy worked. Fifteen percent of whatever Bristol made was a chunk of change, but Lizzy had to pay her own staff, too.

"How's Bristol?"

Annie couldn't stop the smile from slipping into place. "She's wonderful but overextended. I don't know how she's keeping her shit together." She didn't want too many people to know about her and Bristol, so she kept their make-out sessions to herself. Her sister knowing was enough. Privacy was so important to Bristol that Annie felt guilty with her sister knowing as much as she did.

"Well, keep livestreaming your concerts. I'm showing them in the coffee shop. That way, when you return, people will still remember who you are," Charley said.

"I will. And the last concert is going to be amazing. I'll send you the lineup."

"Will you be able to livestream the whole thing?" Charley asked.

"I don't think so, but I'll sneak clips on Instagram. As will tens of thousands of other fans. Okay, go do your thing, and I'll see you soon. Want me to bring back some Portland coffee beans? Isn't that what they're famous for?"

"Bring yourself back. That's what Denver's famous for."

"You're the best, Charley."

"I know."

Getting ahold of Bristol was impossible, and her text messages were short but apologetic. When Annie took the stage that night, Bristol showed up, like clockwork, and sang as though nothing was different between them. She flirted a bit more with Bristol, and the crowd ate it up. Bristol waved and left the stage for Annie to finish. Thirty seconds later when Annie exited the stage, Bristol was nowhere to be seen. People stopped her to tell her it was a great performance, and by the time she got to the dressing rooms, security was standing guard outside Bristol's. With determination, Annie walked up but was stopped short by Bruce.

"I'm sorry, Miss Foster, but I can't allow you to interrupt right now. You'll have to see her after the concert."

"Really? Did she say that?"

"That came from her manager," he said.

"Oh, okay. I understand. Can you tell her I stopped by?" Annie kept a smile on her face as though oblivious to the obvious shutdown.

"Sure thing, Miss Foster. I'll pass along the information. Good singing up there."

"Thanks, Bruce. See you later."

Annie felt defeated. She knew Bristol was super busy, but she could've at least answered her texts with a little more than just *sorry, can't talk* or *I'll see you onstage.* For the first time this whole tour, Annie decided to skip Bristol's concert. She wasn't feeling it, and there was a pretty good chance that Bristol wouldn't even miss her. She grabbed her purse, her pass to get back into the arena, and ordered a Lyft to take her to a popular restaurant.

"Hi. I'm Amber. Welcome to Detention. What can I get you to drink?" Judging by the incredibly large smile on the waitress's face and how she couldn't stop fidgeting, Annie figured she knew who Annie was.

"I'll take an IPA and a cheeseburger, well done, with fries. Oh, and a side of mayonnaise."

"Coming right up, Ms. Foster."

Annie sat back in the booth and pulled up a game on her phone. She knew she was being childish by walking away tonight, but she needed to take a step back. Too many things were happening at once. Plus, she resented how Lizzy treated her. She didn't know why her assistants put up with her crap. Annie wasn't about to start in this business with people walking all over her and bossing her around. They might be the ones with the contacts, but she was the one with the talent. Even if she walked away now, she had a big following on her YouTube channel and could easily do that for a long time. The internet was able to put her in front of more people than a tour could.

"You're Annie Foster, right? Can we get a photo with you?"

Annie looked up to find a family of four standing far enough away to be respectful, but close enough so Annie could hear their request. "Um, sure." She stood and waited for the mother to hand her phone off to somebody at the bar and ask them to take their picture. Several times. Annie's food arrived during the photo shoot. They posed for at least ten pictures.

"You're such a wonderful singer and an inspiration to so many young women out there." The woman's hand was on Annie's arm, and alarm bells started going off. She was entirely too comfortable in Annie's personal space.

"Thank you. Now if you don't mind, I'd like to eat my dinner."

"Let's go, honey." The woman's partner had to pull her away from the table. Honestly, it freaked Annie out. There was normal attention, but then there was this obvious invasion.

"I'm so sorry that happened. We'll make sure you are undisturbed from now on," Amber said. She dropped off the side of mayonnaise and extra napkins and gave Annie a weak smile. Annie asked for the check immediately. She ate half her burger, dropped cash on the table, and ordered another Lyft to take her back to the stadium. If this was what Bristol had to deal with all day, every day, it was no wonder she wanted out.

CHAPTER TWENTY-TWO

Bristol's heart fell when she didn't see Annie in the crowd. She couldn't blame her. Lizzy had asked that they cool it until the end of the tour because they both had big decisions to make. She felt terrible every time she blew off Annie with a text. A month ago, Lizzy was joking about them hooking up, but now she was dead set against it. She insisted it would be easier to make a clean break from Top Shelf if they had fewer entanglements. At the time, it'd made sense.

Being in Annie's arms made her forget that they were on different career paths. Annie was on her way up, and Bristol wanted out. They didn't have a future. Annie didn't strike Bristol as a one-night-stand kind of girl either. As much as Bristol cursed Lizzy's bad timing that night in Bristol's suite, it was a blessing. At least it had seemed so at the time.

Not seeing her face with that beautiful, beaming smile and light blue eyes staring back at her soured Bristol's mood onstage. She had to work extra hard to keep her voice upbeat and a spring in her step as she danced her routines. She couldn't wait for the tour to be over.

"Good job, but not your best," Lizzy said as she handed Bristol a towel and a cold water.

"I'll do better on the encore," Bristol said. Only a few more shows. She took a deep breath and jumped back onstage with the band. The crowd didn't seem to notice that she was out of sorts. They sang the final two songs with her and begged for more when she waved good night.

"Much better," Lizzy said.

Bristol fell into step with her security and followed them out to the buses. She waved to the fans who left the concert early to catch a glimpse of her getting onto her bus. They wanted to hit the road early tonight to set up in Sacramento because Bristol had a signing at a Top Shelf records store at ten, an interview with KIXS radio at one, and still had to get a sound check in before the concert. She could taste the finish line. She popped into the shower and washed off the sweat and bitterness of tonight. Slipping into fresh clothes, she could hear Lizzy barking at somebody. Who? And why? The show had gone off without a hitch. She hated it when Lizzy got overly bossy with people. What she did with her staff was her business, although behind the scenes, Bristol had words with her about being too stern. People, especially the ones at her beck and call, deserved respect. Tours were brutal, and everyone was doing the best they could.

"What's your problem? One minute you're nice and inviting, and the next you abuse me like I'm one of your staff."

Bristol recognized Annie's voice and quickly made her way to the front of the bus. "Hey. What's going on here?"

Annie's chest was heaving as she faced off against Lizzy. "I'm not required to attend every set of every concert. It's a perk, and while I love watching you in concert, I'm getting tired of Lizzy making me feel like crap just because I miss one. I sure as fuck haven't seen Fast Cars in the crowd." Annie's hands were curled into fists and her eyes bright with anger.

Bristol turned to Lizzy. "What did you say to her?"

Lizzy held her hands up. "I just wanted to know why she wasn't at your concert. It obviously upset you."

"She doesn't have to be at my concerts," Bristol said, although she always liked finding Annie in the crowd.

"It's not just Lizzy. What's going on with you? We had a great time the other night, and then your manager shows up drunk and you forget everything that happened. Who blows people off like that? It's rude and childish. If you'd like to say something to me, don't send Lizzy to come at me."

Bristol usually kept calm. She understood this close to the end was hard because people were at each other's throats. The world was small when they toured, and private spaces even smaller. And Annie had it wrong. "I need every single person to get the fuck off the bus right now except for Annie." Her voice boomed in the bus.

Lizzy's assistants scrambled over one another to get out. They'd never seen this side of Bristol before because she hid it, but not anymore. Lizzy's lips disappeared into a straight line before she stood and slowly made her way to the door.

When she turned, Bristol held up her hand. "No." Lizzy shrugged and left. Once the door was latched shut, Bristol blew out a deep breath and turned to Annie. "Please sit down."

"I don't want to." Annie stood with her hands on her hips, still radiating anger.

"Didn't you just give a massive speech about people being adults around here? I understand why you're mad at Lizzy, but why me? What did I do?" Bristol hated that her voice got loud, so she stopped. "Well, I'm going to sit, and I'd like to talk to you about several things. Then maybe you'll understand why Lizzy is the way she is and why I'm the way I am." She sat at the end of the booth and waited for Annie's next move.

"What did I do wrong? How did we go from being fun and flirty to you completely ignoring me? I know you have trust issues, and I completely understand why, but I'm pretty fucking vulnerable here, too. You're Bristol Baines. Me trying to convince you that I'm in it for you and not because you can advance my career is fucking hard."

Bristol felt the sting of tears starting to form so she bit her bottom lip and looked away. "You didn't do anything wrong. Lizzy told me to hold off on talking to you until after the tour ended. I should have ignored her. I've spent the last two days missing you."

Annie's shoulders sagged as she let go of some of the anger between them. "Why did you listen to her?"

"Because she's right about one thing. You're one more connection to Top Shelf. The truth is that I want out." Bristol made a slow, swooping motion with both hands. "All of this. It's killing me. I have no life. Ever since I was sixteen, I couldn't go anywhere without people mobbing me. I've even had people tear at my clothes." Annie's eyes softened at her confession. Bristol smiled sadly. "And you want all of this. We're on two totally different paths, and as much as I wanted to make love to you that night in my suite before bonehead Lizzy showed up, it would have only made matters worse."

"You don't know that." Annie voice was low and not convincing.

"I do. So many people love this life and would give anything to have what I have. The funny thing is that I would give up everything to be like them."

"When was the last time you got out in the real world?" Annie thumbed behind her.

Bristol smiled. "Vegas. And before that was The Night Owl. And before that, it was three months prior where a kid was hurt because a bunch of people rushed after me. I wanted the fortune and fame, and I got it, but it cost me everything." Bristol took Annie's hands, thankful she didn't pull away. "I want you to have everything you want, but just know it comes at a steep price." Annie stared at her for a long time before speaking.

"So rather than tell me, you hid behind Lizzy."

Bristol leaned back in her seat, breaking their physical connection. She was tired of getting pulled in every direction. "I'm really bad at communication. I can't tell you the last time I had a relationship." When Annie didn't say anything, Bristol continued. "I don't really know how to have one. I've been touring for years, and I'm home in spurts. Relationships are new to me."

"But that's an excuse."

"How many relationships have you had in your life? Count them. Don't forget everyone in middle school, high school, college, if you went, after college, last year. Count them out."

"That's not a fair question."

"It is, and I'll tell you why. You still had everything. Awkward school dances, prom, crushes at school. I didn't. I never learned how to date. That's not an excuse at all, but we didn't have the same experiences growing up. I see you, and my palms get sweaty, and I feel weak, and my stomach flops around."

Annie smiled. "That happens when I see you, too. But why wouldn't you want to explore those feelings further with me? We could be great together, or we could crash and burn, but we won't know until we try."

Bristol braced herself for the hardest part of the conversation. She steeled her heart. "I can't be on this journey with you. I think you're wonderful, but your life, your decisions, everything you do in this industry would consume me. I would question your decisions and tell you what to do, and I don't want that for you or myself."

Annie nodded solemnly. "I get that, but you're not giving me enough credit. And I don't understand what this has to do with Top Shelf, specifically. Tell me the truth about them. Right here and now."

"Everyone has different experiences with them."

"Then tell me about yours. No bullshit. Just what happened," Annie said.

Bristol gritted her teeth. "They bled me dry and manipulated me into signing horrible contracts that made them a ton of money and left me with very little."

"But look at what all you have. You have everything."

Bristol's lips curled into an angry smile. "Lizzy had to fight for everything. I didn't start making money until I turned twenty. My first contract was for three albums and three tours, and I saw very little profit. When Top Shelf saw I was on the rise, they bowed to me, but not before taking so much of me." Bristol slid out of the booth to grab waters from the refrigerator. "And they aren't the only ones to blame. I got too big, and now I'm living a very sheltered life. I would love to pump my own gas or go pick up a gallon of milk from the grocery store, but I can't because everyone knows who I am."

Annie put her hands flat on the table. "Don't take this the wrong way, but other celebrities have lives where they get out and do things. Even Leonardo DiCaprio goes to get coffee. And Angela Jolie goes shopping in Beverly Hills. I've seen their pics all over the internet and in magazines. I'm not trying to say you don't have it bad, but I think you have to trust the world a little bit more. And maybe go places where they either know you well enough to leave you alone or somewhere where nobody knows you at all."

"Like where?"

Annie didn't miss a beat. "LA, New York. The same places all those other famous people go out. I'm sorry a child got hurt, but I'm guessing that was in a smaller town where they don't have many celebrities."

Bristol thought about it. Annie was right. "Okay. But there's still paparazzi everywhere."

"You just need somebody to go with you. Lizzy's worthless. I'm sorry, but I feel like a part of her gaslights you so she can always be around to save you. Not a Lizzy fan anymore, by the way."

Bristol had always thought her relationship with Lizzy was solid, but Annie brought up interesting points. She didn't think Lizzy was gaslighting her, but knew she was overprotective. "She's just protecting me, but I get what you're saying. It's time for her and me to take a break."

"Are you really going to walk away from Top Shelf?" Annie asked softly.

She had to trust her. She wanted to trust her. "Yes. They don't know it, but I'm not signing with them. I'm not signing with anyone. I just want peace. Please keep that to yourself. I still have a crew to pay, and Top Shelf owes me money. If they knew I was walking, they would stonewall me, and as much money as I have to sue for what they owe me, they have more." Annie slowly nodded as she processed the info dump. Bristol's anxiety ramped up, realizing she'd just shared very personal information with somebody who was almost in bed with Top Shelf. She trusted Annie, but sometimes things slipped out.

"You really don't trust them, do you?"

Bristol had told her almost the entire story. Annie deserved the rest. "I know you don't like Lizzy, but she saved me. Do you know who Denny Briggs is?"

"Big-shot producer, right? He assaulted that pop star." Annie's veins felt cold at the realization that maybe Denny had assaulted Bristol, too.

"Ruby Delgado. She's the sweetest girl." Bristol took a deep breath. "Before that, there were rumors about him for years. Tyson wanted him to produce one of my albums. When I said I wouldn't work with Denny, Top Shelf forced me to. They threatened to sue over violation of contract. After that, Lizzy never let me record without her present. She wouldn't even let me alone in the building at Top Shelf. She's protective of me for a reason. It might be extreme, but I know where she's coming from."

Annie's eyes grew wide and serious. "Oh, my God. That sounds horrible."

"It wasn't a great environment to produce albums in. I was on edge, stressed, and angry the whole time I was in the studio. I never knew if he would somehow succeed in getting me alone or if he would sabotage my art. Producers have a lot of pull in this industry," Bristol said.

"What happened? How did you finally get a different producer?" Annie asked.

"He was arrested for assaulting Ruby. Sterling put on this whole show like they were shocked."

"Wait. Sterling knew?"

"Oh, yeah," Bristol said.

"I'm so sorry that happened. After spending time with her and hearing all of this, I'm really hesitant about her and Top Shelf. Was she always like that?" Annie asked.

Bristol bit her tongue to keep from spewing out her hatred. "Yes. You know she was my first girlfriend?" Annie nodded. "She broke my heart, but that's not why I dislike her now. I think she uses every means possible to get people to sign bad contracts. She's shady and takes advantage of young, eager musicians. Some people think it's part of the industry, but I don't. At least not an industry I want to be a part of."

"She rubbed me wrong in Vegas, but during the tour of Top Shelf she was really nice. She even introduced me to Willow McAdams."

Bristol couldn't help the eye roll. "Look, I'm sorry, but she's a chameleon. Once she realized you weren't into flirting or impressed by expensive champagne, she changed her approach." Bristol watched Annie's face as she processed their very blunt conversation. It was a lot to digest. "Why don't we take a break? I know we need to hit the road."

"Yeah. I guess I have a lot to think about. Thank you for talking to me."

"I'm really sorry for blowing you off. And I'll talk to Lizzy about leaving you alone. You're the first person I've connected with in a long time, and she's probably jealous. It's always been just us."

"I'm sorry this hasn't worked out the way you wanted it to, but you've been a role model for so many people, and your music has touched the hearts of millions. Know that what you've done in this world is beautiful."

"Thank you for saying that." Bristol was exhausted and wanted her to stay. She wanted to walk into Annie's arms and just be held by somebody who gave a damn about her and not her career, but she didn't know how to ask for comfort. Annie waved good night and walked off the bus as though Bristol hadn't just poured her heart and soul out in the space between them.

"Ms. Baines? Are we ready to go?" Lou knocked on the door that Annie had just closed.

"We're good, Lou. Thank you for waiting." She dragged herself to her bedroom and locked the door. She didn't care who rode with her on the bus as long as they left her alone.

❖

The Angel/Devil tour was finally coming to an end. Bristol looked at the people who hustled around her and realized, as much as she appreciated their efforts, she was fine with not seeing them again for a very long time. Lizzy had given her a wide berth since their blowup and was very cordial and friendly when they did communicate.

None of this mattered anymore. In eight hours, she would be home. She and Lizzy had already discussed bonuses and had deposits ready to drop in everyone's account by the morning. Lizzy had a meeting with Top Shelf after Labor Day to deliver the news that Bristol was dropping them as a label.

"Are you ready for tonight?" Dom asked. She was the only one who either was oblivious to the mounting tension or didn't care.

"I can't tell you how ready I am," Bristol said. She'd stayed close to the tour bus the last few days, not really having a place to land. Once the concert was over and the bands said their good-byes, that was it.

"Do you want to do a farewell video? It might be a good idea to publicly thank everyone," Dom said.

"That's a brilliant idea, and yes. When and where do you think?"

Dom sized her up and looked around. "I mean, we can do it here right now. You look amazing, as always. It might seem more heartfelt, too, instead of onstage in the heat of the moment."

"Good idea. Where should I sit?" Bristol was still made up from a live appearance on *Hollywood Hills* with Lauren Lucas, so there was nothing for her to do other than find a place on the bus with the best background. Dom would set up the ring light, since the lighting on the bus was either too bright or too dark.

"Over there. Get comfortable. I'll set up."

Dom pointed to the chair that was closest to the front of the bus. Bristol looked confused. "Is this the best location?"

"You're on tour. On a bus. It's perfect. Trust me."

Bristol watched as Dom expertly arranged the tripod and light.

She threw out suggestions for Bristol before they decided she should wing it. It would sound more organic coming straight from the heart and not from cue cards.

"Tonight is the last night of the Angel/Devil tour, and I want to thank so many people who made this happen. I have to start with Top Shelf for arranging the tour and putting me in front of fans all over the world. My heart goes out to my manager Lizzy, who made the tour run like a well-oiled machine and for being my strength when I needed it. Where would this tour be without the crew that builds the beautiful and safe sets in every city? Thank you to them and to my stylists and assistants. I needed every single person on this tour, and they did amazing work night after night." Bristol paused, not for effect, but because she was getting emotional. "Thank you to all the bands and singers who opened for me. Fast Cars is an incredible band, and I hope my fans enjoyed their music as much as I did. Ali Hart started the tour with us but had to leave because baby number three decided to show up earlier than planned, but that gave us Annie Foster, whose crisp, clear voice wowed us all. And all of this—the videos, the photos of the tour, the social media posts—are managed by my friend Dom. Come over here, say hi." Dom's eyes widened, but she walked over to Bristol, looked at the camera, and waved. She was quick to duck back out of sight so Bristol could finish. "And my fans." She rested both her hands on her heart. "Thank you so much for your continued support over the years and helping me grow into the person I am today. I love you all, and I hope you enjoyed the tour."

Dom signaled they were done recording and gave her a thumbs-up. "That was beautiful, Bristol. Even though you pulled me into it." She pretended to be perturbed, but Bristol knew Dom loved the attention.

"Thank you for everything you've done on the tour. I know it's hard to be away from your family and friends," Bristol said. Dom was always going to be with her, even if it was in a smaller capacity. She was too good at juggling all the accounts, and she knew Bristol's brand better than Bristol did. She liked posting the little, fun things like the flirting with Annie. What was she going to do about Annie? They'd talked a few times since the big bus blowout, but their exchanges were more cordial than personal, and Bristol hated it. She missed Annie's warmth and her sunny disposition.

"Everything starts early today. How are you feeling?" Dom asked as she broke down the light and packed her messenger bag. As if sensing Bristol's vulnerability, she sat opposite her and waited patiently for Bristol to answer.

Bristol appreciated Dom's attention. "I'm overwhelmed but also excited for it to be over. I get to sleep in my own bed tonight. I'm sure we're all happy to be heading home."

"This was a learning experience, and I got to see the world, so don't think you took anything from me, from any of us. Thank you for trusting me with your online presence. I think everything turned out well."

Bristol squeezed Dom's hand. "Because of you, I have millions of followers. And you really helped promote other musicians on tour with us. I think we all got a much-appreciated boost." She didn't want to get emotional, knowing full well that she would cry onstage. Some part of tonight would break her, but she didn't know what or when. She could feel a vulnerable shift inside. "Now go spend some time for yourself. Thank you for being so wonderful." Bristol got her first heartfelt hug in days and fought hard to keep the tears at bay.

CHAPTER TWENTY-THREE

DJ Spinz Madness was getting the crowd pumped up while Annie hung with Willow backstage. Her anxiety and excitement levels were at an all-time high. It was the last night of the tour. The last night of playing in front of thirty thousand people. Also, the last night of singing with Bristol.

"Have you made a decision about Top Shelf?" Willow had to yell in Annie's ear.

Annie shook her head. "Not yet. I need a manager first, but I have a few meetings next week." As much as she liked Willow, she didn't want more advice. She wanted to enjoy this night and not think about tomorrow. Live in the moment, Sarah always said. That's exactly what she was doing.

"Good for you. Make sure you take care of yourself."

Annie nodded thanks. Suddenly, Willow grabbed her hand and pulled her onstage. "What are you doing?" Annie could only laugh when Willow twirled her and started shaking her hips to the beat. The crowd screamed when they saw them dancing. Annie felt rusty, but Willow was so smooth that Annie was able to slip into a rhythm that was comfortable and fun. She was having fun! DJ Spinz Madness was pointing at them and even mixed in a snippet of one of Annie's songs. Willow's eyes widened when she recognized the music and pointed at her. Annie loved the new arrangement and did a solo dance to it. When it slipped into another popular song, Willow twirled Annie and waved good-bye to the crowd as they skipped offstage.

"That was amazing," Annie said. She hugged Willow. "So much fun."

"I plan on having the best time tonight, and I hope you do, too. I'm headed out on a small tour next week, so this will help me get into the mood," Willow said.

Annie studied her. "How many cities?"

"About twenty-five and I'll be home by Christmas."

"That doesn't sound bad at all." If Top Shelf was working with Willow, they would probably work with her, too. Maybe Bristol's experiences were because of her past with Sterling. Or maybe because Bristol was young when they signed her and they knew they could take advantage of her. That still didn't account for making her work with a dangerous producer though. Maybe they had learned people like Denny Briggs were bad for business.

"Always go for the short tours. They seem to tack on extra shows at the end, depending on your popularity. Since you're hot, they'll want to cut an album quick and get you in front of people," Willow said.

Her voice was so matter-of-fact that Annie started doubting her own doubts. Maybe Top Shelf would take care of her. Maybe signing with them was the way to go. Before she could ask Willow anything else, somebody dressed in black wearing a headset tapped Willow on the shoulder.

"You're up in ten minutes."

"Oh. I'd better grab my guitar. Good luck tonight. I can't wait to hear you live," Willow said.

Annie watched her disappear in the small crowd that had gathered backstage to either watch the show or were busy prepping for it. She was up after Willow. How that had happened was beyond her. Willow was a bigger name than Annie. Fast Cars followed Annie like always, but X-Treem had an hour-long set before Bristol closed out the show. There was talk of all the bands onstage at the end singing something fun for the crowd, but Annie hadn't been notified. She wasn't worried.

"Hello, Los Angeles. Isn't tonight unbelievable?"

Annie smiled as the crowd roared. It was an amazing concert to not only be a part of, but to witness. She whooped with the crowd as they showered Willow with applause and whistles.

"If you don't know this already, I'm Willow McAdams. Maybe you've heard of me."

More screaming and cheers. Annie crossed her arms and smiled hard at the playful banter. She thought she was pretty casual onstage, but Willow gave chill a whole new definition. She played three songs, and right when she started the fourth, Sondra and Lizzy flanked Annie. Sondra handed Annie her guitar.

Lizzy leaned close and shouted, "At the end, we're going to have all the performers go onstage with Bristol. Are you good with that?"

Annie thanked Sondra for her guitar and turned her attention back to Lizzy. "Yeah. That's fine. I'll be here and ready."

Lizzy nodded and hesitated before continuing. "Look. I'm sorry for being such an ass the other day. You've been nothing but great on tour and good for Bristol. I got out of hand. What you do on your time is your business."

Annie could tell she was sincere. "Thank you for saying that. I know touring is tough. I didn't mean to come at you that hard." She still meant what she said, but she could have done it with a little more finesse.

"Here's an access pass for VIP if you want to see the concert from down there. Or you can stay backstage."

"I appreciate it. Thank you."

"Okay." Lizzy nodded. She stood next to her awkwardly for about ten seconds. "You're on in ten. Have fun up there."

DJ Spinz Madness took over during the transition time between artists to keep the groove going. Instead of fifteen minutes to transition, the artists were asked to allow for only five. Annie had only a guitar, so setting up was a cinch. She wasn't going to livestream tonight. It was too nerve-wracking with other artists in the mix, and she didn't want to fuck up.

"Up next is fan favorite Annie Foster! Have a great night!" Willow waved and blew kisses to the crowd.

Annie high-fived Willow on her way backstage. "Oh, my God. You were so good out there." She was beyond nervous. She waited until she heard the beat of DJ Spinz Madness's music fade, took a deep breath, and walked onstage. It was hard not to smile at the energy of the place. "Los Angeles! I've missed you." She found Reece easily enough in the crowd. Vanessa was two seats down. She gave them a quick wave, even though seeing them added weight to her heart. "How incredible is Willow McAdams? She's amazing." The crowd agreed. "I'm Annie Foster, and I'm here to play you a few songs."

The crowd started screaming, and Annie couldn't figure out why.

She knew they liked her music, but this was insane. Bristol moved into her peripheral vision holding a phone recording her.

"What are you doing?" It was incredible how Bristol made every part of Annie blossom, from the huge smile on her mouth to her rapidly beating heart.

"You always livestream your set, and this is a big one to miss. Am I right, Los Angeles?" Bristol shouted.

Annie stared at Bristol. She looked good. No. She looked beautiful. A white lacy camisole with thick straps ended right above the high rise of her tight jeans, affording Annie a peek of smooth skin. She was barefoot with pink toenail polish. It was different than the shade they used in Vegas. Her hair was pulled back in a long ponytail and her makeup very minimal. Annie wanted to melt into her.

"Ack! Now I'm nervous," Annie said. She started strumming her guitar to the first song on her set. Bristol circled her during the chorus, getting the crowd involved and totally flirting with Annie. Annie flirted back and plucked the strings effortlessly. When the song ended, one of the roadies brought out a stand and helped Bristol attach her phone.

"You're still live," Bristol said. She waved to the crowd. "I'll see you in a few songs."

Annie played the next four songs perfectly and even spent an extra minute talking to the crowd. Instead of playing "Waiting All Day" like they usually did, she plucked the first few notes of "Brass in Pocket." Bristol lifted her eyebrow when she joined Annie onstage. She had her guitar this time and added a few notes to enhance the song. Annie liked it. When Bristol leaned forward to share the microphone, Annie almost kissed her out of reflex. Damn, she missed her.

"We love you together!"

Somebody from the crowd yelled during the perfectly quiet moment between strumming and singing, and their message was loud and clear. Annie and Bristol smiled at one another. She felt the flush of excitement as Bristol looked at her like she had the other night when Annie was flat on her back and the weight of Bristol between her legs was the only thing keeping her from floating away. It was hunger. Annie couldn't look away. Bristol's gaze went down to her lips when they sang. If Annie thought they had chemistry before, whatever was happening right now was explosive. She didn't think she was going to survive the song, but she did. Bristol waved to the crowd before leaving the stage for Annie to finish her set.

"Thank you, Los Angeles, for being so welcoming. I'm Annie Foster, and even though the tour stops here, I hope to see your faces at future events. I love you all!" She waved and left the stage. How could tonight get any better?

❖

Annie would never get tired of watching Bristol perform. She was fierce and full of energy on the stage. Her voice was powerful and rich. She didn't even sound out of breath as she danced and sang and gave the crowd the best performance. As much as Annie wanted to stay in the front row to finish the concert with the fans, security arrived to escort her from the VIP section for Bristol's planned encore.

"I'm sorry, Miss Foster, but it's time. Please follow me," Cam yelled.

Annie slipped through the barrier security moved for her and made her way backstage. "What's the plan?" she asked Willow.

"Bristol is going to do one song by herself, and then we're all going to get onstage and sing 'Turn It Up.' I guess there are fireworks, too, so don't get scared when you hear explosions and see bright lights."

"Phew. I'm glad somebody told me."

"She's killing it onstage tonight. Look at her," Willow said.

It was hard to look away. While it was incredible to watch, Annie knew it was because this could very well be the last time Bristol took the stage. It broke her heart how something Bristol was so passionate about had turned on her. There had to be a middle ground. No way would the world allow Bristol Baines to just fade away. Her music was too important. Annie and Willow stepped to the side when Bristol and the band said good night and ran offstage. It was hard not to stare. Lizzy showed up with a towel and a cold water.

"You're amazing tonight," Lizzy told her.

Bristol smiled as her eyes briefly flickered on Annie. She returned her attention to Lizzy. "Thanks. I'm feeling the energy."

"Good job, Bristol." The lead singer of X-Treem patted her on the back.

Bristol gave her a smile. She drank the rest of the water, wiped the back of her neck, and made her way back onstage to the single spotlight. This was her a cappella song. Annie wanted to give Bristol her undivided attention, but one of the stagehands was passing out microphones and stepped into her line of vision several times. DJ Spinz Madness had slipped over to his station in the dark. Once Bristol finished, he was to cue up the beat, and the band would jump in before all the acts joined her onstage. According to the poorly sketched diagram being passed around, Annie was on the far end away from center stage. Her heart sank. She had hoped for time with Bristol, but tonight seemed impossible. There was always the after-party. Annie had a plane ticket for the morning, but she'd rebooked it for Wednesday. She'd agreed to a meeting with Sterling and Tyson on Tuesday. She wasn't planning to sign and expected them to fight her on it, but she also knew to keep a level head. Having everything she wanted sounded great, but Bristol had showed her it always came with a price.

"Let's go," Willow said.

Annie followed everyone out onto the stage and started singing "Turn It Up." Bristol's voice was loudest, but it was hard to hear because so many people were singing at once. It was a hot mess, but the crowd loved it, and Bristol looked happier than she had in a long time. Annie was so proud of her. What a grueling tour, but she'd made it. Near the end of the song, fireworks shot off from the far side of the arena, and fans applauded the bright showers of exploding red, white, and blue stars.

"Thank you to DJ Spinz Madness." Bristol pointed to him at the back of the stage. He waved to the crowd. "And thank you, X-Treem." They waved and trotted offstage. Bristol introduced everyone, until it was just Bristol and her onstage. Annie wanted to cry. Bristol already had tears in her eyes. She pulled Annie into a hug and squeezed her. For a tiny moment, it felt like they were the only ones up there. Bristol's body felt familiar against hers, and Annie leaned into her warmth. Bristol pulled away first. "And Annie Foster. Thank you for finishing out the tour with us." She held up Annie's hand high above their heads as though she'd just won a sporting match. Annie waved. She was sad when she had to drop Bristol's hand to leave the stage so Bristol could finish her encore.

"Good night, Los Angeles. I'm home now, and I hope to see you around."

Bristol dropped the microphone onto the stage, something Annie had never seen her do, and softly jogged backstage. Annie got pushed back into the crowd as people swarmed Bristol, congratulating her on a great concert. Bruce and three of his henchmen whisked her away.

"Hey, the afterparty is at The Cliffs. Do you need a ride?" Willow asked.

Annie had no plans. She had luggage on the bus and nowhere to put it. She tamped down the panic. "Oh, no. I've got a few things to wrap up here. I'll head there when I'm done. Thanks, though. I'll see you there." Annie grabbed her guitar and made her way back to her dressing room. For the first time in a long time, she felt lost. She closed the door, pulled up hotels around the airport on her phone, and booked two nights at the Hilton. Finding a Lyft with everyone leaving was going to be difficult. Better to let the traffic die down. She made her way to the tour buses and had security pull her two bags. She wasn't the only one grabbing their things. She recognized one of Lizzy's assistants, who smiled at her once and avoided eye contact after that. She ordered a Lyft and hung around the bus until her driver was close. She clumsily made her way over, rolling two suitcases in front of her and balancing her guitar on top of the bigger one.

"Is this everything?" he asked.

She nodded and slipped into the back seat, embarrassed to be leaving this amazing tour in such a pedestrian way. By the time she got to the hotel, she questioned whether she should even go out. She dug through her suitcase and was about to throw in the towel and call it a night, when she saw the little black dress she'd picked up at Caesars Palace in Vegas. She smirked. Fine. If Bristol didn't think hooking up was a good idea, then she was going to make damn sure Bristol knew what she was missing.

CHAPTER TWENTY-FOUR

Where was she? Bristol scanned the packed club several times, hoping to lay eyes on Annie. The afterparty was always the best part of finishing a tour. Top Shelf rented out The Cliffs, and getting in was impossible unless you were on the list. Bristol made sure everyone from her tour, including Annie, was on it. She felt like her heart had fallen out of her chest when she heard one of Lizzy's assistants tell them she saw Annie grab her luggage and drive off in a nondescript sedan. Bristol wanted the opportunity to say good-bye to her in person. She wanted time with just her.

Right now, Bristol was surrounded by people she barely knew and others she wanted to get away from. Sterling swung by a few times, but Bristol's table was always full, and it was hard to hear conversations. Bristol shrugged and pointed to her ear, even though she heard every damn word out of Sterling's damn mouth.

"I'm avoiding Sterling, too. She can chat with us when we go in for our meeting this week," Lizzy said.

They watched her work the room, stopping to laugh with the famous people and ignoring people she didn't recognize. "If nothing else, she's a hard worker."

"For what, though? What's the allure at this point? The Mayfields have hundreds of millions of dollars. They could buy a small country somewhere," Lizzy said.

"Too bad she can't go there and run it," Bristol said.

"Should I order us another round?" Lizzy waved over their waiter, whose sole job was their table.

"What can I get you ladies?"

"Bring us a bottle of tequila," Lizzy yelled.

The thought of doing shots made Bristol shiver sourly. "Oh, no. I'll take Disaronno on the rocks. Give her the tequila bottle."

"And lime wedges. We've got the salt here." Lizzy waved the saltshaker at the waiter.

"I should probably make a round just to be social," Bristol said. Lizzy and one of her assistants scooted out of the booth to free Bristol. She got about ten feet before people pounced on her and asked to take selfies. "Maybe later. I have to be somewhere right now." She smiled to soften the blow and headed to the restroom.

Bristol nodded at the security guy stationed outside the VIP bathroom. The private room had its own sink and a counter full of personal-sized hygiene products from mouthwashes to deodorants. She washed her hands, used minty mouthwash, and double-checked her makeup. The jacket she was wearing was hot, but it looked so good on her that she suffered through the discomfort. She wore a thin tank top under it and a pair of ridiculously expensive black pants that clung to her. Her hair was down, but she pulled it up with one hand and fanned herself with the other. She hated that she looked tired. She was going home and crawl into bed and stay there for days until she had to go to her meeting with Top Shelf. She let her hair down, fixed her lipstick, and opened the door. The first thing she saw was Annie sitting on a chaise lounge.

"You made it." Bristol gave Annie a small smile, not knowing where Annie stood on how they'd left things.

"I'm supposed to be at the airport in two hours to catch an early flight out."

Bristol could feel Annie's anger in the space between them, but she felt something else, too. Hope had needled its way into Bristol's heart. Annie was here, was sitting right in front of her wanting something. She was always beautiful onstage, but the Annie in front of her was extremely sexy wearing stilettos with her little black dress. Her curls hung loosely over her shoulders and rolled down her back. She was the most beautiful woman Bristol had ever seen. Her light blue eyes were piercing in the soft glow of the room.

"We can change your ticket."

"I already did."

"Oh?" Bristol took a step closer. Annie didn't move. "You look amazing tonight."

Her shoulders relaxed at Bristol's words. "Thank you."

Bristol stepped closer. "You did a remarkable job on tour. I'm happy you were with us. I know things are off between us, but, Annie, I really hope you get whatever you want out of this." She bit her bottom lip to keep from saying something unsavory about Top Shelf.

"Thank you. I'm still working on the getting-what-I-want part," Annie said.

Bristol didn't know if she should read something into her remark but decided to go for it just in case she wasn't misreading the signs. "Do you want to go somewhere quiet? Where we could talk?"

"You don't have to say good night to anyone?"

Bristol pulled out her phone to send Lizzy a text message.

I'm out. Have a fun night. I'll see you at the meeting.

"That's it?" Annie asked.

Bristol smiled when she felt Annie's fingers on her hand again. "As of two hours ago, I work for no one." Bristol wasn't going to fire Lizzy as her manager because she still ran Bristol's business side of things, but she was going to make it very clear that she was done touring and was never going to sign another contract with Top Shelf again.

"Let's go," Annie said.

Bristol's driver was behind the club in a side alley. Security was standing guard to prevent people from parking in front of him so they could get away quickly. Parking in downtown Los Angeles was a nightmare. A text message from Lizzy popped up, but Bristol ignored it. Tonight was her night.

"We're going to have to sneak out. Hold on to me so you don't slip in those incredible heels," Bristol said.

Annie clutched Bristol's hand tighter and followed her as they made their way down the hallway and through the back of the club to the side door. Bristol tipped the security guy who led them as she and Annie ducked into the limo. Nobody saw them, but when Willie pulled away, tons of paparazzi snapped photos of the moving limo, hoping their flashes would penetrate the privacy glass.

"Can they see us?" Annie asked.

"No. It's reflective, so even if they had a high-powered flash, it wouldn't penetrate," Bristol said.

Annie relaxed against Bristol. "So, what are we doing?"

"Going somewhere to talk."

"We could've talked back there," Annie said.

Bristol leaned forward so she could look into Annie's eyes. "We could've, but I owe you my undivided attention." She paused and tried hard to keep any desperation out of her voice. "Can we just have tonight? Just us? No talk about touring, nothing about managers or the future. Can we just pretend we're two women who are going back to my place to have a glass of wine or breakfast or whatever and get to know one another?"

"But you said you didn't want this kind of relationship. You thought it would be better to stay friends," Annie said.

Hearing her words thrown back at her was hurtful. She understood why Annie was hesitant. "We're just talking. I'll cook you breakfast. You can stay in one of the guest wings until your flight back to Denver. We can even send for your luggage and guitar if you want."

"Guest wings? As in more than one?"

Bristol shrugged. "I'm the only one who lives there, so yes. I promise to behave. I like you, Annie. If nothing else, we can be friends."

Annie leaned back in the seat. "You're right. And I'd love to have my own things here. I'm nervous leaving them in the hotel." The hotel was nice, but it was unsettling having her guitar somewhere else. "Let's go back to your place and see if you really can cook."

Bristol bit her bottom lip, knowing full well she couldn't but would wing it. "Honestly, I don't know if I have any food at the house since I've been gone so long. Worst-case scenario, we can have food delivered. Are you hungry?"

"I'm starving. I haven't eaten since breakfast."

"We can definitely stop somewhere first."

Annie waved off the idea. "It's okay. Let's check your refrigerator first."

Bristol leaned back, and Annie put her head on her shoulder. Both were sending mixed messages, but Bristol didn't know how to stop wanting her. By the time they reached the security gates, Bristol's stomach was nothing but a knotted mess of emotion. The drive to her house seemed to take forever. Annie's look of disbelief at her house made her heart swell with pride.

Willie opened the limo door for them. "Have a good day, Miss

Bristol. I'll drop off Miss Annie's things later this morning." He waited until Bristol unlocked her front door before pulling out of the driveway.

All smiles, Annie turned to Bristol. "This is the most amazing house I've ever seen."

"Would you like a tour?"

"Definitely." Annie slipped off her heels and left them by the front door.

It would have taken Bristol too much time to unlace her boots, so she left them on. They made her tower over Annie, and a part of her liked that. It took thirty minutes to walk through the house, and by the time the tour was over, Annie looked impressed and also exhausted. They ended in the kitchen, where Bristol told Annie to have a seat and she would make breakfast. She was so happy her mother had stocked the fridge. She pulled out ingredients for avocado toast and poured them tall glasses of orange juice. Morning light was starting to erase the darkness.

"Can we eat outside? It's so gorgeous by the pool."

One of the reasons Bristol had chosen this house was the magnificent view, but mostly because it had an infinity pool. She loved to swim. "Definitely."

"At first, I was concerned when you said you were going to stay in your house for three months, but Bristol. This is a beautiful house. You don't need to go anywhere. Ever. This place is amazing."

"It's big enough to have friends over, but not too big."

Annie looked at her in disbelief. "How many square feet?"

"I think seventy-five hundred," Bristol said.

"Let me put this into perspective. I have a one-bedroom apartment that is six hundred square feet. And I share it with a cat. Over seven thousand is mind-blowing."

It occurred to Bristol that Annie misunderstood why she had all of this. "I bought this house not because it's seven thousand square feet or has an amazing workout room or has the best view of the city. I bought this house because it's safe. I don't need all of this. I paid a lot of money for my safety and privacy. The house just came with it."

Annie must have sensed she'd hit a nerve because she reached over and touched Bristol's hand. "It's incredible what you've done with your life. You deserve all of this, especially the safety and privacy. Please don't think I'm teasing you because I'm not. Even though we don't know one another well, I'm proud of you. Is that weird?" Annie crinkled her nose during her confession. It was utterly adorable.

"I felt proud of you, too, when you were onstage. You had some great shows on tour."

"Thank you. It was the best experience of my life." Annie hid a small yawn with the back of her hand.

"Listen. Why don't I give you some clothes to sleep in and set you up in one of the guest wings? We can have a nice day after we've both slept."

"That sounds good. Thank you for getting me away from the party. Watching the sunrise with you in your home was the perfect way to end my tour."

Bristol pulled Annie into a hug but stepped away when it was apparent they either needed to kiss or separate. "Get some sleep."

"Thank you, Bristol. For everything. I mean that," Annie said.

"Thank you, too. I'll see you later." Bristol went to the master suite, stripped off her party clothes, and showered before crawling into bed. She felt comfort in knowing Annie was close. It was exciting, too, but gave Bristol a sense of peace she hadn't had in a very long time.

CHAPTER TWENTY-FIVE

Annie woke and immediately knew where she was. The posh digs, the softest sheets in the world draped around her, and the unbelievable quiet. She looked at her phone. "Holy shit!" She'd been asleep for eleven hours. Slipping from the warm bed, she padded over to the bathroom and turned on the shower. Bristol was probably downstairs pacing, wondering if she was still alive or had split in the middle of the night. When she saw the stack of fresh clothing on the counter, she knew Bristol had checked on her. The bathroom had everything she needed. New makeup, hair products, face lotions, and the fluffiest towels Annie had ever wrapped herself in. She slipped into shorts, a T-shirt, and a hoodie. When she made her way downstairs, Bristol was on the couch reading a book. She stood when Annie walked in.

"I'm so sorry I slept that long." Annie covered her face with her hands. "I'm so embarrassed."

"Don't be. You needed the sleep. I only woke up an hour ago. How are you?"

"I feel amazing. That bed is so comfortable."

"Are you hungry?" Bristol asked.

Annie nodded. "I could cook for us this time."

"Or I could order takeout if you want to sit and chat for a bit."

"Chat. Okay. That sounds nice," Annie said. She fell on the couch next to Bristol and took her hand. It gave her comfort to have a physical connection, even if she hadn't sorted through the reasons why.

"Tell me about a day in the life of Annie Foster."

Annie pursed her lips and shrugged. "It's pretty normal. I get up about nine and work on jingles if I have a project. If I don't, then I work on songs. I perform Tuesday, Wednesday, and Sundays at The Night Owl."

"*Coffee & Chords* on Wednesdays, right?"

"Yes. It's so much fun. There's so much talent in Denver."

"Lizzy found you at the hospital, of all places."

"Why was she there?" Annie asked.

"For hydration therapy. Sometimes she gets dehydrated on the road. We aren't the best eaters or drinkers," Bristol said.

Annie noticed that Bristol looked away when she spoke about it, so she gingerly changed the topic. "Let's see. I sing songs for the kids in the cancer ward. It's so rewarding. They have so much fun on music days."

"I'm sure they love it," Bristol said.

Annie nodded. "And most of my evenings are spent at The Night Owl, even when I'm not performing."

"What do you do for yourself?"

"I play my music."

"When was the last time you dated anybody long-term?"

"Maybe a year ago? You?"

Bristol threw her head back and laughed. "It's been years."

"So, do you ever hook up with groupies? I mean, I know that sounds so stereotypical rock star."

Bristol thought for a moment. "No groupies. I want someone who's into me, not my fame. That's my problem. I never know who's in it for me or just who I am."

"Why can't it be both? You are a pop star, and you're also a softie with a big heart. Why can't people find the balance?"

"I can't answer that question. I want to, but I can't."

Annie moved closer. "So, wait. You haven't had sex on this tour at all?"

The blush that crept up Bristol's neck was adorable. "Have you had sex on this tour?" Bristol asked.

Annie laughed. "Only with myself, and only in the privacy of a hotel room."

Bristol stood and fanned her T-shirt out in front of her. "How about we order dinner?" She led Annie to the kitchen. "We can share a bottle of wine beforehand. What are you hungry for?"

It was the perfect opening for Annie. She could have said what she wanted for dinner, and they could've perused online menus of local restaurants, but Annie was tired of this polite game they were playing. She walked over to Bristol and took her hands. "I'm hungry for you."

Bristol's mouth dropped open a tiny bit. And maybe it wasn't fair of her to take control, but when Bristol's breathing became heavier, Annie slid her hands from Bristol's shoulders up to her face and held it gently in front of hers.

"Don't be afraid." She moved her hand and put it right above Bristol's heart. "I'm here for you. For what's inside your heart. Not for what you can do for me. I know you think there's no future for us. Even though you're wrong and I want more, I can't walk away from the possibility of showing you how amazing you are. Give me this."

Bristol closed her eyes at Annie's words, and just when Annie thought she'd overstepped, Bristol pulled her close and kissed her soundly. It was the kind of kiss that made Annie forget where she was or how long they'd been kissing, and wonder why she was still upright. There was no learning curve with them. Bristol knew exactly how to kiss Annie, and if kissing made her knees weak, what would having sex do? Annie almost came from the feeling of Bristol pressing her hips into her soft core. Her knees buckled as a rush of excitement exploded in her.

Bristol lifted her so she was sitting on the marble kitchen isle and stood between Annie's knees. When Annie felt Bristol's hands move underneath her shorts, she whimpered and scooted her hips closer to Bristol's hand. She wanted Bristol inside her. She wanted to feel her fingers pressing her into an orgasm, but the angle was wrong. She broke from their kissing frenzy.

"Can we go to your room?"

"I'm so sorry." Bristol blushed and moved just enough for Annie to slide off the counter and down the length of her. Her hand was back under Annie's shorts, teasing her. Her mouth was hot on her neck. Annie clutched Bristol's shoulders and moaned her impatience. Bristol grabbed Annie's hand and led her to the bedroom. Annie ripped off the hoodie and stood in front of Bristol wet and panting, wearing tiny cotton shorts and a tank top. Bristol sat on the edge of the bed, and Annie straddled her. She rolled her hips, wanting friction from any part of Bristol.

"Are you sure about this?" Bristol asked.

Annie barely heard her. "What? Yes. I'm a thousand percent sure. I've wanted this since the first time we were onstage together." She moaned when she felt Bristol's fingers move closer to her throbbing pussy. She hadn't been wearing any panties last night, and even though she felt sexy wearing her little black dress and heels, something about wearing Bristol's clothes and getting her shorts wet from wanting her so much made this moment even sexier.

Bristol stopped kissing Annie to look at her when she slipped two fingers inside. They both moaned at the intimacy. Annie threw her arms around Bristol's shoulders and leaned her forehead against Bristol's.

"Yes," she whispered against Bristol's cheek. She'd never known how tender and vulnerable Bristol was until this moment. She kissed Bristol again. She tugged at her bottom lip with her teeth and slipped her tongue inside her mouth. Her hips started moving against Bristol's hand. She wanted more, but was she taking too much too soon? Was her greed a turnoff? Annie didn't know if they would have more than this one night, and she didn't want to miss a single moment but didn't want to come off too strong. She wanted no regrets in the morning when life returned to normal and they went their separate ways.

"We have to get these off you." Bristol flipped Annie so she was on her back. She wasn't gentle when she pulled off the shorts. A thrill shook Annie from the inside out, and she quickly removed her tank top. Bristol knelt above her, looked at her, then back into her eyes. "You're perfect. Absolute perfection."

It was as though the clock had stopped and they were cocooned in this perfect moment. Bristol slowed everything. She kissed Annie softly on her mouth and made a trail of wet kisses down her neck, across her collarbone, and settled on one of her erect nipples. The pulsating pleasure Annie felt with every tug of Bristol's mouth was almost unbearable. She grabbed Bristol's clothes, desperate to feel her warm flesh against hers. It wasn't fair that she was the only naked one in the room. Bristol got the hint and slid off the bed to strip.

Annie swallowed hard. Bristol was both hard and soft and the most beautiful woman Annie had ever seen. She pulled Bristol back between her legs and closed her eyes when Bristol kissed her way down to the apex of her thighs. Annie spread herself when she felt Bristol's hot breath on the soft, sensitive skin above her clit. When Bristol's lips pressed against her wet slit, Annie moaned over and over. She couldn't speak. The euphoric feeling of Bristol's mouth on her pussy was too much. She let the pressure build, and instead of focusing on slowing it down, she let it take over and explode. Bristol continued to lick and suck until Annie's legs shook and she had to pull away. Annie curled up and hid her face in the crook of Bristol's arm while she caught her breath. She didn't know what to say after that explosive orgasm. Was she supposed to thank her?

Bristol pulled Annie closer into her arms. "Why are you hiding? Is it too bright in here for you?" Bristol asked.

Annie shook her head and looked at Bristol. "No. I like the light because I get to see every part of you this way."

Bristol smiled and placed a small kiss on Annie's lips. Annie wanted more. She sucked on Bristol's bottom lip and slipped her hand between them to cup Bristol's full breast. Bristol's sharp intake only intensified Annie's need to have more. She ran her thumb over Bristol's erect nipple, wishing she could slide down and swirl her tongue over its hardness.

As if reading her mind, Bristol leaned up on her knees and elbows and gave Annie the space she craved. She wasted no time moving down Bristol's body. Bristol moaned the lower Annie kissed, and when her head was between Bristol's knees, she grabbed her hips and brought Bristol's swollen pussy down onto her mouth. The pure sexiness of the moment almost made Annie cry. Bristol's vulnerability and trust made her heart soar.

An unfamiliar, intense feeling burst inside as Annie held Bristol's hips until she was at the right height for Annie to taste her. Bristol was warm and wet against Annie's mouth. She swirled her tongue around Bristol's swollen clit, gauging the right pressure from her sharp intakes of breath and loud moans. Bristol shook and shuddered when Annie slipped one finger inside. It was a difficult angle, but Annie needed to be inside her. She moaned at Bristol's smooth, slick walls and how she tightened around Annie's finger. The slow pump of her hips informed Annie to keep the pressure the same. She could tell Bristol was close. Her entire being vibrated with pleasure. This first orgasm was pure lust. It was figuring out the fastest way to give Bristol immediate pleasure.

The next one would be slow after Annie touched every single part of Bristol's beautiful body. She was going to take her time making love to her. Annie braced her free hand against Bristol's hip as the orgasm worked its way through her. Bristol slowly rolled over and dropped to the mattress. Annie was immediately beside her, holding her until her shakes subsided. She couldn't tell if the speeding heartbeat she felt against her chest was hers or Bristol's.

"I…I don't know what to say." Bristol's voice cracked.

Annie was speechless. She couldn't describe what had just happened with words. She and Bristol were so in tune with one another that they completely skipped over the fumbling part of first-time lovers. Annie ran her fingers through Bristol's hair. "You don't have to say anything."

"Bristol? Honey, are you home? Where are you?"

With almost no time to spare, Bristol pulled the covers up over them right before Vanessa sailed through the bedroom door in search of her daughter.

"Oh, my God. I'm so sorry," Vanessa said before bolting back out of the room.

Bristol groaned and pulled the covers completely over her head. "That did not just happen."

Annie was embarrassed but also had to laugh. She leaned over Bristol. "At least she didn't walk in five minutes ago."

Bristol groaned even harder. "Why is my mother here?"

Annie pressed her lips against her shoulder. "She's probably just making sure you made it home okay."

"Well, now she knows I'm home and not alone."

"We're all adults here. Come on. Let's get up and say hi. The sooner she knows you're okay, the sooner she'll leave us alone," Annie said.

"Fine."

Neither one moved. "I'm going to need something else to wear. I mean, the tank and hoodie are fine, but the shorts are…well, I'm just going to need something else," Annie said.

Bristol turned so she could look at Annie. "I'll get you another pair." She leaned up and placed a hard, fast kiss on Annie's lips. "You're right. The sooner we greet her, the sooner she'll leave." She stood and reached for Annie. "Let's find you something to wear for the next fifteen minutes."

Annie smiled at Bristol's enthusiasm. Tomorrow would be a different story, but they had at least twelve hours ahead to remind them that it was okay to take chances and the future was never set in stone.

CHAPTER TWENTY-SIX

Bristol walked into the kitchen as her mother was placing a note on the table next to the box of Primo's.

"Sweetheart, I'm so sorry I interrupted you. I hadn't heard from you since last night, and I was worried."

Bristol couldn't do anything about the heat on her cheeks. She smiled softly. "Sorry about that. I was avoiding Lizzy, and my phone is somewhere around here." Bristol pretended to look around the room, even though she knew it was on the couch. Anything to avoid this conversation with her mom.

"Oh, hello, Annie. It's so nice to see you. How was the afterparty?"

Annie slid into the room wearing a fresh pair of shorts and the same hoodie from earlier. "Hi, Vanessa. It's good to see you." Bristol's mouth dropped open when Annie hugged her mom. "I wasn't there long. But it was okay. Not really my scene."

"Bristol's always saying she hates everything that doesn't involve playing her music in front of people."

"I one hundred percent agree. I've only had a taste of it, and while it's kind of cool that people want to know you, I get why Bristol wishes there was an off button after performances."

Bristol rolled her eyes. "I'm right here, and I can hear everything."

"It was a great concert, baby." Vanessa looked at Annie. "By both of you. All of you. The final song was amazing."

"I'm glad Willow gave me a heads-up about the fireworks, or else I would've hit the floor, thinking they were gunshots."

"That's so sad," Vanessa said.

"I'm from Colorado. Everyone has guns," she said.

Bristol looked at her. "And here I was thinking of visiting Vail because you thought it might be a safe place. Never mind now."

When Annie moved closer and brushed her lips across Bristol's mouth, Bristol turned beet red. She had never introduced somebody she was seeing to her mother. Annie acted as though it was normal, and so Bristol rolled with it, too.

"Does that mean you won't come and see me?" Annie asked.

"I don't know. I'm pretty sure all the places you suggested I check out now that I'm done touring are in Colorado," Bristol said.

Annie playfully pinched her. Bristol looked at her mother for the first time since Annie breezed into the room. Her mother winked at her. She approved of Annie, but that wasn't hard. She was perfect.

"I'm going to leave and not barge in again. Annie, it's so good to see you here with my daughter. Have a good evening," Vanessa said. She hugged Bristol.

Bristol felt the extra squeeze in her mom's hug. "I'll come see you tomorrow."

"Annie, you take care. I hope to see you again very soon."

When Vanessa left, Bristol leaned her head on the counter. She was beyond embarrassed. She heard Annie laugh and felt her arms circle her waist.

"I think your mom knows you're almost thirty and this happens."

Bristol stood and faced Annie. "You're the first woman I've brought home, so I'm still working through this." She placed a small kiss on her lips and draped her arms over Annie's shoulders. Annie tried hard not to look surprised, but Bristol saw it in her eyes. "One day you'll believe me."

"I believe you now. Also, I need to show you something," Annie said.

Her expression was serious as she pulled Bristol back to the bedroom. Alarms went off in Bristol's head. She'd been away for so long that she thought maybe something was wrong with the house. Annie pointed to the bed.

"What's the matter?" Bristol asked.

"You're not in it."

Bristol bit her lip to keep her goofy post-orgasmic smile from giving too much away. She was completely charmed by Annie. "Do you want me to stay like this?" she asked and pointed down at the outfit she'd donned to greet her mother.

Annie pulled off her hoodie. "Do you want me to stay like this?"

"Good point." Bristol got rid of her shorts and T-shirt before grabbing Annie and falling onto the bed with her.

"Can I tell you how sexy you are? I mean, I knew you were gorgeous fully clothed, but seeing you in just panties and a bra? Knowing full well what's underneath?" Annie kissed Bristol hard and flipped her. "Just plan on my hands on your body for the next twelve hours."

Bristol lifted her arms above her head and pressed her hands flat against the padded headboard. It was unlike her to give up control, but she trusted Annie. "I'm yours." It was a small thing to say, but it spoke volumes.

Annie lifted her brow but didn't say anything. She simply sat back and ran her hand over Bristol. She brushed the valley between her breasts with her fingertips and gently placed her palm on Bristol's stomach.

"You're so warm," she said.

Bristol felt like she was going to explode just from Annie's slow, torturous touch. She spread her legs apart, wanting Annie to touch the soft skin of her thighs and everything in between. Her eyes fluttered shut when Annie's fingers trailed over her panties and slid down to the inside of her thighs.

"Especially here."

Bristol opened her eyes when Annie shifted on the bed. She watched as Annie caressed her thighs with both hands, moving closer and closer to her silk panties. Every time Annie got close to Bristol's pussy, Bristol lifted her hips, hoping this time Annie's fingers would slip under the elastic and push deep inside her.

"Will you please take them off?" Bristol asked.

Annie kept eye contact with her the entire time she slid them down. Bristol loved how light Annie's eyes were, especially darkened with desire. It was empowering to know she had this effect on her.

"Better?" Annie asked.

"Your hands aren't on me, so I'm going to say worse." Bristol bit her bottom lip to keep from begging.

"You're right."

Annie crawled between Bristol's legs and lightly traced a path to the top of her thighs and back down. She briefly grazed Bristol's swollen pussy and the inside of her thighs. Bristol was almost panting with need.

"Is this better?" Annie asked.

Bristol reached down and ran her finger up and down her slit while Annie watched with surprise. "This is better." She slipped one finger inside and moaned, lifting her hips to get deeper. Usually, Bristol didn't do that when she masturbated, but with Annie watching, she felt bold and sexy.

"Oh my God." Annie watched as Bristol finger-fucked herself. As if she couldn't stand it any longer, Annie touched Bristol's hand and helped push her finger deeper inside. They both moaned.

When Bristol finally moved her hand away, Annie wasted no time slipping a finger inside. "You're so tight." She closed her eyes and swallowed hard. "So unbelievably tight."

Bristol lifted her hips slightly, wanting Annie to go deeper. Annie slipped two fingers inside and pulled them out quickly. Bristol almost wept at the extreme pleasure of how Annie filled her, followed immediately by intense disappointment at the loss of Annie's touch. Annie did that several times, building her up. Bristol could feel herself getting wetter. She moaned and greedily pushed her hips against Annie's hand when Annie added a third finger.

"Is this okay?" Her voice was low and full of concern.

Bristol licked her lips and nodded. "Please don't stop. You feel so good."

Bristol tried to relax as Annie fucked her harder and faster, but the orgasm rushed her, taking her by surprise. Bristol arched her back and cried out. She never yelled when she came. She was always quiet, and her previous lovers never knew if she orgasmed or not. Today, the whole world probably heard. Annie stayed inside and used her thumb to rub Bristol's sensitive clit. It took only a few strokes before she came again. Her whole body shook with pleasure. She felt like she was falling apart as each aftershock ripped through her.

Annie slipped out of her and lay next to her. Bristol could feel her excited energy but was too spent to do anything but hold her close.

Annie kissed her temple, her shoulder, her neck, and eventually her mouth. It was the kind of kiss that promised more to come.

"We should probably order some food because I plan to do this all night, and I'm going to need some serious carbs," Annie said.

Bristol gave a half-laugh. She was still pinging with tiny waves of pleasure, so the sound that came out was unrecognizable. She nodded instead. "I don't want to leave this bed until we have to. We can sustain ourselves on the carbs from doughnuts, right?"

"Let's have food delivered. What are you hungry for? Please say pasta and bread." Annie grabbed her phone.

Bristol told her the name of a restaurant to look up, and they placed an order for an obscene amount of pasta and bread. She called Mac at security and told him to expect the delivery in forty-five minutes. She didn't waste time sliding back into bed and pulling Annie into her arms. Annie kissed her shoulder and ran her fingertips up and down the valley of Bristol's breasts. It was a powerfully tender moment, and Bristol felt the sting of tears but kept them from falling. She felt so much for Annie, and to let her go was going to destroy her. She leaned up and looked at her. "You know, we have a lot of time before the food gets here." Bristol stretched her body across Annie's. "I have a pretty fantastic idea of how we can kill it."

Bristol woke tangled in Annie's arms and legs. It wasn't quite dawn, but she knew the sun would wake them up soon. She'd forgotten to close the blinds last night but didn't want to leave Annie's warm embrace to do it. She listened to Annie's even breathing and slow, rhythmic heartbeat until the panic of knowing she would be leaving in a few hours set in. She slipped out from her embrace and curled up behind her like a big spoon. The cute sighs Annie made when Bristol ran her hands over soft, sensitive spots on her body made her smile. She wasn't sure when Annie woke up, but she smiled when she felt Annie respond to her touch.

"Good morning," she whispered in her ear before biting her soft earlobe. Annie moaned in response. Bristol nipped the back of her neck and grazed her shoulder, biting gently into the soft muscle. Annie stretched out on her stomach, and Bristol took the opportunity to lie on top of her, spreading her legs with her knees. "Are you awake?"

Annie nodded and wiggled underneath her. Her voice was still gravelly with sleep. "Yes."

Bristol ran her tongue down Annie's back and kissed the two shallow dimples above Annie's tight ass. Annie tensed up but didn't stop her. Bristol crawled up and whispered in her ear again. "Are you ready for me?" She reached down between them and rubbed Annie's slit, which was already wet and engorged. "Oh, look. You are." She placed most of her weight on her knees and braced herself on her palm. With her free hand, she slipped two fingers inside. Annie arched her back and moaned as Bristol moved in and out, using her pelvis to thrust her hand even harder. Annie clutched the sheets and pressed into Bristol's hand.

"More," she said.

Bristol's heart jumped at the request. She'd never had three fingers inside anyone before. She gently added a finger and waited until Annie got comfortable. Her moans were different, and her hips pushed hard against her.

"Fuck me, Bristol," Annie said.

Bristol was on her knees in a matter of seconds. She spread Annie's legs farther apart and moved her hand gently at first. Annie's moans were intoxicating. There was no doubt that she one hundred percent gave herself to Bristol. Bristol gently added one more finger and wiggled them side to side, afraid she would hurt Annie if she pulled out and pushed them in again. Annie threw back her head and cried out.

"Yes, Bristol, just like that. Just like that."

Their lovemaking was primal and decadent, and even after she felt Annie's pussy clench at her orgasm, she didn't slow down. She didn't want to. She wanted to give her everything. Another orgasm hit, and another. It was the most amazing sexual experience of Bristol's life. When Annie finally pulled away and dropped to the mattress in a sweaty mess, Bristol held her. There were no words. She couldn't let Annie walk away from her, but she couldn't ask her to stay either. Annie's career was about to take off, and she would only be dead weight.

"That was the best way to wake up in the history of ever," Annie said drowsily.

Bristol felt like her heart would burst if she stayed in bed with Annie a minute longer. She kissed her cheek and slid out of bed. "I'm going to shower. Go back to sleep. It's not even six."

She pulled the covers over Annie, closed the curtains, and slipped into the bathroom. She was finally alone with her thoughts. The tour ending was both a high and a low, as expected, but she wasn't prepared for the high and low of Annie agreeing to spend time with her. She thought she would be able to hold her emotions in until Annie left, but her heart burst, and she slid down the wall of the shower, hoping the spray of the showerheads drowned out her sobs.

CHAPTER TWENTY-SEVEN

Annie walked away from Top Shelf with a smile. She changed her flight again from Wednesday morning to Tuesday afternoon. It didn't make sense to spend additional time in Los Angeles. She was eager to see Raven and her family, and get the SUV in front of her sister.

Annie needed to hear a friendly voice, so she called Charley in the Lyft on her way to the airport.

"So, it's all over. How was the final concert?" Charley asked.

"It was the most amazing thing ever. I'll never forget it."

"Tell me the afterparty was mind-blowing. Tell me everything," Charley said.

Annie didn't want to tell her everything. Even Charley wouldn't be able to help her process it. "There were fireworks at the end, and all the bands and singers sang the last song with Bristol. It was so much fun. I didn't stay long at the afterparty. I had to get my luggage off the bus and find a place to put everything, and by the time that was done, it was super late."

"My friend, the rock star," Charley said.

"I'm not a rock star, but I did learn so much on this tour about the industry and about myself," Annie said. Her thoughts drifted back to her time spent with Bristol. Their good-bye had been swift. So many words and feelings weren't said, but Annie knew Bristol wanted space.

"Do you need me to pick you up?" Charley asked.

"No. I've already scheduled a Lyft. I'll swing by tonight though."

"Can't wait to see you. I'm glad you're coming home."

"I miss you, too."

Annie avoided talking to her sister because she was emotionally drained from the tour and would probably end up ruining the surprise. She ended up scrolling through social media and liked several posts from fans on Instagram. She jumped over to TikTok to follow Reece, because in his videos she would see glimpses of Bristol's life. The kid had posted at least two dozen videos since the one he and Bristol made on the tour bus.

Her flight was at one thirty and would get her into Denver at five. She had an appointment at the dealership at six and was hoping to be at Sarah's by seven thirty, right before Peyton's bedtime. Peyton started all-day kindergarten today. Annie knew she would be wound up wanting to talk about it until she dropped off to sleep, exhausted.

She got to the airport, took a few selfies with fans who recognized her, and slipped into first class without any problem. She slept the entire trip, waking only when the tires bumped on the tarmac. Everything about today felt rushed.

At 7:14, Annie pulled up in Sarah's driveway and honked. She had stopped a block away to throw on the giant red bow the dealership provided. The SUV was charcoal gray with heated seats that Annie tested on the drive over. Strange that it was still hot in California but there was already a chill in the Denver evening. Sarah opened the door and stared.

Annie jumped out of the car and yelled, "Surprise!"

"You're home." Sarah ran down the steps and hugged her.

"I'm home," Annie said.

"Did you get a new—wait a minute." Sarah took several steps back when she noticed the red bow and Annie dangling the fob in front of her face. "No! Shut up. Seriously?"

Annie couldn't stop the tears that rolled down her cheeks. "It's what you asked for and the very least I could do." She thrust the fob into Sarah's hand. "She's all yours."

"Auntie Annie!" Peyton pushed open the storm door and squealed when she saw Annie. She was already in her pajamas and carrying her elephant stuffed animal that she slept with every night.

"Peyton! Come here!" Annie braced herself as Peyton flung herself into Annie's arms. "I've missed you. How was your first day of school?"

Her blue eyes widened with excitement. "It was so cool. I had the best time."

Annie hugged her tightly as more tears welled in her eyes. It was amazing how much she'd missed her family. "I was going to call you, but then I thought you would be busy with homework, so I thought I would wait until I knew you were done." Peyton's tiny giggle made Annie melt.

"I don't have homework. I'm only five." She held five fingers up to reiterate her age.

"What's going on out here?" Chase walked down the stairs and hugged Annie. "Welcome back. Did you get a new car?"

"No, but I did!" Sarah said. She waved Annie over. "Get in. Let's go for a drive."

"Can I come?" Peyton asked.

"No, sweetie. We need to put in your booster seat. Besides, it's bedtime, so Daddy needs to take you inside and read you a story. We'll be back before you fall asleep."

Annie gave Peyton one last hug and transferred her to Chase's outstretched arms before crawling into the passenger side.

"I want the full story, so be back in ten," he said.

"Years! Ten years!" Sarah yelled and waved as she slowly backed down the driveway. She stopped at the bottom and hugged Annie hard. "You didn't have to do this."

"I wanted to, and I promised you that I would. The paperwork is in the glove compartment. The check for the sales tax is in it, too. The only thing you need to do is get it insured and registered."

Sarah cupped Annie's face. "I'm so proud of you, sis. You did it. You hit it big."

"It's only a car. Besides, I have an idea for what I want to do next."

"You're going to get a manager, right? And then sign with the biggest record label, right?"

Annie shrugged. "I met with Top Shelf this morning, and they promised me everything I wanted, but it didn't feel right. I know the importance of going on tour and staying in front of an audience, but I like my life. I like what I'm doing. And with the added boost of having been on tour with the most famous pop star of our generation, I've gained followers. A ton of followers." She emphasized the word *ton*.

Sarah pulled back into the driveway after the slowest drive around the neighborhood and put her new car in park. "I'm overwhelmed with everything. You're home again. You bought me a car. A fucking car! Peyton started school today. Where did the time go? I just don't know where to land right now."

Annie hugged her sister again. "I get it. But everything is good. I'm good, your daughter is good, you have a job you love, you have a new car, and you don't have to check on Raven for a long time."

Sarah pointed at her. "That cat hates me. Like it wants to slice my throat when she sees me walk into the apartment."

Annie sighed. "If she had opposable thumbs, we'd all be dead."

"I won't tell anyone if you give her back," Sarah whispered.

Annie laughed. "Back to the streets? Nah. I love her too much. That little psycho kitty. Let's go inside, tuck Peyton in, and then I'm going to need a ride home."

"I love you."

"Because I'm the best."

"Because you're the best," Sarah said.

❖

"It's Annie Foster, back from tour, and I'm here to sing a few songs and answer some questions." It had been a week since the tour ended. Annie had met with Mountain Entertainment but didn't feel a real connection with them, so she left without signing.

She was off. Nothing felt right since she left Bristol. Her first question during the livestream popped up. Annie repeated the question and answered it.

"How did I like the tour? It was amazing. One of the best experiences of my life." She strummed a few notes before jumping into the biggest hit she'd had on tour. She scrolled through the questions and answered the ones she wanted to. "What was Bristol Baines like?" Annie felt both sad and elated at the question. "She's such a wonderfully kind and gentle person. She always made me feel like I was good enough to be on tour in front of thousands."

She sang a few more songs, answered more questions, and before she even realized it, the hour was up. Her tip jar brought in more money than any jingle gig. She was done writing them. Not talking to Bristol was driving her crazy, but she had to respect Bristol's wishes. She was at a complete loss.

"Okay, let's make a list," Sarah suggested when Annie dropped by that night.

"What do you mean?"

"We need to figure out what makes you happy." Sarah was the only one who knew the truth about what had happened in Los Angeles after the tour. She didn't know the specifics, only that she and Bristol hooked up one night and that was it.

"What do you mean?"

Sarah grabbed a notebook and drew a line down the center of a blank page. "On this side we're going to write down everything that makes you happy. And over here we're going to write down what doesn't and talk about it when we're done. I'm going to start."

Annie watched her write down Peyton, Sarah, Chase, Raven, Charley, and Bristol in the left column. In the right she wrote down being away from family, followed by being away from Bristol.

"Have you talked to her at all?"

Annie shook her head. "No. I'm honoring her wishes."

Sarah rolled her eyes. "Not even a text?" She gave a low whistle. "I love you, but you are a genuine idiot." She ran her fingers through her hair and sighed. "Here's the real question. Are you ready?" At Annie's nod, she asked, "Do you love her?"

Sarah's words were a sucker punch. Annie leaned over and rested her head in her hands. "It never occurred to me. I mean, Bristol Baines. She's untouchable."

"But she's capable of love, and if she's as torn up about being apart as you are, then you have to talk to her. She's a person, sis. I mean, she's used to being alone, but maybe that's not what she wants."

Annie had suppressed all emotions the minute she got into the car Bristol had ordered for her the morning after. She couldn't even cry because then the driver would know that something had happened, and it would be on all entertainment news outlets. She kept her head high, slipped on sunglasses, and listened to music to drown out her thoughts. She didn't collapse until she was safely in the airport-lounge bathroom.

Twenty-eight glorious hours. She was with Bristol Baines, in her arms, in her bed, for a solid day. Annie had never given herself so freely to another person. The only reason Bristol had her guard up the next morning was because she thought Annie was going to sign with Top Shelf and go on a path that was completely different from hers.

"Things are different now." Annie suddenly sat up. "Sarah, things are different now."

"What do you mean?"

"I don't need to be on the road. Yes, the tour was great, but there was nothing wrong with what I was doing before."

"As long as you're happy, you do whatever you want. I'm proud of you regardless."

Annie chewed on her bottom lip for a long time. Life was full of change, and big decisions didn't come very often. "I have a lot to think about, don't I?"

Sarah held Annie's hand. "There are direct flights to Los Angeles daily. I'll even watch Raven another week or for however long it takes. Just make sure Bristol isn't allergic to cats, because that's a deal breaker right there."

Chapter Twenty-eight

"As long as I'm not fired, we're good," Lizzy said.

Bristol's cheeks were still burning after ending her toxic relationship with a company that cared only about how much money she could bring to the table. The meeting had been moved to Friday at nine. It was cordial and friendly at first, but once Lizzy dropped the news, the gloves came off, and they called in their team of lawyers. It was after noon when they were done. Lizzy had her team of entertainment lawyers on standby in case Top Shelf threw them a curveball, but after pointing out that Bristol had fulfilled her contractual obligations, they had no choice but to accept her resignation.

Bristol should have felt elated, and a part of her was, but she was also melancholic. Half of her life was Top Shelf. Every major milestone had happened when she was with them. First girlfriend, her parents' divorce, learning to drive, first platinum record, first world tour, first Grammy, first ulcer, first nervous breakdown.

Bristol stopped. "Oh, no. You're not fired. You're too good at managing everything else of mine. Just don't ever come at me with a music contract."

Lizzy held her hands up. "Never again. I'll maybe tell you about an event, but I won't book anything unless you give me the okay."

They had never talked about Bristol leaving the afterparty early or what had happened after. It wasn't Lizzy's business, and now that they weren't on tour, Bristol had the upper hand again.

"Want to do lunch next week?" Lizzy asked.

Bristol slipped on her sunglasses as they walked out of the building and shook her head. "You're lucky I left the house for this one."

Lizzy rolled her eyes. "It was necessary. Also, can we talk about how Sterling almost popped a vein when you told her you were done? Tyson had to loosen his tie. Oh, shit. That was priceless."

Bristol smiled for the first time in hours. "It was pretty incredible." Her driver waved her over the moment they stepped out of the building. "Listen, if I go dark for a month, don't worry. I'll check work emails regularly, but don't text me unless it's an emergency."

"Reach out if you need me, and sleep a lot. Get caught up. Maybe get back into a comfortable routine," Lizzy said.

Bristol didn't want to tell Lizzy she was writing new music because she would subtly push and force a deadline. Bristol didn't want that. Writing music was always cathartic, and she had a lot of new emotions to work through. "Oh, getting back in a routine will be nice. Pilates, maybe I'll start cooking. I mean, I have a massive kitchen and don't know how to use most of the appliances." She stood outside her limo and hugged Lizzy. "Go home. I'll call you next week if I'm in the mood to be around people."

"I know I'm not perfect, but thank you for being a friend. And for keeping me around," Lizzy said.

Bristol wondered if she would even reach out to Lizzy in the next month. Everybody from the tour was playing catch-up with life except Bristol. She was hiding from it. Her mother and brother had come over one night for dinner earlier in the week, but that was it. Bristol worked out, spent a huge amount of time in her studio, and binge-watched shows that people had recommended over all social media platforms.

Her mother wasn't giving up on her and Annie. She pressed Bristol about the two of them every time they got together. Bristol said it was just a one-time thing and for her to let it go. Tonight was different. For the first time ever, she gave Bristol love advice.

"Maybe Annie's okay with your choices and your lifestyle."

"How could she be, Mom? She's destined for stardom. People love her onstage. If she wants the success I have, she has to go in a completely different direction than I'm headed. Watching somebody I care for experience even a little of what I did would be too brutal for me. I would speak my mind, and we would end up fighting and resenting one another. I want to be a part of Annie's life. In a good capacity. If that means we'll only be friends, that will have to be enough."

"Even if that means giving up somebody you've come to love?"

Bristol turned quickly away from her mother to hide the tears that sprang to her eyes. She let them fall when she felt her mother pull her back into a hug.

"She's the real deal, honey. I can tell. She's not using you at all. I think if you opened yourself up, you would find that she picked you, not your success. I saw the way she looked at you. You can't fake that."

Bristol turned to face her mother. "It's too late, Mom. She signed with Top Shelf."

"How do you know? Did they make an announcement?"

"No, but one of their assistants told one of Lizzy's assistants that she was there earlier in the week."

Vanessa scoffed. "That doesn't mean she signed."

"Well, she's not here, is she?"

"Well, you're not in Denver now, are you?"

Bristol sat at the kitchen table. "No, I'm not."

Vanessa set down her mug of coffee and sat across from Bristol. "Love is the best reward, baby. Nothing else matters." She grabbed Bristol's hands and squeezed them. "I can't promise that it won't hurt or tear you apart inside, but it will also make you feel amazing things and lift you up so high. You deserve true love. Hopefully it's with Annie, but if it's not, just be open to the idea."

"How do I know if I'm in love?"

Vanessa smiled at Bristol. "You'll feel like your world has been turned upside down and the only thing that makes sense is the person who occupies so much of your head and heart. When they are with you, everything seems perfect." She finished her coffee and stood. "You'll figure it out. I trust you. Now, I have to make sure your brother doesn't sleep the day away. It's been a rough week getting him out the door and to school on time."

"Good luck there."

"How did two completely different children come from the same womb?"

Bristol held up her hand. "No. I refuse to believe that. He's adopted."

Vanessa cupped Bristol's chin and pushed her hair behind her ear. "But he looks just like you."

"Purely coincidental, I swear."

"Get some rest. I'll call you tomorrow."

Bristol washed their cups and wiped down the counter. She had nothing to do. Nothing needed her immediate attention. Bristol's financial advisors had instructions on what to do. All her emails had been answered by Lizzy's team. They forwarded any that they felt required a personal touch. She was officially bored. It had been a week. One week.

When the doorbell rang, Bristol laughed. "Mom, you can use your key. I promise it's okay." She opened the door and had to hold the handle to keep from falling to her knees. She couldn't find her words. She could only stare.

"How do you feel about cats?" Annie stood in the entryway with a guitar and a small rolling suitcase.

"What are you doing here?" Bristol asked.

Annie didn't falter. "How do you feel about cats? This is a very serious question. This could make or break us."

Bristol teared up and laughed. "I think cats are amazing. I've never had one, but I hear they're sometimes a lot of fun."

"Would you be okay with one who maybe wanted to kill you in your sleep?"

Bristol pulled Annie close. *She was here. She came back.* "We could give that cat an entire wing of the house. I mean, maybe we'd see her sometimes, but we'd keep her out of the kitchen, well, because of knives." She hugged Annie tightly. "You came back. How did you get through security?"

"Your mom told Mac to let me in. And yes, I came back. Can I come in?" Annie asked.

Bristol grabbed Annie's suitcase and rolled it inside. She quickly shut the door and reached for Annie again. "What's going on?" She couldn't stop touching her.

"Can we sit down? It's been a long day already."

"Of course." Bristol didn't let go of her hand until they sat on the couch.

"I've been thinking about everything. The tour, what you said, what I want. As much as I loved being on tour and getting all the attention, I didn't love being away from the important people in my life. There are other ways I can succeed as a musician."

"Did you find a manager?" Bristol asked.

"I'm talking to one. I would be his first client. He knows what I want, and having spent a great deal of time recently on the Angel/Devil tour, he knows it's not for me."

Bristol frowned. She had no idea who Annie was talking about. "Who? I mean, most of the guys were stagehands."

Annie smiled. "Vaughn. He quit Lizzy's firm and asked if I would be his first client. Who better than somebody who just witnessed what went down the last eighteen months for you and everybody?"

"I should probably check my emails more." Bristol couldn't believe that Annie was here. Or that Vaughn had struck out on his own.

"I know we're talking about my professional future, but we're forgetting about the most important part."

"Which is?"

"Us. I want there to be an us. The time we had together made me realize that what I really want isn't a world tour." Annie looked at their hands. "I want you, Bristol. Time spent with you was the best time of my life." She put her hand on Bristol's heart. "Not the famous international pop star, but Bristol Baines, the shy woman who has the biggest heart and would do anything for anyone. The woman who helps people out because she can, not because she's contractually obligated. And the woman who is playful and fun and likes to eat ice cream in bed and watch bad television from the eighties." Annie moved closer. "The woman who makes my heart feel like it's going to burst out of my chest whenever I see her." Tears welled in the corner of Annie's eyes. "Just hearing your voice makes me want to curl up in your arms and stay there for as long as I can."

Damn all the tears today, Bristol thought. She dabbed the corners of her eyes with the sleeve of her sweatshirt. "Are you sure about this?" Her heart sounded like thunder in her chest as she waited for Annie's answer. She was rewarded with Annie's full lips pressed against hers.

"I want us. More than anything else. I want to see you when I want, and I want to see my family when I want. I don't want to miss Peyton growing up. I can still have a music career."

Bristol wanted to believe her. Everything inside her wanted to fall into Annie's arms and never leave, but she'd been hurt before, and it was hard to trust people. Annie said this now, but what if she was wrong? What if she resented Bristol for giving up on her dreams?

"Bristol, look at me," Annie said gently. She dropped to her knees in front of Bristol. "I know we haven't spent a lot of time together, but that's why I'm here. I love you. Do you hear me? I love you. I don't have to compromise anything. I can have you and my music and my family. I don't need to sign with a huge label to have the career I want. I might not be as famous as I could be, and I'm one hundred percent okay with that."

Bristol broke. She dropped her head into her hands and cried. She cried because for the first time in a very long time, she was happy. She felt complete with Annie in her life. Her mother had just told her that the only thing that would right her world was love, and she was correct. Annie straddled her lap and moved Bristol's hands away from her eyes. She kissed the tears on her cheeks.

"Bristol, I love you. We can have this together. I know we can. We can still have careers, and I know you're worried that I won't be happy in the future, but I was happy before. You gave me the opportunity to shoot straight to the top in the business, but you also gave me love. And I can have both. I want both. Not everybody can handle your level of success, but I can handle what I've been given because of you. Does that make sense?"

"Repeat the first part."

Annie laughed. "I'm running on caffeine and emotion right now. I can't remember what I said, but in summary, I love you, and I'm here to make it work."

"You love me." Bristol wasn't being snide. She was repeating words she didn't think she would ever hear from Annie.

Annie nodded and smiled. "I definitely do. I mean, not only are you incredible in everyday life, but twenty-four hours in your bed solidified my opinion." She playfully fanned herself with her hand.

Bristol had never blushed more than when she was with Annie. The fact that Annie brought up their lovemaking made her feel invincible, empowered, and loved. She pushed aside the cautious words that threatened to spill out of her head and instead let the ones from her heart speak up. "I love you, too, Annie Foster."

"Woohoo!" Annie threw her hands up. She would have fallen off Bristol's lap had Bristol not grabbed her thighs. "I knew it." She cupped Bristol's face. "Nobody fucks like that without being in love. That's how I knew."

Bristol feigned shock. "Ms. Foster. That mouth of yours."

"Needs to be all over your body. Why are we still here and not back in that giant bed of yours?" Annie asked.

"Good point. Less talk, more kissing." Bristol grabbed Annie's hand, turned on the security system in case her mother decided to swing by unannounced again, and led Annie back to her bedroom. Bristol had thought about her life over the past two months. She had gone from being depressed to finding the love of her life. Maybe she'd needed to walk away from the only life she ever knew in order to appreciate Annie and accept the love she offered.

"I really do love you," Bristol said.

Annie stopped and held Bristol two steps from the bedroom. "I know. I knew before you did. I wouldn't have been brave enough to come here if I didn't believe it."

"What did I ever do to deserve you?" Bristol asked. Her arms were still wrapped around Annie. She was afraid to let her go.

"You gave me a chance, Bristol. A chance at a career, but more importantly, a chance at you."

Epilogue—One Year Later

"Why does she hate me?" Bristol stood in the kitchen doorway with her arms crossed. Raven was skulking around the island growling and making angry cat noises with every step.

Annie put her arms around Bristol's waist. "She doesn't hate you, babe. She hates change."

"She's lived here before. This is her home," Bristol said.

"She's heavily medicated and was just on a plane for three hours. I'm a little crabby, too."

Annie smiled at how Bristol was so concerned about Raven's disposition. They both knew that by the end of the night, Raven would be curled up in bed wrapped in Bristol's hair. And she knew Bristol wouldn't move until Raven was done sleeping. It was adorable how close they'd become.

After Annie showed up and confessed her love to Bristol, they were inseparable. Three weeks later, Annie moved in with Bristol. She took a week to pack up her apartment and get her affairs in order. Charley was ecstatic and told her she would still have open-mic nights on Wednesdays. When Annie missed her family, they flew to Denver to be with them. Since it happened frequently, they bought a house in Denver. Splitting their time between California and Colorado seemed like the best option. The only one who struggled was Raven.

"I just want to make sure she's okay."

"I love that you love her," Annie said and tucked herself under Bristol's arm. She was so happy. She and Bristol had started Serendipity, a small record label where they found new-to-the-scene musicians and got them in front of people. Annie posted videos of new acts to her

YouTube channel, which had grown exponentially since the world found out she and Bristol were together.

"I'm so proud of you," Bristol said. She leaned her head against Annie's.

"We've come a long way, haven't we?" Annie asked.

"A true power couple," Bristol said. The tabloids called them Bristannie, which was completely ridiculous, but Lizzy managed to start an online merch store where fans could buy T-shirts, hoodies, and coffee mugs with #Bristannie stamped on them. Bristol insisted all proceeds go to music programs for schools. They worked with organizations all over the country to get instruments back in the hands of children and teens who otherwise wouldn't have the opportunity.

Raven yowled at them again.

"Knocked down to reality by a cat." Annie laughed.

"Tragic, but true." Bristol tightened her hold on Annie. "What do you want to do tonight?"

"Hang out with you and our cat. Did you have something else in mind?"

"What do you say to your own private Bristol Baines concert? It's been a long time since I sang to you."

Annie laughed. "We literally just did a mini concert for my family last week."

"But it wasn't just for you. You deserve your own performance," Bristol said.

"I can't turn down an offer like that." Annie smiled.

Bristol held up two fingers. "I have two conditions."

"It was your idea. Now you have conditions?"

Bristol nodded seriously. "One, the event has to take place in the bedroom. The acoustics are best there." Annie rolled her eyes at the obvious lie. "And two, you have to sing with me. We make the best music together."

"Deal."

Bristol held her finger up for Annie to wait and returned with her Preston Thompson guitar. "Any requests?"

"All of them."

Annie sprawled on the bed and listened to Bristol play the songs that had made her fall in love with her. Bristol's words took on a different meaning now that they shared hearts. She smiled when Bristol started strumming her massively successful hit "Forever." She wanted to sing with Bristol but stopped when she realized the words were different.

You're here with me always and forever.
I can't believe this is my life.
Will you marry me, Annie Foster,
And do me the honor of being my wife?

About the Author

Multi-award-winning author Kris Bryant was born in Tacoma, WA, but has lived all over the world and now considers Kansas City her home. She received her BA in English from the University of Missouri and spends a lot of her time buried in books. She enjoys hiking, photography, and spending time with her family including her world-famous dog, Molly.

Her first novel, *Jolt*, was a Lambda Literary Award Finalist. *Forget-Me-Not* was selected by the American Library Association's 2018 Over the Rainbow book list and was a Golden Crown Finalist for Contemporary Romance. *Breakthrough* won a 2019 Goldie for Contemporary Romance. *Listen* won a 2020 Goldie for Contemporary Romance. *Lucky* was a 2020 Forward Indies Finalist. *Temptation* was an Ann Bannon finalist and won a 2021 Goldie for Contemporary Romance. Kris can be reached at krisbryantbooks@gmail or www.krisbryant.net, @krisbryant14.

Books Available From Bold Strokes Books

A Good Chance by Ali Vali. Harry, Desi, and Desi's sister Rachel are so close to getting everything they've ever wanted, but Desi's ex-husband is coming back to get his revenge and rip apart their chance at happiness. (978-1-63679-023-7)

A Perfect Fifth by Jaycie Morrison. Streetwise pianist Zara Keller and Lady Jillian Stansfield couldn't be more different, yet their connection brings a new awareness of who they are and what they truly want in their lives—including each other. (978-1-63679-132-6)

Catching Feelings by Ana Hartnett Reichardt. Andrea Foster expected to catch a lot of pitches from the Alder Lions' star pitcher, Maya, but she didn't expect to catch feelings. (978-1-63679-227-9)

Defiant Hearts by Lee Lynch. In these stories, you'll find your lovers, friends, and lesbians you wish you knew—maybe even yourself. (978-1-63679-237-8)

Love and Duty by Catherine Young. All Princess Roseli wants is to marry her three lovers, but with war looming, she must instead marry Princess Lucia to establish a military alliance between their planets. (978-1-63679-256-9)

Serendipity by Kris Bryant. Serendipity brings jingle writer Annie Foster and celebrity pop star Bristol Baines together, and their undeniable attraction keeps them close, but will their different paths drive them apart? (978-1-63679-224-8)

The Haunted Heart by Jane Kolven. A ghost, a ring, and a quest to find a missing psychic—it's a spell for love. (978-1-63679-245-3)

The Rules of Forever by Nan Campbell. After reconnecting at their high school reunion, Cara and Lauren agree to embark on a textbook definition friends-with-benefits relationship, but trying to keep it uncomplicated is harder than it seems. (978-1-63679-248-4)

Vision of Virtue by Brey Willows. When virtue and desire come together, be prepared for sparks in this next installment of the Memory's Muses series. (978-1-63679-118-0)

The Artist by Sheri Lewis Wohl. Detective Casey Wilson and reclusive artist Tula Crane are drawn together in a web of passion, intrigue, and art that might just hold the key to stopping a killer. (978-1-63679-150-0)

Cherry on Top by Georgia Beers. A chance meeting leaves Cherry and Ellis longing for a different life, but when Ellis's search for truth crashes into Cherry's insta-filter world, do they have any hope at all of a happily ever after? (978-1-63679-158-6)

Love and Other Rare Birds by Angie Williams. Ornithologist Dr. Jamie Martin and park ranger Rowan Fleming are searching the Alaskan wilderness for a bird thought to be extinct, and they're about to discover opposites really do attract. (978-1-63679-108-1)

Parallel Paradise by Mayapee Chowdhury. When their love affair is put to the test by the homophobia of their family, community, and culture, Bindi and Rimli will need to fight for a chance at love. (978-1-63679-203-3)

Perfectly Matched by Toni Logan. A beautiful Cupid named Hannah, a runaway arrow, and just seventy-two hours to fix a mishap that could be the best mistake she has ever made. (978-1-63679-120-3)

Slow Burn by Missouri Vaun. A wounded wildland firefighter from California and a struggling artist find solace and love in a small southern town. (978-1-63679-098-5)

The Inconvenient Heiress by Jane Walsh. An unlikely heiress and a spinster evade the Marriage Mart only to discover true love together. (978-1-63679-173-9)

The Value of Sylver and Gold by Michelle Larkin. When word gets out that former Boston Homicide Detective Reid Sylver can talk to the dead, the FBI solicits her help on a serial murder case, prompting Reid to assemble forces once again with Detective London Gold. (978-1-63679-093-0)

Wildflower by Cathleen Collins. When a plane crash leaves seven-year-old Lily Andrews stranded in the vast wilderness of Arkansas, will she be able to overcome the odds and make it back to civilization and the one person who holds the key to her future? (978-1-63679-244-6)